IN THE TIME OF
KINGS

Also by N. Gemini Sasson:

The Crown in the Heather (The Bruce Trilogy: Book I)

Worth Dying For (The Bruce Trilogy: Book II)

The Honor Due a King (The Bruce Trilogy: Book III)

*Isabeau: A Novel of Queen Isabella
and Sir Roger Mortimer*

*The King Must Die:
A Novel of Edward III*

*Uneasy Lies the Crown:
A Novel of Owain Glyndwr*

IN THE TIME OF

KINGS

N. GEMINI SASSON

cader idris
press

*For anyone who has ever loved another
with all your heart.*

Author's Note

The first time I set foot on Scottish soil, I felt like I'd arrived home, even though I'd never been there before. I was overcome with a sense of belonging, of 'knowing' the land deep in my soul.

Since then, five of the novels I've written are based on the lives of Robert the Bruce, James Douglas, Queen Isabella and her husband Edward II, as well as their son Edward III. It wasn't until a year after the last of those books was published that I began to research my genealogy further and discovered I am a descendent of several of the people I had written about.

My previous historical novels are all based on rigorous research of factual events. This book, while it does center around a short period in Scottish history ending shortly after the Battle of Halidon Hill, is largely fictional. I have borrowed names from the past and created some characters purely from my imagination. At the end, I've included a Historical Note regarding some of the events of the time.

I had many starts and stops while writing this book. In the end, it was a matter of understanding *why* I had to write it. Insight can come in a sudden seismic shift or gradually like the tide wearing away at the shoreline, as our subconscious grapples to replace old concepts with new ones. For me, the answers came in their own time, as so many things do.

But when the answers do come, when you meet that special

'someone', you just … know. Your soul knows. Trust it.

Enjoy the journey,

N. Gemini Sasson

PROLOGUE

LONG, LONG AGO

<u>Scotland — 1333</u>

NOT YET NINETEEN AND already she had lost a husband. Only lately had she begun to love him.

Perhaps if she hadn't, if she had remained strong, God would not be punishing her like this.

They had said he was a heretic. She believed them now.

The cold of the chapel room flagstones seeped into her flesh, chilling her to the bone, even though it was still summer. How long she had lain by the altar she did not know. All she was certain of was that the sun had set many hours ago; its light had been intrusive and she was glad to see it gone.

She welcomed the night. Embraced the stillness. Immersed herself in the nothingness. Somehow, the darkness seemed more familiar, more … protective. Like a burial shroud.

Grief filled her, consumed her. Throughout the corridors, the sounds of keening echoed, although it brought her no solace to know she was not alone in her loss.

Her heart was as hollow as a tomb robbed of its corpse. She could never love again. Why, then, even live?

She stared past her outspread fingers. A threadlike shadow caught her eye, small and nimble. The spider scampered toward her, but she did not move, could not. Her strength had fled along with her hope.

The spider skittered across a patch of sunlight, paused, and then retreated into the shadows.

Sunlight. Shadows. Was it dawn already?

Slowly, she lifted herself up — onto her elbows first, then her knees. Hugging the column closest to her, she stood. Not until her legs stopped shaking did she take the first step. When she reached the arched doorway, she clung to its frame for a long while, uncertain of where she was going or what she would do. Nothing had purpose to her anymore.

From an open window somewhere, the low roar of the sea beckoned, whispering her name in a throaty rasp.

She moved through a dim corridor, each step as forced as the one before. Faces, blank to her, turned to watch. Ghostly voices came to her as if muffled through wool. Hands grazed her arm, grasped at her shoulder, but she shirked them away and continued. Her left hand trailing along rough stone, she descended the tower stairs, her steps coming faster now.

Shoving the door open, she inhaled the air, suffused with the smell of salt and moss. The sky's brightness drew her onward. A hundred steps more and she was at the furthest point of the headland. Wiggling her toes, she looked down. The wind rushed upward, making her skirts billow and snap. She could see little of the cliff's rugged face, so sheer was the drop. Waves thundered against the jagged rocks below, their impact sending the spray up so high she could taste the sea on her tongue.

Wind tore at her hair, red as a stormy sunset. She lifted her tear-swollen face to the sun, now fully risen above an endless sea.

"Mariota," it called."Mariota!"

"I am here. Here!" she cried. Then more softly, "I am here."

Her arms wide, she surrendered.

PART I:

*"Oh that 'twere possible
After long grief and pain
To find the arms of my true love
Round me once again!"*

From Alfred, Lord Tennyson's *Maud*

1

NOT SO LONG AGO

Balfour, Indiana — 1990

*L*arge, calloused fingers curl over mine. The grip is firm, unrelenting, in the way that a carpenter would grasp a hammer.

"Hold on real tight, Ross!"

My scrawny legs dangle from the edge of the seat. Flakes of green paint cling to the crackled surface of the swing set's frame, begging for small fingers to peel them loose. I look past scraped knees and bruised shins at dusty red sneakers. On each shoe are matching holes where my big toes have worn through.

My mom waves to me and I smile. This is the best day of my life.

Tied to the handle of our picnic basket, a helium balloon bobs at the end of its blue ribbon. Inside the basket are the strawberry frosted cupcakes my mom made for my sixth birthday. She snaps the red plaid blanket out, then begins laying out the plates and food.

I kick impatiently and clamp my hands tighter on the chains.

"Push, Daddy. Push!"

He nudges me forward. Gently at first, so the ground rocks beneath me, like when Mom used to hold me in her arms, my head tucked against her shoulder, and sing me to sleep. Metal creaks against metal. A warm breeze whispers across my cheeks, my arms, my shins. For a split second, I hang at the pinnacle of my ascent, suspended in the heavens. My stomach somersaults into my heart.

Then gravity yanks me backward and the world reverses. A whoosh of air races by and parts the hair at the back of my head. The packed dirt of the ground looms far beneath me and I erupt into laughter, knowing I'm safe.

I beg for more; my dad pushes me higher, higher, higher. Sky blends with earth, blurring the horizon. A lemon-yellow sun darts erratically amidst swirling clouds like a bee in search of nectar. I imagine that I can fly. And I can — but not in the way you'd think. Because in that moment something ... shifts. Time shifts.

Salt spray spatters over my forehead. I hear the raucous cry of seabirds. Startled, I close my eyes to wish it away. Yet my face dampens more and the shrieking intensifies, piercing my eardrums. Cautiously, I raise an arm to shield my face and look again.

Crescents of white flash across my vision. Moments later, I realize I'm standing on a cliff watching a flock of gulls explode upward. Below, sunlight glints copper off an angry sea.

Bewildered, I blink several times. Still, I see it, as real as the rust staining my palms and the metal links pinching my fingers.

I gape at the glittering water, awed. I've never seen the ocean before. How is it that I can see it now?

But I do. I do! I'm there. Then. A long, long time ago. I sense it all around me: the deep expanse of sky and sea, the rush and retreat of waves upon the shore, the scent of saltwater and damp

IN THE TIME OF KINGS

stones, and the wind scrubbing at my face.

And then, there is the girl. No, not a girl. A woman. Her reddish-gold hair whips in the wind. My arms are around her, holding so tight she must know in that moment that we will always, always be together.

For those few moments — or are they minutes? — I'm someone else, in some other place and time. A grown man who's lived a life full of adventure and danger.

The woman in my arms murmurs and steps away. Fingers spread wide, I reach toward her, wanting to draw her back, afraid of losing her forever. I speak her name, but she keeps walking, the distance between us small, yet gaping. Desperate, I leap forward, my balance pitching with a gust of wind, and —

That's when I slip. Not in that time, but in this. The wooden seat of the swing flips from beneath me and thunks against my spine. As I slide, my T-shirt snags against an exposed bolt on the seat, scraping skin raw. The back of my ribs burns. I flail a hand, but can't grab the chain. As my body twists toward the earth, my arm catches between the seat and the S-hook where the chain attaches. My knees plow into dirt, but my torso continues to pitch forward. I hear the 'pop' of my shoulder being wrenched from its socket.

For what seems like a very long minute, I don't cry or scream. I just stare at my arm, turned in a position I'm sure it's not supposed to go.

A shadow moves across the sun. His lip twitching in annoyance, my dad stands over me. "Clumsy jackass. I told you to hold on."

2

HERE & NOW

<u>Scotland — 2013</u>

"HAM AND EGGS, SIR?"

The shade on the airplane window snaps open. I blink at the watery brightness pouring in through the small glass square and nudge my glasses back to the top of my nose. Everything comes into focus. A rising sun fans its amber rays above the cloud tops, heralding morning. Where had the night gone?

"Ham and eggs?" a distinctly British female voice repeats. A simple phrase and yet it stirs so many unwelcome memories.

A stewardess — far too pert for this ungodly hour — locks the cart wheels into place. The flight has been so smooth and the infant seated with its mother in front of us so quiet that I had actually fallen asleep. Then I realize I haven't slept all that long, given that we've lost five hours of daylight in the time zone jump.

Claire tugs at my sleeve. "Ross, did you forget to tell them?"

I stroke her wrist, feeling her tendons taut beneath my thumb.

"You know I always do. It seems perfectly normal to me."

She gives the stewardess a saccharin-sweet smile. "He's a vegetarian. The biscuits will be fine. And a fruit cup, if you have any."

"The same for you, miss?"

"That's misses," I say. Happy doesn't begin to describe how I feel these days. Claire's my wife now. My *wife*.

"Ms.," Claire corrects politely, winking at me. She had kept her maiden name. Before the wedding, we took bets on which of us would get called by the wrong last name first. I'd lost when the DJ at our wedding introduced us during our first dance as Mr. and Mrs. Forbes.

How lucky I'd been to grow up next door to this gorgeous creature. We started as friends, two kids passing the summer wading in the creek, turning over rocks to hunt for crawdads. We shared our dreams and finished each other's jokes. Her secrets were mine, mine were hers.

The day she announced she was moving away during our freshman year in high school, as nonchalant as I tried to be about it, the news had left me feeling like some evil superhero villain had just sucked my intestines out through my belly button and danced on them.

It wasn't until I cracked a filling and dragged myself to my dentist's office one Monday morning, writhing in pain, that we reconnected almost fourteen years later. The regular dentist was out with bronchitis, they told me. 'No problem,' I mumbled, clutching my jaw, 'anyone will do.' I had to defend a research grant request to the head of the Biology Department in eight hours and it wasn't going to go well if I had a screwed up look on my face. Not that mumbling through the proposal with a numbed tongue was going to go that great, but at least I could do it with a smile of relief.

When Claire — *Dr.* Claire Forbes — walked in, I suddenly forgot my agony. Five minutes later, I asked her out. Five months after that, we were married beneath the sandstone overhang at Ash Cave in Hocking Hills, the waterfall so close I felt its mist on her lips when I kissed her. It might have seemed like a short engagement, but that connection between us had never truly been severed.

Our parting, in a way, had been a blessing, because when we saw each other again it was in a very different way. Still friends, yes. But ... suffice it to say that at the age of fourteen I had never looked at the freckled, pig-tailed tomboy Claire and said to myself, "God, I want to wake up next to that hot body every day for the rest of my life."

"Oh, no, no," Claire says, yanking me out of my reverie. "Ham and eggs, please. They smell great."

The stewardess lays the cellophane-covered plate on Claire's tray. "I'll have to bring the fruit later. I'm sure we have some. Meanwhile, would you like some juice?"

"Grapefruit?" I unwrap the plastic utensils on my tray and arrange them on either side of my plate: fork on the left, knife and spoon on the right.

"I'm sorry. We only have orange. Will that be all right? Or would you prefer coffee?"

My fingers tighten around my plastic fork. Coffee and orange juice. Another painful reminder of my father's senseless rituals. I slip my fork beneath the tray and grip the handle so tight it bends, threatening to snap. Quickly, I place it back on my tray. I'm a grown man now. On my own. I really need to stop letting that kind of crap bother me. "Hot tea. Earl Grey if you have it. Extra hot. Plenty of sugar. Hold the milk."

"I'll take an orange juice." Claire shoots me a sideways glance and shifts her plate over to make room.

"What? I was going to ask for a spiced chai."

She rolls her eyes at me.

After our drinks are served and the stewardess is a few rows back, Claire spears a forkful of scrambled eggs. "You're *so* particular."

"Yet you still love me." I plant a kiss on her cheek, then blow a puff of air into her ear.

Giggling, she jerks her shoulder up and leans away. "I do. God knows why. You're a cat-loving, meat-loathing botanist — and there's irony there, if you think about it — who'd rather spend his Saturday afternoon snorting paper dust at the university library, than go dancing with me."

"That's not true." I tap a finger on her tray edge. "We danced at our wedding, remember?"

"Oh … yeah."

"Sorry about your toe."

"You didn't break anything. It was just a bad bruise. But the cake —"

"My fault for stepping on your foot. Besides, the icing matched your dress perfectly."

"I promise never to ask you to do the chicken dance again." She kisses the tip of my nose, smiling. "But you'll still slow dance to Sinatra with me, right?"

"Every chance I get. Although we never seem to make it past the second song before things …" — I wink at her — "well, you know."

"Why do you think I keep a playlist of him?" She pulls her iPod out of her purse and flips through the icons. But instead of song titles, she's staring at pictures of her dog, Dahlia.

Dahlia is a wicked smart Border Collie who likes to unnerve me by staring at me as if trying to transmit ESP messages while getting hacked off that I can't understand her. What really perturbs me is that Claire can tell the difference between her 'I need to go out' look and her 'Throw the ball, you moron' look. They all look the same to me.

"Oh Ross, do you think Dahlia and Pirate will get along when we get back and you move your things in to my … I mean, *our* house?"

"If they don't, you and I will have to split up." Pirate is the one-eyed cat I found in the dumpster behind the science building four years ago. He was probably ten then and frankly I'm concerned about how he's going to adjust to new surroundings, never mind the dog. I wink at her, but she's not laughing. "I'm kidding. We'll figure it out. So will they. Anyway, this is going to be the most romantic, adventurous honeymoon ever. All your hygienists are seething with envy at this very moment. In a few hours, we'll be landing in Glasgow. I've got it all planned out. By tomorrow afternoon, we'll be on our way through the Highlands. Then, a short ferry ride around the Orkneys. A jaunt or two to some historic sites. I've even booked us a stay in a castle along the coast later."

"Yes, I saw your itinerary. It sounds a little ... exhausting." She arches an eyebrow at me. "Was it necessary to plan it down to the quarter hour, Ross? I mean really, a little spontaneity wouldn't hurt."

"Neither does a little organization. We only have so many days and I want to make the most of them. Remember all those hours I spent on the genealogy site? Well, I've run into some dead ends and I'm hoping this trip fills in some gaps."

My internet contacts had put me in touch with a man named Reverend Murray, who is in charge of the archives in a little village outside of Berwick. I'd traced my roots all the way back to the fourteenth century and a less prominent branch of the house of Sinclair. Given the history of the time, I thought I might learn some interesting facts about my ancestors that I could one day tell our kids about. We still aren't in agreement about the number of kids we'll have — Claire wants two, I want three or four. But we can tackle that detail later. I might change my mind after the first one.

"Look, let's just have fun," I say. "Take it all in. If you feel worn out at any point, let me know and we'll slow down, alter our plans, okay?"

"Now that's why I love you, Ross Lyndon Sinclair. You know when to give in."

She's more forgiving of me than I deserve sometimes. "You couldn't *not* love me."

"You're right." Faking a stern look, she points at me. "And remember I said that. I don't plan on repeating it often in the future." She reaches across the armrest and laces her fingers inside mine, then lays her head on my shoulder, sighing. "Isn't it funny how we were parted and then found each other again later, totally by accident? Almost like we were meant to be together."

I squeeze her hand and turn my face toward her, my lips brushing her hairline. "Yeah, what are the odds?"

After we finish eating and the flight attendants collect our trash, the speakers crackle and the captain's voice emanates from all around us: "Ladies and gentlemen, we're now beginning our descent towards Glasgow. Today's forecast is a warm twenty-seven degrees Celsius here on this sunny July day. Or for those of you from the west side of the pond, shorts and sandals weather. You know the routine: trays up, power down your electronic devices, and strap yourselves in."

Claire bristles with excitement like a five-year old seeing Main Street in Disney World for the first time. "It's really happening, isn't it? We're almost there."

"Yeah, babe. Almost there. The beginning of the rest of our forever."

3

HERE & NOW

Glasgow, Scotland — 2013

BY THE TIME WE land in Glasgow, it's late morning and we're both charged with adrenalin. The jet lag will hit us later. Like all the other impatient travelers, we rush to the baggage carousel only to stand around for twenty minutes watching the conveyor belt spit out somebody else's black bags. Finally, the neon green shoestrings I'd wound around our luggage handles signals that our wait is over. Claire grabs her pull-along and I collect the other three — two of them hers. No matter which way I arrange them, I'm weighed down unevenly on one side. I scan for a cart, but they're all taken.

Somehow, we straggle to the curb, me working up a sweat and her clipping along at a brisk pace. Claire hails a taxi, and I heave the bags in the car with a grunt of relief. Apparently, when I suggested that she pack light, I neglected to define what that meant.

"Holiday Inn Express, Riverside," I tell the driver.

He peers at me through the rearview mirror, his bushy black

eyebrows rising up to meet the brim if his tweed cap. "You must be American."

It's a statement, not a question. I'm not sure whether or not I should be offended. Before I've even leaned back in my seat, the driver punches the accelerator and the car jerks forward.

By the time we step out of the taxi, my breakfast is one brake-slam away from decorating the vinyl upholstery of the backseat. The taxi peels away, leaving a trail of exhaust in its wake. I grab a lamppost to steady myself. Claire grips my arm so tight I wince. "Ow!"

"Do you think he was trying to kill us?" She lets go of my arm and extends the handle on her pull-along.

My glasses have so many fingerprints on them from trying to keep them from sliding off my face whenever he took those wild turns that I fold them up and slip them in my pocket. As long as I don't have to read any road signs or fine print, I'll be okay until I have time to clean them. "I think he figured that a couple of tight-fisted Americans weren't going to tip him much anyway, so he might as well set a land speed record and get back to the terminal for more passengers."

"We're taking the train from now on, right?"

"Right."

AFTER CHECKING IN AND taking a quick shower, we head out to look for lunch. With Claire's arm hooked around mine, we wander down Argyle Street. We cross a few busy streets and turn too many corners to count. Claire calls out the landmarks to help her remember the way back, while I clutch a photocopied map and trace our path with a pen so we won't end up completely lost. All the while I keep thinking there's probably an app for getting around Glasgow. For now, it's fun going wherever our feet lead us.

By 2:00, I'm starting to feel my blood sugar level drop. We stagger around a corner and are confronted by a congested street lined with narrow shops and international take-away.

"There!" She points at a doorway with a little sign swinging over the street that says: 'Jeet, Good Indian Cuisine.'

"Just 'good'?" I quip. "Why not hold out for 'great' or 'excellent'?"

"Do you want to eat or not?"

She spins on her size five ballet flats. I grab her hand before she can disappear into the press of Glaswegians and hang on for the mad dash.

We duck through the doorway and nearly plow into the back of a wide-shouldered man in stained coveralls reeking of engine oil. He wheels around, and I snatch Claire's arm to hold her back, expecting a scowl and a terse reminder to heed his personal space.

Instead, he flashes a gap-toothed smile at us. "You should blow in at a proper mealtime. Line goes out the door and around the corner."

"So we've come to the right place?" Claire stands on tiptoe to get a clearer view of the menu posted on the wall. The man in coveralls shoves a beefy arm between the patrons ahead of him and pulls a smaller printed version of the menu from beside the cash register.

"'Ere y'go." He thrusts the rectangle of paper at Claire. "Bit spicy for me, but the wife likes it."

Unfortunately, there are only four stools and one small counter in the place and those are filled with what look like college students. I need to sit down and soon, before I fall over. My stomach rumbles every time someone drifts past with a paper bag filled with takeaway. I can smell the spices through the containers. After we get our food, we take our little paper boxes and a couple of Cokes and make our way to George Square. It's evidently a gathering place for indolent students, young mothers pushing prams and business people needing a break from their cubicles, although half of them are texting away on their smartphones.

"Look at those two, would you?" I poke Claire in her ticklish spot, at the base of her lower back.

She flinches, then smacks me on the arm so hard it stings. "What? Who?"

Canting my head to the left, I smirk at the teenagers making out on the park bench: the girl with pink hair sitting on the boy's lap, her tight-fitting miniskirt inching up as she scoots herself up over his groin. They're all over each other, hands roaming, tongues rammed down each others' throats.

"Where are the cops, anyway?"

"Oh come on, Ross. Are you that big a prude? Just a couple of teenagers doing what comes naturally." Stopping in front of me, she gives my butt a suggestive squeeze. "They'll probably be doing the same thing later on that we'll be doing."

"They can't be more than sixteen."

"Yeah, well, I was sixteen when —"

"Claire, don't." I stop her before she can spill the details. I don't want to be reminded that I wasn't her first, even though she was mine. In fact, she's the *only* woman I've ever been with.

"I was going to say I had urges, Ross. That's all. I wasn't going to elaborate on it. Certainly not name names."

"Oh. Really?"

"Yeah, really."

"Look, I'm sorry. I just want you to myself. I always have." Shoving my hands in my pockets, I scuff my shoes over the concrete. Then I let my gaze sweep over her body in a much more grown-up, suggestive way. "I want to be next to you, kiss you all over, touch you in places no one but me knows of, make love to you all night long, first thing in the morning, halfway through the afternoon, in your dentist's chair, behind my lectern. I'd rather do you than eat, drink, or sleep."

Crossing her arms, she cocks her head at me. "Is that the only reason you married me?"

"No, I married you because I can't think of being with anyone else, ever. I married you because you're my reason for being. I married you because when I saw you again, after all those years, I knew what true love was. And I knew what 'forever' meant."

Her stance softens. Playfully, she presses a fingertip against my sternum. "How can I stay mad at you when you talk to me like that?"

Our lips meet in a kiss as she raises herself on tiptoes. I draw her against me and she tilts her hips, pressing them against mine.

"I can't wait until we're alone," she whispers, her tongue flicking over my teeth playfully. "And I don't care who sees us right now or what they think."

I moan at the promise, my kisses growing more passionate.

Suddenly, a big claw slams squarely into my back, crushing the air out of me. Claire and I topple to the ground. A long, slobbery tongue scrapes against my cheek, leaving a trail of slime.

"Sorry, sorry!" A middle-aged woman wearing a red jogging suit jerks at the leash to rein her leggy mutt in. Reluctantly, the playful Great Dane lopes away beside her, nudging her sideways with its oversized muzzle.

Had I not realized how ridiculous I looked, sprawled out there on the cement with dog drool dripping down the side of my face, I might be mad at Claire for laughing so hard. Instinctively, I check for my glasses. They're still there, although slightly askew. I finger the frames to make sure they're not bent.

The two teenagers are gawking at us, now. Claire is still laughing. I scowl at her, but notice she's holding up the plastic bag with our lunch inside it.

"Look, I saved it." She wipes at my face with a stiff paper

napkin, then helps me to my feet. "There's a good spot over there."

We squat at the base of Sir Walter Scott's imposingly tall statue and are immediately surrounded by a mob of pigeons, cooing and strutting in a tightening circle.

"Here? Are you sure? I don't like how they're looking at us, Claire."

"Who?" She scoops a pile of rice into each of our meals and digs in. It always amazes me how she can wolf down more calories than I can, even though I'm a good fifty pounds more. The woman has the metabolism of a hummingbird on diet pills.

I point with my plastic spoon and whisper, *"Them."*

She stops in mid-chew, swallows. "Birds? Oh my God. You're serious, aren't you?"

"Just look at them." I wave my spoon back and forth, thinking they'll take it as the threat I intend it to be. Instead, four more glossy-feathered gangsters land nearby and the level of cooing rises to a din that drowns out the Maroon 5 song from the iPod of the chick nearest us who's sporting three nose rings and a neon blue Mohawk. "It's like they're conspiring. Waiting for the right moment to —"

A sticky lump of rice mixed with saag paneer smacks me in the temple, slides down my cheek and drips onto my shirt collar. Claire grins wickedly, one hand gripping the handle of her spoon and the fingers of the other one cranking the business end back with a fresh load of ammunition. "There's more where that came from if you don't stuff that overactive, paranoid imagination of yours."

I crane my neck toward her to give her a peck on the cheek, signaling my submission. Just as my lips brush her face, the flap of wings startles us and we gasp in unison. A pigeon dives in and gobbles up the rice.

"See," I say. "Told you they had a plan, didn't I?"

Leaning our foreheads together, we laugh until our stomachs ache and our eyes swim with tears. If anyone is watching us, wondering if we're deliriously drunk or just plain mad, we don't give a rat's fanny.

Fifteen minutes later, too stuffed to move, we recline against the base of the statue, fingers woven together, comfortable in our silence. An old couple now shares the bench that had belonged to the teenagers, who scurried off with worried looks after the girl got a cell phone call — probably one of her parents asking her where the hell she's been. The old man still has a full head of steel gray hair, but judging by the many lines in his face and the liver spotted skin, he has to be in his mid eighties. Beside his wife rests a polished ebony cane, the end carved into the figure of a swan so that the neck serves as the handle. She lays her head against his shoulder and puts her hand in his. They talk for a long time, laughing at one another's jokes, each taking a sincere interest in what the other has to say. Whenever they fall silent, there is always a look of serene contentment on both their weathered faces.

"Sixty years from now," I say wistfully, "I want that to be us, Claire."

"Why do you say that?"

"Because they're happy just being together. My parents … they were never happy."

"I don't think that was your mom's fault."

"Me either. But I feel like I'll live my whole life trying to make you happy, just because of all the fighting I saw growing up."

"Ross, don't worry. You don't have to prove anything. You're nothing like your dad."

"I hope you're right. I mean, I know you are. But that old couple there, they deserve to be together for a long, long time. As much as I miss my mom, maybe it was a tiny blessing that she died when she did. Looking back, I can't understand why she didn't just leave him. Maybe she could have had a few happy years, if she had."

"Maybe she saw something in him no one else does? Maybe he

used to be different?"

"Yeah, well, life is full of 'maybes'. I can only work with the facts and the fact is he's a jerk, to put it mildly."

The old couple bends forward to go, but the woman struggles to stand. Her husband gets up, his back hunched, and gives her his forearm. When she's steady, he helps her shift her weight to the cane, then moves to her side. It must take them ten minutes to move from their bench to the sidewalk and begin down the street.

"Promise me something, Ross."

"Anything."

"If, for some reason, we don't both make it to that age, promise me you won't mourn me forever. That you'll find someone else to make you happy. I can't stand the thought of you being alone."

"That's a weird request to make on our honeymoon, don't you think?"

"I just want you to be happy, that's all. It's important to me. Promise?"

"Sure, I promise. Same goes for you." I give her a peck on the cheek. "Besides, you're not allowed to die. Ever. I won't allow it."

"Hate to break it to you, honey, but people don't live forever. Love, though ... *Love* never dies."

Our fingers interlace. In that moment, I'm aware of nothing but the sound of her breathing, the heat from her hand and her thigh pressed against mine.

When you love someone with all your heart, the only thing that matters is being with them. You always think that love means forever, but the truth is you don't really know.

Because in the blink of an eye, everything can change.

<u>Western Highlands, Scotland — 2013</u>

THE RUGGED LANDSCAPE OF the Western Highlands races by, stone-capped peaks parting filamentous clouds of ivory. Red shaggy cattle wander in loose clumps through the valleys, while curly-horned sheep cling to higher ground. I rest my cheek against the glass of the train window, my view obscured by the smeared fingerprints of previous passengers. The constant 'thunk-thunk, thunk-thunk' of the wheels on the tracks jars my skull, so I slide down further in my seat and lean my head back. I pull out the printed pages I've been carrying with me and unfold them: copies of the Scottish side of my family tree. I can't lay claim to any royal ancestry, but there are several prominent families on it: Gordon, Graham, Campbell, MacNeil, Sinclair …

While I'm no more than an amateur genealogist — hundreds of ancestors just a few keystrokes away — the idea that some of my forebears played pivotal roles in history is a rush, however vicarious. The past first took on meaning for me when I started sorting through my belongings in preparation for moving in with Claire and pulled out the partial family tree my mom had given me before she died. It only went back to the mid 1700's, but one long weekend later, I had made it four centuries further back. There were plenty of branches that ended abruptly, but naturally I'd taken the most interest in the Sinclairs. Trying to figure out that one piece of the puzzle made me realize I could spend years researching this and never have all the answers.

Beside me, Claire naps contentedly, her navy blue hoodie wadded up and tucked against her shoulder for a pillow. I envy her that ability, being able to sleep anywhere. I stir at every sound, as if I sense some primal need to keep vigil in case of attack.

Through the window, the ruins of a square keep crown a distant crag. One corner of its curtain wall has completely collapsed, making me wonder whether siege engines or time alone ravaged it. People once lived there, far above the surrounding mountains and deeply carved glens, and within its stone embrace they found shelter — from the elements, from their enemies. For awhile, at least.

"Sinclair, Gordon, Campbell, MacNeil ..." Claire sits up and taps the papers, tracing a finger from left to right until she comes to a dead end. "Geesh, 'Unknown' sure shows up a lot, doesn't he? Or she?"

"Hey, babe. I thought you were asleep?"

"Was. But that sunlight was like a crowbar between my eyelids. I think it's the first time we've seen any sun since we got here." She yawns, stretches her legs. Her shins bang against the framework of the seat in front of her and she lets out a tiny 'Ow!' before pulling herself upright. "So, you've been studying that a lot. You aren't going to drag me around to a bunch of grave sites, are you?"

"Of course not."

A look of relief passes over her face. "Good, because they make me sad."

"Just one," I say, which earns me a frown. "But it's a battlefield. And you don't have to go if you don't want to."

"No, I'll go. I can tell it's important to you." She squeezes my forearm. "Anyway, where is this place and when are we going there?"

"Outside Berwick. A site called Halidon Hill. And it won't be until the tail end of our trip. There's a retired Presbyterian pastor out that way who promised to look into some things for me."

"Like what?"

I don't answer immediately. Claire has never shown an interest in genealogy or history before. Normally, she'd switch the subject, so the fact that she's even asked is a shocker.

"Well, there's a William Sinclair here, see?" I point to the name. "It says he was born in 1334, but I can't figure out who his father or mother were. There's another William Sinclair I found, but he died a few years earlier, so he couldn't have been *this* William's father. Maybe he had a brother and that brother named his son after him? It's all so confusing, but I'm curious who these people were."

"So this is why you wanted to come to Scotland, huh? To chase ghosts. Here I thought it was for the romance." She winks at me and I smile back. "What does all this have to do with this Halidon Hill, anyway?"

"I think some of my ancestors may have died there. In fact, I'm sure of it. At any rate, it was a big battle. Huge. Tens of thousands of casualties that day, almost all Scottish. Can you imagine? The entire male line of families wiped out in just a few hours? A lot of people say it didn't have to happen. That it could have been prevented. You see, Berwick was under siege by Edward Balliol, who'd laid claim to the Scottish throne, and the King of England, Edward III. Sir Archibald Douglas, who was the Guardian of Scotland, came to the town's defense, but it was all too little, too late."

Claire mouths an 'Oh'. Her eyes are taking on that same glazed over look I give her whenever she comes home talking about a disgusting case of tooth decay in a Mountain Dew addict. I can't help myself, though. I've spent hundreds of hours online the past year and I find it exhilarating, like a detective following leads in a murder investigation. Luckily for her, Claire is spared further details when the train's velocity begins to slow and a white sign with black lettering speeds by just outside our window: Ft. William.

After a filling dinner and an overnight stop in Fort William — where Claire wears me out by ducking into every shop on High Street — we're off again. A perilous ride on the steam train takes us to Mallaig and from there we hop a ferry to Skye. Our B&B host on the island, a bent-spined lady with a blue bouffant hairdo, raves about the stables near the shore that offer pony trekking.

Claire turns those doe-like brown eyes on me, her lower lip jutting. "Can we?"

"One word: hives."

"Oh yeah, I forgot."

"Just be glad I'm not allergic to dogs."

She wrinkles her nose at me. "If you were, I'd keep the dog and kick you out."

4

NOT SO LONG AGO

<u>Balfour, Indiana — 1996</u>

"*R*oslin!"
    I startle awake, shivering with sweat. Several minutes pass before my heart calms.

Watery sunlight filters through threadbare curtains. Yawning, I stretch my arms, grab my glasses off the nightstand and stare at the bright red numbers on my radio alarm: 7:02 a.m. I kick the sheets off and pad to the bathroom. Five minutes later, I'm dressed in cut-off shorts and a striped polo. It's too hot for shoes. I'd go shirtless if my mom wouldn't screech at me to put a shirt on.

Still barefooted, I sneak down carpeted stairs to the kitchen. Tilting the sugar container, I scoop out three spoonfuls, sprinkling each one over my bowl of Kix cereal. Then, hunching over my breakfast at the table, my mouth pressed to the rim of the bowl, I shovel down the sweet goodness and wait for the jolt of energy to enter my bloodstream.

It doesn't dawn on me until I eat the last spoonful of cereal that my dog Ivanhoe hadn't been asleep beside my bed last night or followed me downstairs. I lower the bowl, peek under the table, and give a low whistle. Silence.

I check the laundry room, the basement, the garage. If Ivanhoe annoys my dad by scratching at fleas or getting underfoot, he's been known to lock the dog up in any of those places and completely forget about him.

There's one more place to look. The moment I step into the backyard, I see Ivanhoe stretched out in the long morning shade of the boxelder. Mom must have let him out in the yard earlier, as she sometimes does. I call his name, but Ivanhoe doesn't stir.

"Geesh, you are getting old, boy. Can't hear a thing, can you?" I jog across the yard, dew soaking my feet. "Come on, boy. Maybe Claire will want to go to the pond with us and you can chase the ducks like you always —"

I reach out to shake him, then jerk my hand back. Ivanhoe's orange-freckled legs are rigid, his swollen tongue protruding from between a jumble of yellowed teeth.

"No," I whisper as I shake my head. "No, no, no." Twining my fingers in the tassels of hair that cover his floppy spaniel ears, I sink to my knees and bend forward until my forehead touches his furry topskull. I try to swallow the lump in my throat, but a fountain of grief bursts from deep in my belly and I begin to sob. Great, heaving sobs that rack my whole body and rise in a long, pitiful wail.

"Ross!" my dad bellows from the kitchen window. "What the hell are you doing? I don't need the cops showing up here because you were raising a ruckus at 7:30 in the Goddamn morning."

"It's Ivanhoe," I blubber.

"What?"

I drag a forearm across tear-soaked eyes. "He's dead. Ivanhoe's dead."

He scoffs. "It's a dog, Ross. They don't live forever."

With that, he slams the window closed.

"But he's my friend," I whisper, my hand now resting on Ivanhoe's back. "I love him."

For a long time, I stroke and stroke and stroke, as if I can somehow revive him. But he remains still, his body losing warmth, his legs growing stiffer by the minute.

My dog, my buddy, had been alive longer than I had. He had always been there throughout all of my twelve years. I think of all the days we'd spent together — his short legs spinning over gravel roads as he trailed after me when I rode my bike out toward the hidden pond. There, beyond the railroad yard, I battled imaginary dragons with a trash can lid as my shield and a rusty piece of rebar as my sword. Ivanhoe was my faithful squire, ready to alert me to danger with an excited bark if a stray cat wandered near or lick my face clean if I stumbled while clambering up the sand hill. Before we returned to the house, I would always pick the burrs from his hair. As he got older, I'd walk my bike home while he lagged behind, his steps unsteady, his breaths coming heavily. Eventually, I had to put him in my Radio Flyer wagon, the bottom lined with an old blanket, and pull him behind me.

"Ross?"

It's Claire. She comes through the gate and squats beside me.

"I'm sorry. Really sorry. I'll miss him, too." She bends down and kisses his muzzle. "He was the best dog ever. Nobody could ever take his place."

For a long while we sit with him, neither of us saying a word as the neighborhood stirs to life on that lazy summer morning. A car with a noisy muffler rumbles by. The Bradford twins from across the street squeal with glee as they roller skate down the sidewalk. Somewhere, the deep 'woof, woof' of a German Shepherd guarding his territory booms.

"We should bury him," I say.

"How about here — under the tree? You could come out and talk to him whenever you wanted that way."

I contemplate it. Mom won't care. But Dad ...

"By the pond," I say. "He'd like it there."

Even though I've made the decision, I remain where I am. Any minute, I'm sure he'll wake up, yawn, and gaze at me with those cloudy eyes. I'm not ready to say goodbye. Not yet. Certainly not forever.

I meet Claire's eyes. She understands.

"Here." She lays both hands across Ivanhoe's ribs. "Do like this. We'll help him pass over. Do you want me to say the blessing?"

I nod and she closes her eyes, so I do the same. She says a bunch of words I don't understand, sometimes pausing as she struggles with how to say them.

When she's done, I fetch the wagon and she helps me put him in it.

"What language was that?" I say.

"Latin," she answers. "I'm not sure if anyone speaks it anymore, but the priest at my church is the only one I know who uses it. I think it was the right thing to say."

Claire's family is Catholic. My dad says if her parents were good Catholics, they'd have more kids than just her and her brother. I never really understood that and always meant to ask him if we weren't good Lutherans then, because there was only me.

"I know this won't make it hurt less," she goes on, "but when

my grandpa died I asked my grandma if she was sad. She said what made it easier was knowing she'd see him again someday. She didn't know when or where, but she was sure of it."

"In heaven, you mean?"

"In her next life." She wrinkles her nose. "Crazy, I know."

Maybe, but I'd like to believe it's true.

5

HERE AND NOW

Orkney Islands, Scotland — 2013

T HE FERRY RIDE ACROSS the tranquil, steely waters of Pertland
Firth is both soothing and eerie. A thick mist had drifted around
us soon after our departure at sunrise from John O' Groats at the
northernmost tip of Caithness — although 'sunrise' in this case is a
figurative term, since the sun has yet to make an appearance. We'd
had to get up at, as Claire liked to call it, O-dark-hundred just to
catch the bus from Inverness for our day trip to the Orkneys. The
steady churning of the water behind the boat, the chug of its engine
and the pea soup fog give a very surreal feel to our adventure, as if
we're slipping into some long ago time.

Claire is asleep, her head resting against my arm, pressing on a
nerve there. The numbness is spreading downward from my
shoulder, so I shift, but the guy next to me is dozing soundly, too,
and I don't want to be responsible for waking both of them up. So I
suffer, trapped between them, until I can't feel my fingers anymore.

Occasionally, gulls cut through the veil of drizzle to buzz our intrepid little craft, but upon discovering it's not a fishing boat and there's no lunch to be had, they flap away into the sea's breath, squawking their complaints. Soon, the low hum of the engine and monotonous slapping of the waves against the hull lull me, too, to sleep.

A BELL CLANGS TO my left, startling me awake. Our meager crew springs to life, tramping over the deck and unraveling ropes as thick as their arms. The ferry drifts on black water toward the dock, the fog parting to reveal a canopied welcoming area. Beyond it, I can see a small, touristy village, its main street lined with the requisite eating establishments, a post office, and a chemist. The side roads are lined with stone houses with white-paned windows. Even in the glum light of a cloud-laden day, their black slate roofs glisten with dampness.

After rousing Claire, who immediately exclaims her hunger, we chow down at the pub closest to the dock and then dash through the shops. Soon, we're on our way again, the little ferry boat putt-putting along, the skies finally beginning to clear at noon. To the east, dark waters stretch endlessly beneath a blue dome of sky. Our path begins to curve westward, where the isle they call Mainland rises. Colonies of terns dot the shoreline. Seals with their mottled pale brown coats are sunning themselves on the rocks. They stretch their whiskered noses and bellow at our passing. Every time a clump of seals appears, Claire rushes to snap pictures. There will be hundreds to sort through when this trip is over.

After disembarking at Kirkwall, we're directed to a gathering tour group. As the guide circulates through the crowd to collect her fee, I pull out my wallet.

Claire flaps a map at me. "Let's go off on our own, okay?"

I finger the brightly colored bills. "Hmm, I don't know, honey.

I'd hate to get lost and end up missing the boat back to the mainland. Our luggage is still in Inverness."

Sighing, she turns pleading eyes on me. "Ross, we've been surrounded by people since we got on the first train. I've been forced to converse with more retired Floridians than I ever met at home in the States. I just want to be alone with you for awhile." Her lower lip juts out. "Pleeease?"

The tour guide halts in front of us, wiggling her fingers. "Coming along?"

"Not today, thanks." I stuff the bills away and slip my wallet into my back pocket before offering Claire my elbow. "You lead the way."

EXHAUST FUMES SPEW FROM the tailpipe of a sputtering green tour bus parked on a side road. We squeeze between it and a low stone wall topped with wrought iron, but are waylaid by a stream of tall, fair-haired women chattering excitedly in either Swedish or Norwegian. They congregate next to a gate, where an English-speaking guide with a thick Scottish accent welcomes them and waves them through.

I start to follow, but Claire clamps a hand on my forearm and shakes her head.

"Can we at least go around the corner?" I say. "The fumes are making me sick. I don't think you want me to hurl right here next to a church in front of all these nice people."

We slip past the last of the tourist group and swing around the corner. Her finger glued to the map, Claire stops dead, then glances up at the front of the church.

"This is it? St. Magnus Cathedral? I'm ..." — her nose twitches — "underwhelmed."

I pluck the map from her hands and flip it over to the brochure side. "Says here that construction was begun in 1137 A.D. How can you be underwhelmed? Nearly nine hundred years old and it's still standing."

"I just meant that it's so plain for a cathedral. I guess I was expecting something more like Notre-Dame."

"Believe it or not, they were begun at roughly the same time, but Notre-Dame was designed with higher, thinner walls, which completely changes the look. The flaw in that was that its architectural limits were stretched and cracks developed, so they added the flying buttresses later out of necessity. When you consider that, St. Magnus here was actually the more practical structure and —"

Her extended sigh tells me I'm overloading her with information. Yet how can she not find details like that fascinating? When we were kids, I was the one rushing home to my encyclopedia set to identify the water beetles we'd seen skimming across the pond; she was the one who'd lie back in the grass, stare at the clouds as they whisked overhead and tell me to stop worrying about whether they were stratus or cumulus, to just enjoy the fact that it wasn't raining. Even as different as we are, we complement each other perfectly.

Still, I can't help but marvel at the sight before me. It's a wonder they had the means to build structures like this in a time before there were power tools and heavy equipment.

Rough sandstone blocks reflect sunlight in bands of pink and amber. Although a fairly large structure, it's true what she said — there isn't much fancy about it. No spindly buttresses, intricate spires or armies of perched gargoyles adorning its exterior.

I grab her hand and pull her up the stone steps. "Let's see what's inside."

One of the massive doors is propped open, letting the faint sea breeze waft in. We stand at the threshold, dazzled by the sunshine streaming through high windows. Light spills across the tiled floor in alternating stripes of gold and shadow. Two long rows of tall, thick columns flank a central aisle where row upon row of wooden chairs face the far away altar. There, a stained glass window soars, its uppermost panes forming a rosette. The lower section of the great window is a quartet of pointed arches, each containing various stone-carved religious figures in their robes and short tunics.

From a hidden recess comes the brogue of the Scandinavian group's tour guide, followed by gentle murmurs and the ringing of many feet padding across the tiles. I try to listen to the guide, but her words are too muffled to make them out.

"You see, this is when I wish we'd gone on the tour, Claire. I could've asked who those statues —" Suddenly, I realize I'm talking to myself. I've spent so long gazing at the towering arches and bulging columns and marveling at the rainbow of colors emanating from the stained glass that I didn't notice Claire drifting down the aisle. Halfway to the altar I catch up with her. Her steps quicken.

Abruptly, she stops in front of the altar to gaze at the trio of carved wooden statues behind it and then up at the angels and saints etched on the glass. After several minutes of her standing there in a dazed stupor, I tap her on the arm.

Flinching, she whips her head sideways and looks at me for a second as if she doesn't recognize me.

"What is it?" I say.

She shakes her head. "Nothing. Just a weird feeling. Like I've been here before."

"Yeah, well, we're going to be here for a long time if we don't scoot. We have less than ten minutes to get back to the ferry."

Her gaze drifts upward again to take in the vaulted ceiling and pointed arches between the columns. I hook a hand around her elbow and tug her toward the door, as I remind her that if we don't make it back in time for the ferry's departure, our whole schedule will be blown to smithereens.

TO MY AMAZEMENT, CLAIRE stays awake the entire rest of the day. Our whirlwind tour takes us to the Standing Stones o' Stenness, where massive upright slabs ring a wind-scoured patch of grass, and to the ruins of Skara Brae, where primitive people once dwelt in earthen mounds whose interior walls are lined with stone slabs. I loiter to inspect the tiny alpine flowers along the footpath and the golden and sage-colored lichens encrusting the scattered stones. Even on the monotonous bus ride back to Inverness, Claire remains atypically silent, gazing out the window to where the sea batters the shore, just as it has for millions of years.

Whatever is on her mind, she isn't going to share voluntarily. I'll have to drag it out of her.

"How're you doing, sweetie?" I pass her a bottled water from the snack tray the guide is toting down the aisle. "You've been, I don't know, quiet? Are you tired?"

"Not really. Just a little ear ache, maybe. I think that cold wind was blowing in my ear this morning. My head hurt a little earlier, too, but it's better now. Don't worry about it."

"You're positive?"

"Yeah, I'm fine, really."

"Something on your mind?" Truth be told, I'm afraid *I* have done something wrong — which is entirely possible. I've learned it's better to get these things out in the open at the first hint, grovel profusely and move on.

"Do you believe we have souls?"

"Whoa," I say. "That was out of left field. Why do you ask?"

"I can't explain it. Something about being at that old church in Kirkwall. It was like I could sense the people who had been there before."

"It's a big tourist draw, I imagine. At least in Orkney terms."

"No, I mean people from a long time ago and, well, it made me wonder if when we die, we really do just turn to dust, or if our energy ... our souls, somehow carry on or come back or ... I don't know. It just doesn't seem like when our hearts stop beating that we're really gone, for good."

I gaze out the window at the darkening sky. On the horizon's silhouette, a scattering of lights outlines the perimeter of a town just off the motorway. "I'd like to think we get a chance to live again and get things right that we screwed up before."

What I don't tell her is that I believe I've lived before. Hell, I've never told anybody about my dreams, or memories, whatever they are. For all I know, I just had an active imagination as a child.

And that's why I have to go to Berwick. To see Halidon Hill. Because once I stand on that ground, I'm sure I'll know.

6

NOT SO LONG AGO

Balfour, Indiana — 1994

I skid to a halt on the green-flecked kitchen linoleum. Ivanhoe, an unkempt mop of orange and white tangles, scoots out of the way with a yelp. An old dog with a pot belly and a fear of cats that makes him tremble uncontrollably whenever he sees one, next to Claire he's my best friend — and my trusty squire. Although his sight is dim and his hearing nearly gone, he trails after me constantly and sleeps by my bed at night, faithfully keeping the closet monsters at bay. Yesterday was his twelfth birthday — or so we guess, because we don't really know. I'd chosen a date one month after my own birthday (I turned ten myself last month) and every year I celebrate by giving him a wedge of Velveeta between two slices of Wonder Bread. The tradition started when he stole my cheese sandwich off the coffee table once and ran away with it. So I figured he really liked cheese sandwiches, because the prize *was worth the scolding he got.*

I bend over and scratch the mutt behind his worn leather collar, which sends his leg thumping.

"Cut it out," Dad snaps.

Pulling my hand back, I straighten and clench my baseball bat before me. "I am Sir Ross, the king's champion!"

I mean it, literally, although I'm not sure which king I'm talking about.

Mom snorts coffee onto her good buttercup yellow blouse and laughs like it's the cutest thing she's ever heard. "Aren't you simply darling?"

Scoffing, my dad flicks open his Bic lighter and torches up a Marlboro.

"Get over yourself, boy." He sucks in a lung-filling drag. The end of his cigarette glows orange. Eyeing me cynically above black-rimmed bifocals, he exhales a cloud of smoke and taps gray ashes into the empty saucer beside his coffee cup. "You ain't that important. Just a dumb nobody like the rest of us."

"Jack," my mother chides, "he's a child. He has an active imagination."

"He's making shit up, that's what he's doing."

I shrink beneath my cloak and it slips sideways with the slump of my shoulders. Well, it's not really a cloak. More like a blue satin jacket that I'd claimed from the depths of the hall closet. I tug it back into place. The sleeves are tied loosely around my neck, a gaudy piece of Grandma Gordon's old costume jewelry pinned in the middle to keep the ends together. On my head sits a scuffed batting helmet — no visor, but at least it will protect my scalp from arrows. A pair of old gardening gloves which reek of insect dust serve as my gauntlets. Defeated, I lower my arm and schlep off, dragging the bat behind me.

Furry paws scrabble after me as I head out the back door. Crumpling on the stoop, I tear off my cloak and fling it behind the forsythia bushes next to the garage.

"Just a dumb nobody," I repeat. A sob wells up in my throat and threatens to tear loose, but I swallow it back, determined to be strong. They're just words, anyway. What is it Mom used to tell me? Nobody can make you feel bad unless you let them. It makes sense, but it doesn't seem to work that way.

Ivanhoe nuzzles my hand until I reward him with a pat on the head. The dog sneezes twice and curls his body around to squirm beneath my arm. His brown nose quivers as he sniffs at the sword... the bat, really. I pick it up and hold it straight out before me. Make-believe, that's all it is.

An ache begins to spread from my right shoulder down to my elbow. That arm has been weak ever since the accident with the swing set.

The bat grows heavier in my hand. I flick my wrist, trying to let go of it, but the handle is molded to my palm as if it's Super Glued there. My vision blurs, clears, and then blurs again. With my left hand, I rub at my eyeballs, but as I do so, the handle wobbles in my palm. My arm dips as if being pulled downward. Clutching tighter, I dare a look. No, it isn't my eyesight that's blurring, it's the ... whatever it is I'm holding.

The longer I stare at it, the more it changes in shape and the more defined it appears. The grip becomes a hilt, bound in worn leather. At its bottom is a round knob decorated with red-eyed snakes of gold. Above my knuckles, a curved crosspiece flares. The column of wood is gone, replaced by a shining length of metal: an iron blade. Midmorning sun flashes off the sword. The edges are nicked in a few places, but the blade is freshly polished.

A rumble of voices fills the air. Standing, I look up and see, not my backyard, but a valley, bigger than even the soccer field complex at Eldred Yoder Community Park. Gone are the silver maples and privet hedges of my neighborhood and all the brick ranch houses of suburban Balfour. Instead, broad hills ring a low-lying expanse. A wind, warm and heavy, ripples over a sea of grass that stretches from horizon to horizon. In the distance, a city enclosed by high walls stands beside a broad river.

Crowning one of the hills, a jagged line of spearheads points heavenward. Sunlight captures distant flashes of metal: helmets, swords, axes. Behind the spearmen, armored knights sit upon impatient mounts. Banners of gold, green, azure and scarlet flutter in the breeze.

To the front, the most terrifying sight of all: archers. Each has an arrow nestled to the string. As if they're one, they all raise their bows, seeking their marks, and wait. Arms cock back. Then a command, the word indistinguishable above the buffeting wind, emanates from somewhere in their midst.

Fingers twitch. Slashes of black cut across the sky: silent, deadly, sure.

Below the rain of arrows, an army plunges into the valley, oblivious to its fate.

I close my eyes and plop my bottom down on the stoop, slapping my left palm against the cool surface of the cement steps.

No, this isn't my imagination. Can't be. If it is, I'm already going crazy and I'm too damn young for that. Darn, I mean. Mom says I'm not supposed to cuss, even though my dad does it all the time.

I grip my right hand tighter, raise my arm. Feel the weight of the sword in my grasp. My right shoulder throbs, the pain burning so intensely I can hardly bear it. I let my arm drop to my side. Why aren't I riding with them?

My ears are filled with the roar of battle cries as soldiers rush into the gaping valley. The hiss of feathered shafts. The howls of the dying as arrows rip through flesh. The deafening clang of metal as the survivors collide with the enemy's front lines.

The smells that fill my nose make me want to puke. It's the scent of iron. And blood.

"Sir Ross," comes a voice, sweet and light as cotton candy, "what are you waiting for? You were s'pposed to come over an hour ago."

Nearly tumbling forward, my eyes fly open. I flip the sword behind the closest bush and look around. Claire Elaine Forbes sits astride a bough of the boxelder tree, looking down on me from the other side of the leaning picket fence.

Damn, she's pretty.

7

HERE & NOW

Inverness, Scotland — 2013

MY PLAN WAS TO stick to trains and buses for the rest of our trip, but Claire can't stand the slight swaying motion of the trains and bus fumes make me nauseous. So we rent our own car in Inverness with the understanding that for a drop-off fee we can return it to the airport at Glasgow. That totally busts our budget for a castle stay, but there's no sense in either of us being miserable on our honeymoon. After signing away the inheritance of our firstborn, we march out to the parking lot with our keys.

I pop open the trunk and toss our bags inside. Before I pull open the door handle, Claire clears her throat.

"So you're driving the whole way, right?" she says.

"It's a stick shift, so yes, I am. You never learned how, remember?"

"And they drive on the other side of the road, correct?"

"Well, yes." I wait for more questions, but she simply stands there wearing a little smirk of amusement. Fine, I'll show her how it's done. I yank open the door and slide into the seat. *Crap.* The steering wheel is on the other side. And the gear shift ... is left-handed. You'd think I'd have caught on to that by now.

Claire bursts out laughing. With as much dignity as I can muster, I get out, go to the other side and get back in.

The engine hums as I turn the key in the ignition.

She hops in the passenger seat. "Are you sure you don't want to go back and get an automatic?"

"I asked. They were all out. We're stuck — unless you want to take another train?"

"Not a chance." Claire clicks her seatbelt. "Tally ho!"

Highlands, Scotland — 2013

WE CUT ACROSS THE teeth of the desolate Grampian Mountains — a landscape so rugged and sparsely inhabited, it sometimes feels more like we're on the moon than somewhere in the British Isles. After a harrowing near-miss with a Bentley when we crest one of the narrow, winding roads, I pull off to the side and get out. My knuckles are white from gripping the shifter and my shoulders are so tense it would take one hell of a massage to unknot me.

The first thing I notice is the wind. I hadn't been prepared for the drop in temperature since we'd started our drive three hours earlier.

"Recovering?" Pulling her sweatshirt on, Claire leans against the hood of our car. "Or taking in the view?"

"Both." I curl an arm around her and go to kiss her, but her mouth is firmly closed. She's chewing something.

"Crisps?"

"Huh?"

She crinkles a foil bag between us. "Potato chips."

I dig my fingers in and pull out the last two, then pop them in my mouth. "Is that all?"

"Sorry, I was starving. All this globe trekking is making me hungry lately. How far to the next town?"

The road goes on as far as I can see, a black ribbon twisting over stony mountains bare of trees. Granite crags embrace purple swaths of heather and feathery clouds whisk across a crystalline sky. Thank goodness I've brought a map along, because the GPS doesn't work out here. "Hours."

"Oh. Then I'm really sorry, because I ate yours, too."

She's not, but it's hardly worth arguing about. "We'll have to skip the castle stay."

"It's all right, Ross. We've seen so many already I think I'm having castle-saturation. So what's next?"

"Balmoral. We can take a long walk in the gardens, stretch our legs a bit."

"Do you think we'll see the Queen?"

"Absolutely. I sent her our itinerary well ahead of time so she could clear her schedule."

"Good. I hope Prince William tags along. I'm still mad he hooked up with Kate." She winks at me. Prince William is her royal celebrity crush. "And after that?"

"The Drumtochty Highland Games. Sword dancing, caber tossing, kilted pipers. Plenty of photo opps. After that, I want to swing by Berwick to speak with that retired cleric about my family tree. Then we have a day and a half to shop in Edinburgh before heading back to the airport in Glasgow."

"Fabulous!"

"I knew you'd think so." I retrieve two water bottles from the car and hand her one. "So, are you having fun? I mean, given the rigorous schedule I planned out and everything?"

She hugs me tight. "It's perfect, Ross. You're here. I'm here. I'll never forget a day of this trip. It couldn't be more perfect."

"It just got more perfect."

"Huh?"

I point to a place halfway up the mountain closest to us. There, next to a narrow rock-strewn stream, is the biggest red stag I've ever seen. I can't count the number of prongs to his antlers from here, they're so many. He dips his great rack as he drinks from the water, then lifts his head to stare at us with sorrowful dark eyes. And then, it gets even more interesting. A doe appears over the rise and joins him. Her hide is a touch redder than his, less brown, but I'm guessing from the dull patches in his fur that he's still shedding his winter coat. They stay like that for a long time — watching us watching them.

Finally, Claire breaks the silence. "I thought the males were solitary."

"Usually they are, but those two look like a pair. Like they've always been together."

"Like us. There's something about this moment. It feels like … like it could go on forever." She tucks her cheek against my chest and murmurs over my heart, "Remember it, Ross. Remember how it feels."

"I will." I hook a finger under her chin and kiss her gently, her breath mingling with mine, our hearts beating in unison. "Believe me, I will."

Near Berwick, Scotland — 2013

SPRAWLING FOR ACRES AND acres, Balmoral Castle is opulent beyond imagination. While standing in the ballroom — which is the only place inside the castle the public is allowed — I remark, "How many rooms does one person really need?"

Meanwhile, Claire spins in a circle, alternately making an ugly face at the stags' heads mounted up high and then ogling the artwork hung on the walls, her mouth open in awe as she utters, "Wow, oh wow, just … wow." I patiently follow her around while she reads the plaques next to the clothing displays. When her hour is up, I drag her outside to visit the gardens. She's exceedingly tolerant of me reciting the Latin names of all the herbs, shrubs and flowers. Afterward, I go to the snack bar for some drinks and return to the bench where I left her. Her eyes are closed, her cheek propped on her fist.

I nudge her shoulder. "Have you recharged yet? I need you to talk to me on the drive so I don't nod off."

If we've missed any culture yet, we soon get our fill at Drumtochty. We park our car in a muddy field and hike to a row of pavilions. Claire gets her shopping fix, while I marvel at the strength of the men balancing tall poles and heaving them end over end. If that isn't enough machismo, as soon as that competition is done, they have a contest tossing a stone weight the size of my head over a bar twenty feet off the ground. I dart off to the little city of tents, hoping to find Claire and whisk her away before she discovers the kilted tough man contests and asks why I don't start lifting weights.

By the time we cross the Forth Bridge and are headed down the A1 past the Lammermuir Hills, we're both exhausted, but it's an exhilarated kind of exhaustion, the kind where you're flying on adrenalin, knowing you're going to sleep like the dead when you finally get home. Miraculously, Claire stays awake by drinking black coffee and her light speed chatter keeps me more than alert.

I pull into a parking lot and kill the engine. Claire's head swivels around.

"Why are we in an empty church parking lot?" she says.

"They call them kirks here. This is where I'm supposed to meet Reverend Murray."

"And who is he again?"

"The gentleman I've been in contact with. He's retired, I think, but he's from the village we just passed, Aberbeg, so he helps take care of this place."

She tips her Styrofoam coffee cup back and taps on the bottom. "All gone." She sets it down in the cup holder. "Okay, so why are you here to see him?"

I take the sheets of paper out of my jacket pocket. "To help me with this. Look, why don't you just sit here and take a nap? I won't be more than half an hour — and if I am, you come in and drag me away by the earlobe, okay?"

"Sure, I'll just inspect the inside of my eyelids while you're jabbering away with someone about dead people. Works for me."

Before she can slather on the guilt trip any thicker, I hop out of the car and look around. The tang of salt air hits my nostrils and I realize we're less than a mile from the shoreline. As I follow the walkway around to the front, I notice one other car parked on the opposite side of the building. The front doors are locked, so I continue around the building until I see a door to the rear. I grab the knob and turn, but it won't give. So I wrap both hands around it and just as I push, someone yanks it open from inside. Letting go, I fall on my butt with an '*umph*'. My glasses fly from my face and land on the walkway. I pick them up and inspect the lenses for cracks. None, thank God. I put them back on and look up.

"Oh dear," mutters the man in the doorway, "I didn't realize anyone was out here."

He's wearing a black cardigan and a black button-up shirt

underneath. On his nose sits a pair of silver wire-rimmed glasses with lenses so thick you could use them like a magnifying glass to start a fire. My vision isn't great, but he must be almost blind.

"Reverend Murray?" Standing, I pound the dust from my pants, then extend my hand. "I'm Ross, Ross Sinclair."

"Mr. Sinclair!" His eyes light up. He returns my handshake with remarkable strength. Although his spine is crooked and his hair white as snow, he's spry and healthy for his age, which has to be something well past eighty. "Do come in."

I scurry to keep up with him, even though he walks with a limp.

"I was expecting you earlier," he says. "I must have written down the wrong time. Typical of me these days."

"You didn't. We were delayed by an accident just south of Edinburgh. I left a message on your phone."

"Oh, that explains it." He flips a switch as he enters an office and the overhead light clicks on, emitting a low hum as it warms up. In the middle of the room sits a very old mahogany desk piled with papers and behind it is a bookcase crammed full that spans the length of the wall. The room smells of old leather and moldy parchment. "That was my home phone number. I should have given you the number for here. I don't have a mobile phone. Never felt the need for one. At any rate, I made use of the time. Have you been to the battle site yet? Seen the castle?"

"Neither. I scheduled that for tomorrow afternoon. Then we have just enough time to visit Edinburgh before leaving."

"We, you say? Is your wife with you? I'll go invite her in."

"Don't worry about it. She's probably asleep in the car by now. I've been wearing her out on this trip." I readjust my glasses. The frame seems twisted. Distracting, but not anything I can't live with until we get home. "Did you find the information you were looking for?"

"Curious thing about that. I did come across some documents

that might help. Then again they might be full of useless information." He rifles through one stack of papers, then another, finally shoving them both aside. "You mentioned there were some discrepancies?"

I spread the paper on his desk and smooth out the wrinkles.

He pushes his glasses further up the bridge of his nose and traces a finger over the names, pausing at each one to impart bits of history. Most of it is irrelevant to the real reason I've come, but I absorb every word like a sponge. His knowledge of the complexities of Scottish history is nothing short of amazing: the unification of the thrones of Scotland and England, the tragic death of Mary, Queen of Scots, John Knox and the Protestant Reformation, James IV and the Battle of Flodden Field ... Two hours later, I realize we still haven't gotten back past 1400.

"Most people remember him for his end, but James IV was quite a forward-thinking man. In fact, alchemy was one of —"

"Excuse me, Reverend Murray, but we got such a late start and I really need to take my wife out for a bite to eat."

"I've been babbling. I do apologize."

"Not at all. I've found it all very fascinating. I'd love to hear more. Would you join us for dinner?"

He checks his watch. "Dear heavens, I hadn't realized the time. I have a ... an appointment. My neighbor is recently widowed and he invited me over this evening to watch some telly. He very much needs the company. Do you have time tomorrow to stop by? Is 10 a.m. all right?"

"I'll be here. Not to press you, but you did find something, right?"

"I believe so, yes. The father of this William Sinclair, here, born in 1334," — he taps on the paper — "I'm quite certain he died at Halidon Hill."

"Then he was born after his father's death."

"That must be."

"But what was his father's name? There was another William Sinclair, but he died in 1330."

"That William may have been a brother, then. There have been a lot of men by the name William Sinclair." He tilts his head in thought. "Now I remember where I left those papers — in plain sight on my hallway bookcase. It's been a hectic day. I'll bring everything tomorrow, I promise. See you then?"

We walk out together and say goodbye. It's almost dusk and the sky is lightening to a pale silvery-purple. The first stars wink faintly in the east. Since the summer days here are so long, I have no idea what time it is. I flip open my phone and upon seeing the time realize the only place we'll be able to grab any food at this hour is at a pub. Reverend Murray is already pulling away in his car when I slide into the driver's side of ours and poke Claire in the ribs.

Her eyelids flap open. "Has it been half an hour already?"

"About that. Let's go find our bed and breakfast. Maybe the owner can point out a cozy pub in the village for a bite to eat? We'll immerse ourselves in the local customs — you know, sample some whiskey and get foolishly wasted."

"Get drunk? That's so unlike you, Ross." She tweaks my nose. "Sounds perfect. Anyways, I'm famished. I wasn't expecting to like Scottish cuisine, but I can't get enough of those scones and shortbread. It's a good thing we're headed home soon. My waistband is getting tight." Puffing her cheeks out, she pats her stomach. "Oh God, Ross, do you think I'm getting fat?"

"The answer to that is *always*: No, you're not." In fact, she couldn't be more perfect.

"You still love me then?"

"I will *always* love you."

"Forever?"

"And ever." I kiss that pouty lip of hers. Her tongue darts out in response and slides between my teeth. I tug at a button on her blouse and hear it pop open. She giggles and wraps her arms around my neck to pull me in closer. If it weren't for the fact that the windows are partway down, we'd be steaming them up right now.

Twisting onto my hip, I lean across the —

"Ow!" I yelp.

"What?"

Pressing a hand to my ribs, I rock back into my seat. "The gear shift. It's in the way."

She starts laughing first. Then me. Five minutes later we mop our tears dry and look at each other, still smiling.

"Let's go get a room," she says.

I turn the key and the motor hums to life.

As LUCK WOULD HAVE it, our car begins to make an odd thumping noise just as we roll into the outskirts of the village. I know the sound. Luckily, Aberbeg has no more than a dozen streets to it. I coast into the driveway beside our B&B, then get out and inspect the tires to see that the rear right one has leaked out nearly all its air.

Claire bounces out and pulls the luggage from the backseat. "What is it?"

"A flat." I pop open the trunk, only to discover there's no spare, not even a donut tire. And here I thought I was going to be so manly. Fixing a tire is the one mechanical thing I do know how to do. Slamming the trunk, I grumble. This is going to put a wrench in my plans. Claire sits on the stack of suitcases, frowning. After digging in the glove compartment, I find the number for the car rental place. I dial it and get a message about the office opening at 7 a.m.

"Just great," I mutter. I should have known everything was going too well.

"What's that?" She's now standing by the side door to the house, a quaint two-story brick Tudor with overflowing flower boxes at all the first floor windows.

"No one there. I'll have to try in the morning."

"Maybe there's a garage in town? Even if we have to foot the bill, I'm sure they'll reimburse us." She inclines her head. "Come on. If we don't eat soon, I'm liable to pass out."

The owner turns out to be a short, middle-aged bachelor named Dermot. I suspect by his accent that he's Irish, but don't ask. He could be Welsh or Manx or Cornish for all I know. I'm not good at telling the difference. He shows us to our room, hands us the key and asks if we need anything else before he retires for the night. When I mention the flat tire, he waves his hand, cutting me short.

"Me cousin owns a garage t'other end of the village. I'll give him a ring first thing in the morning for you."

"Are you sure?" I say. "That would be wonderful if you could."

Claire leans against me, one hand rubbing her stomach. "Could you tell us where we could grab a bite to eat?" she says." We know it's late, but we've had a long day and —"

"To the right, Mrs. Sinclair, seven blocks. Big sign out front: The Finch and the Frog. Can't miss it. Not much of a selection on the menu, but it'll keep you till morning. 'Tis a lovely evening for a stroll."

She smiles, not bothering to correct Dermot about her name. "Come on, Ross. Let's take in some of the local flavor. I'd like a nip or two of the Scotch before we leave."

"May I recommend the Glenfiddich?" Dermot suggests with a wink. "And trust me, you won't stop at a nip."

Hand in hand, Claire and I stroll along curvy streets to the other side of the village. Quaint little shops hug the main road, some with hand painted signs dangling from a metal bar and hooks above the narrow sidewalks. We're hungry, road weary and ready to head home, but the air, tinted with sea breeze, refreshes us.

The side road Dermot directed us to follow crosses the road to the motorway, opening the view to the vista beyond. Miles away, Berwick's lights wink in the darkness. Claire slides her arm around me and tucks her head against my shoulder. We stand like that for minutes, not saying anything.

When we get back to Ohio, it's not the castle ruins and uncluttered scenery of the Highlands I'll remember so much as perfect moments like this. Just Claire and me, together.

8

NOT SO LONG AGO

Balfour, Indiana — 2001

*W*hile most other seventeen-year olds I know are sleeping in on weekends, every Sunday morning at promptly 8:00 a.m., I have to have breakfast on the table for my dad: ham and eggs, a glass of orange juice, no pulp, and a scalding cup of black coffee. The routine never varies. I make the meal, serve it, and sit across from him for fifteen excruciatingly long minutes, just the two of us, neither speaking. Then I clean up while he plods his way through the Sunday paper, occasionally commenting on the war in the Middle East, the capture of a serial killer, the unemployment rate or some other morbid news.

"Geez Louise." He slurps his coffee, then pushes the cup across the table at me. "Gas is over $1.50 a gallon in Chicago already. It's gonna be so damn expensive to fill the tank, we'll be eating pork and beans until the day we die."

I pour his coffee, sit the cup to his left, just like he's always told me to, and stare at him until he looks up.

"You got something to say, boy?"

That's what I am to him nowadays: boy. Not Ross, not even 'son', but 'boy', like I could be anyone's stray kid he came across on the street.

"Josh Thompson took a job at the gas station."

"That so? Why should I care?"

"I asked the manager at the drugstore and he said I could have Josh's hours now, too. That means stocking the shelves on weekend mornings. I have to be there on Saturdays and Sundays at 7:30 in the morning." I'm lying. Mr. Harris, the manager, told me 8:30, but I want to get out of the house before this charade of a family tradition is supposed to begin.

"Whoop-de-doo. Think you're gonna buy a fancy car or something with all that extra cash?"

"I'm going to go to college. I've been saving for over a year now and I figure by —"

He snaps his newspaper open. "One year and you'll be so broke you'll come crawling home, begging for a place to sleep and a job at the machine shop. Meanwhile, I guess we'll be up bright and early on Sundays now, won't we? Things are different here since your mother left us. I expect you to do your share around the house. Remember, I like my ham thick-sliced and my eggs over easy."

I should have kept my mouth shut.

9

HERE & NOW

Near Berwick, Scotland — 2013

URNING OVER, MY RIGHT shoulder throbs with a habitual ache. I try to sit up, to open my eyes, but I flail where I lay, enveloped by darkness.

"*Roslin?*"

The voice is but a whisper, as airy as spider web.

"*Roslin?*"

This time, it's louder, clearer, beckoning me. But where is it coming from?

I inhale again, long and deep, letting air fill my lungs, an assurance that I'm awake and not dreaming. The smell of ham and eggs frying hits me full force. I pry one eyelid open, then the other.

A slat of morning light pierces the dusky room, dust motes sparkling in a haze of suspended diamonds. Before me, a crumpled form writhes beneath the sheets. I curl an arm around Claire's waist and slide closer. She kicks me in the shins with her heels, not hard enough to bruise, but sharp enough to warn me to tread slowly. Claire was never a morning person, but I have plans for today. I'll insist. Politely, of course.

"Morning, Sunshine." Gently, I tuck the knotted mess of her hair behind her ear and nuzzle her neck, sniffing. "Do you smell it? Dermot's serving up breakfast for us. I think that's our signal to roll out of bed and start another glorious day. If you listen, you'll hear the sizzle of ham in an iron skillet. I requested it just for you."

A small groan — or maybe it's a moan, I can never tell with her — thrums at the back of her throat.

I trail light fingertips down her back, then curve my palm over the rise of her hips to pull her snugly against me. Amazing how just her nearness stirs me to desire. Last night had been a wild ride. The walls are probably thin. I'm sure we'll get a grin or two from Dermot this morning. Newlyweds. He'll understand. The more I think about it, the more turned on I become. She must have noticed by now.

She jabs an elbow in my stomach. Guess she did notice.

"I take it you're not in the mood, then?" I say.

"Aw gawd, Ross. I have a terrible, *terrible* headache." Flopping over, Claire clamps her head between her hands and twists her mouth. "Must've been the Glenfiddich. Remind me that as of this morning, I've sworn off drinking."

"Hammered, were you?" I kiss her lightly on the knuckles, then pull the sheets up around her before sliding out of bed myself.

"I had one shot glass. One. I'd forgotten what it did to me."

I slide my jeans on and bend over to dig a fresh T-shirt out of my bag. "I don't know. I kind of like what it did to you. You were so … so … uninhibited. I had no idea you knew how to —"

A pillow whacks me in the back of the head with so much force I topple over. On hands and knees, I slink back to the bed and peer cautiously at her over the edge of the mattress. "What was that for?"

"Just shut up, Ross. You're talking too loud."

"Right."

After I finish dressing, mindful of every sound, I creep to her and say softly, "I'll bring you back something to eat."

She shakes her head once. "No food, no."

"Coffee? Double cream and one sugar?"

"Extra strong."

"Was that a dig at my watered down swill?"

"Shhhh!"

I lower my voice even more. "Aspirin or acetaminophen?"

"Both."

"Back in ten." My glasses are sitting on the bedside table. The frames are definitely bent. Must have happened when Reverend Murray flattened me with the door. I leave them where they are and reach toward the bottom tab on the shades, thinking to let in the daylight, but draw my hand back when she flips the covers over her head. Even with a hangover, she's so damn cute. I want to ravish her several times today, but I think my chances are slim. Still, it's all I can do not to rush back to her and tell her so.

The tumbler in the door lock clunks as I close it behind me. The floorboards in the hallway groan like arthritic old men and the stairs squeak like gerbils at feeding time. This building has to be four hundred years old. I expect to see ghosts around every corner. From the floor below comes the sounds of a cat being tortured — that or it's the murder of "Morning Has Broken" by a tone-deaf leprechaun. As I near the bottom, the odor of pork fat overpowers me. I push two fingers to my lips, trying not to vomit. Usually I'm okay when meat's cooking, but this smell is overpowering. Dermot appears at the landing, humming, a smile as wide as the Firth of Forth on his cherubic face. In one hand, he balances an iron skillet; in the opposite, he waves an oversized fork like a conductor's baton.

"Did me singing wake you?" he chimes in his lilting accent.

"*You* were singing? I thought a chorus of angels had gathered at the front door. I only came down to let them in." I take a quick look outside the front door, then close it. "No one there. Looks like everyone else has already headed out for the day. Just you and me then."

He leads the way into the breakfast nook: four small round tables draped in white linen, each with a centerpiece of freshly plucked daisies. "Will Mrs. Sinclair be along soon?"

"*Ms.* Forbes, actually. Modern woman, you know? We both agreed that Claire Sinclair sounded kind of hokey. But please, just Ross and Claire will do." I sit at the table closest to the window to soak up the morning sunlight. "Anyway, she has a pounding headache. I thought I'd run to the chemist's after this for some medicine."

"No need for that, Mr. ... Ross. First door on your left by the entrance. Just about any remedy you can think of stashed in the cabinet there."

"I'm sorry if you went to the trouble of cooking up something specifically for her. I'm sure she'll be better by tomorrow morning."

"Ah, just a couple of thin slices of ham with an egg on the side." He pats his round stomach. "It won't go to waste. Nearly my lunch time, 'tis. Been up since sunrise. The Pattersons had to be off early to catch a plane. You're here for one more day?"

"Two, actually. Then back to Glasgow and headed home."

Moments later, Dermot places a scone and bowl of fruit and yogurt in front of me, then pours a cup of coffee from a silver pot.

"Tea for me," I say, "but would you mind if I took my wife this cup when I'm done here? I know you probably don't prefer guests to take food and drink back to their rooms, but —"

"No worries! Go right ahead. Will you be relaxing here today or doing a wee bit of sightseeing?"

I glance down at my bare wrist, realizing I've left my watch in the room. "What time is it, Dermot?"

"Half past nine, I reckon."

"Already?"

"Aye, 'tis."

"Damn ... I mean ... I'm going to be late. I forgot our rental car had a flat and I have an appointment at ten o'clock."

"Where at?"

"Oh, I'd say it's no more than five or six kilometers from here. South of Aberbeg. A little kirk called St. Joseph's. I'm meeting a man there named Reverend Murray. Said he might have some information on my genealogy."

"Ah, aye, I know the place. Stone wall about so high" — he holds a level palm to his hip — "covered in ivy? Gravestones all 'round? Giant yew tree out back, looks like it would smash the roof in if a good wind came along?"

"That's right. Said he had an early appointment before that and had to be off for Dunbar for the rest of the day. If I don't catch him at ten, I might not at all." I take a few sips of black tea, burning my tongue in the process, devour a scone laced with walnuts and gobble down several spoonfuls of yogurt, nearly choking on the chunks of fruit I had forgotten were there.

Dermot drifts back in from the kitchen. "I'd offer you a lift, but I have to take me mum to the doctor's in an hour. Do you know the way? You can borrow me bicycle. Wee bit o' rust on the frame, but I keep the gears oiled and plenty of air in the tires."

"Yeah, I suppose I could make it if I leave in the next few minutes."

"Your ancestors are from around here, then?"

"Not exactly. They took part in the Battle of Halidon Hill, though." I don't bother to tell him they probably died there. That's a given.

"Never been much interested in my own ancestry," Dermot muses. He hands me a fresh mug of coffee, then scoots the sugar and cream closer. "But I'm sure there are a fair amount of skeletons rattling around back there. If they could only tell their stories ..." He chortles to himself, his cheeks reddening. "Then again, maybe there are a few things we're better off not knowing, aye?"

"Maybe, Dermot. Maybe." I stir Claire's coffee and push my chair back. "I'll just grab a few pills, take this up to my wife, ride out to the kirk and be back by noon." Wishful thinking, I know, but it sounds like a good plan. If Reverend Murray has somewhere to be later today, I can only spend so long with him — which is a blessing, considering the talker he seems to be.

"I'll fetch the bicycle from the shed and prop it next to the side door for you, then."

"Thanks, Dermot."

I duck into the bathroom by the front hallway and pop open the medicine cabinet. I have to hold the bottles at arm's length to read the labels, but I finally decipher what's what. I pour a handful of aspirin into my palm. Then, not wanting to take advantage of Dermot's generosity, I count out four and put the rest back. There are only two acetaminophen capsules left, so I take the bottle, reminding myself to buy him a replacement when I return later.

Again, the stairs creak under my feet on the way up. I'm more successful in opening the door quietly this time, though I expect to find Claire curled up under the blankets, dozing off her potent Glenfiddich. Instead, I hear her in the bathroom, puking up last night's dinner of haggis and rosemary potatoes. I warned her. Waiting until I hear the toilet flush, I set the coffee on the bedside table and go to look in on her, like any good husband would.

She's donned one of my ratty old college T-shirts. Hair springs raggedly from her loose ponytail, one unruly lock covering her left eye. Pushing it out of the way, she rolls back onto her bottom, then leans her head against the wall.

Extending my palm, I offer her the pills and a glass of water.

"You really are a mess."

"I've felt better." In two quick gulps, she downs the pills. "Better hurry up. You're going to miss breakfast.

"Already back from there." I run a washcloth under cool water and dab her forehead, then press the cloth into her hands. "You know, I was going to meet with Reverend Murray this morning, but I'm not sure I should leave you like this."

"Oh, Ross, I'm so sorry. I'm ruining our honeymoon already."

I sink to my knees on the glossy tiles. "You're not ruining anything. I just want to make sure you're okay."

"I'll be okay once I can hold the pills down. Mostly it's my head that hurts. I feel better just having emptied my stomach." She screws her eyes shut, then covers her entire face with the washcloth. "Really, not much you can do here, except watch me hurl some more and maybe take a nap, if I'm lucky."

"You sure?"

Her head bobs in a feeble nod behind her terrycloth veil.

"Don't be mad at me if I tell Dermot to look in on you, okay? I'll be back in a couple of hours. Well, three at most, knowing Reverend Murray — I promise. I'll have my phone with me."

She flaps a hand at me.

"You sure?"

"Go, before I throw up on you."

MY TRANSPORTATION, MISSING ITS kickstand, is propped against the brick wall along the driveway. When Dermot said there was rust on his bike, he wasn't kidding. It looks like a relic from the days of the Wright Brothers' cycle shop, with big, knobby tires and an oversized seat. A basket is strapped to a wire platform over the back tire, big enough to transport a few days' worth of groceries. The original color was once royal blue with white trim, but oxidation has taken its toll, splotching the frame with patches of deep red rust. The inner tubes may have been well inflated, but fine cracks in the tires' rubber hint at the beginnings of dry rot. I push down on them several times, expecting the telltale hiss of a leak. If they go flat, the worst thing that will happen is that I'll have to walk back. Luckily, it isn't that far. I've been telling myself I need to start an exercise program. Maybe today's the day. I hike a leg over the seat and glance down to notice a big smear of oil from the chain streaked across my pants leg.

"Just great," I mumble.

"What's that?" Dermot says from behind me.

Looking over my shoulder at him, I fake a gracious smile. He's drying his hands on his apron. Since I didn't know he'd followed me out, it's a good thing he spoke up or else he would've heard a string of cuss words next. "This is great. Thanks, Dermot."

"Just put it back in the shed when you return. Do you need me to call the car rental company for you? Or run the tire over to me cousin's?"

"Thanks, but no, I can take care of that later. Should be back around lunchtime, or a little after. If you could stop by the room sometime ..."

"Don't worry, don't worry. I'll look in on her before I head out to pick up me mum." He unties his apron and tucks it under his arm, then points down the street. "Take the main road that way. When you come to the edge of town, you'll see a petrol station. Go left. There's a stone bridge about three kilometers from that. After you cross the bridge you'll take the second right. Just past the fourth house, turn left, go up the hill and —"

"Wait." I interrupt him before he can confuse me any further. "You lost me at the petrol station. We went by the kirk yesterday on our way here. I'm sure it wasn't that complicated."

He rubs at his nose. "Just trying to keep you out of traffic. If you want, you can take the main road most of the way, but mind the automobiles. They don't pay any heed to the speed limit. When you see the sign for Paxton, follow that. You should see the kirk just over the hill there. Careful of the lorries, though. They're even worse. Think they own the bloody motorways."

I pat my pockets to make sure I have my phone and speed away — speed being a relative term, in this case.

SINCE MOST PEOPLE ARE already at work, the roads are fairly clear of traffic and I zoom into the parking lot less than ten minutes later. The kirk looks as though it has seen better days. Ragged patches of gray stone show through where its limewashed walls are chipped. The slate roof is in better condition, although the north side is half covered in algae from the frequent rains and the sprawling shade of the giant yew tree that prevents the sun from ever drying it out. Weathered headstones, mottled with lichens, are scattered over the lawn to the west of the building, the names they bear long since faded into oblivion. My guess is that more people are laid in the ground outside the old church than now make use of its interior, a theory confirmed when I realize that the gravel car park is overgrown with weeds that are now kept in check by frequent mowings.

There is no evidence of Reverend Murray, no car, not even a bicycle. Maybe he walked here? I rest the bike against the stone wall that encloses the cemetery and walk toward the side door. As I approach the bright red door, I notice a yellow square of paper tacked to it, its edges fluttering in the breeze. The words are blurry, but the reverend's writing is neat enough that I manage to piece the message together.

Dear Mr. Sinclair,

Sorry to have missed you. Called away unexpectedly. Come again tomorrow, if possible. Same time. I have interesting news for you.

Blessings,
Reverend Murray

What kind of emergency could a retired pastor possibly have? Damn it. Tomorrow won't exactly be convenient, since we have to take off for Edinburgh, but by then we'll have a working car. At the bottom of the note, he has scrawled his office phone number. I stuff it in my front pocket and jog back to my nineteenth century wheels.

A low rumble rolls across the land. In the west, heavy clouds are gathering — and they're moving quickly my way. I swing a leg over and imagine myself on the last stage of the Tour de France, the finish line in sight.

I'VE JUST REACHED THE edge of Aberbeg when my phone rings. Raindrops the size of marbles pelt me.

Barely avoiding an accident with a sign post, I veer off into a narrow alley and pull out my cell. "Claire?"

"No, Dermot here." His voice is muffled by the pounding of rain. "Sorry to disturb you, Mr. ... Ross, but I think you need to come back. I checked in on your wife for you, and ... she looks *quite* ill."

Guilt shoots through me. I should have ignored her insistence that I go anyway. Claire was never one to want to be fussed over. "Is she still throwing up? Does she have a fever?"

"No, but the pain's worse, she said." Over his words, I hear a long moan.

"Was that her?"

"Aye."

"Call an ambulance, Dermot. I'll be there in a few minutes." I snap the phone shut and pedal as fast as I can.

BY THE TIME I skid to a halt in Dermot's side driveway, chased there by the wail of a siren, my clothes are drenched. A burst of flashing red lights reflects against the windows as the ambulance turns the last corner. I plunge inside the house, then race up the steps three at a time.

Claire lays curled up on her side in the middle of the floor, her fists balled to either side of her head and her jaw clenched in agonizing pain.

Just inside the door is Dermot, wringing his apron in his hands. "I'm sorry. I tried to help her, but she wouldn't let me. When she said she felt like her head had exploded, I called you."

Dermot continues to apologize, but I stop listening. Something is terribly wrong with Claire. She'd suffered from the occasional migraine before, but that usually only resulted in her closing the bedroom curtains, popping a few pills and burrowing beneath the covers to sleep it off. The way she has her head clamped between both hands and is wailing, you'd think someone has driven an ice pick into her skull.

Footsteps pound in the stairway. Before I can even go to her side, the EMTs have pushed past me and are taking her vital signs.

"Hello, miss," one of the EMTs says calmly, as he pulls up one of her eyelids and shines a penlight in them to check her pupil dilation. "My name is Thomas. That's Andrew and Harry with the stretcher. We're here to take care of you. Can you tell me where it hurts?"

Water is collecting in a puddle beneath me. I shiver from the dampness seeping into my bones. Even though I'm aware how cold and wet I am, I'm transfixed, wanting to help, yet not wanting to get in the way.

As Thomas takes Claire's jaw in his hand and positions her head to check her other eye, she whips her face sideways and lets out a scream. She gulps in air, sputters. "My head, my head, my —"

She cries out again, the pitch rising until it comes out as a screech.

Thomas tosses a commanding glance at his coworkers. Seconds later, they're carefully hoisting her onto the stretcher. I snatch my glasses off the table and follow them.

At some point, one of them asks who's with her and I mumble, "I am."

Beyond that, I don't remember any details about the ambulance ride to the hospital, the questions they ask me or even how long it takes to get there. I can only think of Claire, and how scared I am.

This is our honeymoon. Things like this aren't supposed to happen. This is the beginning of our forever.

10

NOT SO LONG AGO

Balfour, Indiana — 1999

"*Twenty-five hundred dollars?*" *Dad smacks the piece of paper against his palm, then tosses it onto the writing desk next to the rotary phone. "And our insurance doesn't cover one cent, Goddamnit! They said it was an experimental procedure. Tell me where we're supposed to get the money from, Rachel. Where, huh?"*

Mom looks down at her lap, twisting a tissue between her hands. Mascara is smudged beneath her eyes. A white streak runs down her cheek where a tear has washed away her foundation. She keeps her voice low, her tone apologetic. "I don't know, Jack. But what was I supposed to do?"

She looks so ... I don't know. Forlorn, maybe? Yes, that's the word. Like she's lost her last friend. Like she's all alone, without hope or comfort. I want so badly to run to her, wrap my arms around her and tell her it's going to be okay, just like she'd done for me so many times. But I'm scared. Scared to know what they're talking about. And scared of my dad. He's never raised a hand against either of us, although I often wished he had. Then I could go to the police and have him thrown in jail. What he does every day is worse than beating us. He doesn't leave bruises or broken bones, things other people can see. Proof. Just scars on our hearts.

Mom glances my way. Her lips curve into a tepid smile, but her chin quivers. "Ross, I didn't see you there. Go on in your room and I'll be there in a minute to help you with your homework."

"I don't have any homework." I grip the doorjamb, more to stop myself from going into the dining room and giving my dad a good shove than to keep myself upright. "It's Saturday."

"Of course it is." She fakes a laugh. "How silly of me. Can't even remember what day it is. Working those extra hours at the store sure has me mixed up. Well then, go ride your bike. A growing boy like you needs his exercise."

The firm set of her jaw tells me to stay out of it, she'll handle things. I glare at my dad, but his back is turned to me, like he's purposefully ignoring me. Shoving my hands in my back pockets, I leave the room. I don't bother to tell her there are six inches of snow on the ground and the road is a river of slush dirtied by car exhaust.

She doesn't notice much these days. It's like she's not completely with us. Like she'd rather be somewhere else. Like she's already gone.

11

HERE & NOW

Berwick, Scotland — 2013

I WAIT FOR THE second hand of the clock on the wall opposite me to sweep around past the '12' one more time before I separate myself from the furniture and stomp to the desk.

"Have they figured out what's wrong with my wife?"

The station nurse lays her pen down and pushes aside the paperwork she's been examining. The cap on her head sits askew, her sweater is rumpled and the bags under her eyes tell me she's probably nearing the end of a twelve-hour shift. She gives me a patronizing smile. I clench my fists at my sides. This may be the tenth time I've bugged her since they sat me down on that green vinyl couch three hours ago, but somebody needs to fill me in.

With my hair plastered to my head and my clothes still not dried out, I probably look like a deranged wreck, but I don't care. Too many scenarios are crowding my head. If this woman puts me off one more time with some trite response, I'm going to reach over the desk and choke her until someone gives me the answers I need.

"As far as I know, sir, they're still running tests. I'm sure as soon as they have anything to tell you, they'll be right out."

"Is she okay?"

"Again, as soon as they —"

"Can I see her? Where is she? I think it would help if she had someone with her, don't you? I mean, she's probably pretty scared right now and I just want to tell her it's going to be okay, you know?"

At that point, I'm begging. Patience and politeness haven't gotten me anywhere so far. This is my wife they're keeping from me, damn it, and I deserve to know what's going on.

"Let me see what I can do." She lifts a hand toward the waiting area. "Meanwhile, please, have a seat."

There's more command than request in her voice. I comply, but not without a glare of insistence.

She taps at the keys on the phone, talks to someone for a minute, then clicks it back into its cradle. When she scoots her chair back and rises, I stand, sure she has news for me, but she calls another patient to the desk. A young woman goes forward, a crying infant clutched to her chest. Another nurse escorts them to an examination room. Instead of sitting back down, I pace back and forth past the automatic glass doors, making an arc in front of them after they whoosh open the first time.

Nine more minutes slog by. Outside, rain falls in marching walls of gray, slapping against the sidewalk and then bouncing up knee-high before coming back down again. Righteous anger fades to concern. I feel sick to my stomach with worry. I haven't called Claire's parents or her brother yet. What would I tell them? Why cause concern if she's okay, if it's just some random migraine that will pass?

But if that's all it is, why haven't they let me stay with her? Why keep me here, fretting like a sailor's wife?

Somehow I find myself swallowed up by the vinyl couch again. There are other patients and their families waiting here. I'm aware of them, I hear them talking, some crying, but very little registers in my brain. Claire is all that matters. I can't think of anything else.

I dig my hands through my hair. My forehead sinks to my knees.

"Mr. Sinclair?"

I lift my head just enough to see a pair of sensible white shoes in front of me.

"Are you Mr. Sinclair?" A woman wearing blue scrubs extends her hand. Several pens are jammed into the hip pockets of her lab coat, looking like they might all spill onto the floor at any moment. Her rich brown skin and ebony eyes indicate she's of Indian descent. She can't be much older than me. A surgical mask hangs loosely from around her neck.

My grip is feeble as I stand, place my hand in hers and shake it. "How's my wife?"

Her smile is sympathetic. "I'm Dr. Nehru. Will you come with me, Mr. Sinclair? I think it would be better if we discussed her condition alone."

Oh God. Why not just tell me?

My knees almost give out on me. In a daze, I follow her, a white-coated figure gliding through corridors of pale green, while machines beep from open doorways.

Suddenly, I'm not sure I want to know just how bad off she is. Still, there's a little twitch of hope deep inside my gut that won't let me believe she's going to be anything but okay. I have to hang on to that.

12

NOT SO LONG AGO

Balfour, Indiana — 2000

*H*er skin is a translucent gray, thin as wet paper. I'm almost afraid to touch her, scared I might tear her open and all the life will pour right out of her. Her hair has thinned noticeably, little patches missing where clumps have fallen out from the ravages of the cancer. In a few short months, my mom has aged decades, not just in appearance, but in the way she moves and speaks. Gone are the smiles she saved for me alone, the praise she poured out over my grade card when my father has left the room, the easy conversations about everyday things. She barely eats, has quit her job, talks only when she has to, has even stopped arguing with Dad. I know she's given up and is just waiting for the end. More than anything, it kills me that even I'm not reason enough for her to fight this terrible disease.

Her cancer has metastasized to multiple organs. There is no

hope. That bleakness pervades my life. Fills every breath.

She opens her palm for me to hold her hand. I curl my fingers inside hers: warmth against the coldness. Her thin bluish lips tilt upward as she tries to smile, but the tubes coming out of her nose surrounded by white tape make it impossible and her mouth slips back downward.

Her voice is as faint as a memory. "Someday you'll understand, Ross."

The white sheets crinkle as I lean against the edge of the hospital bed, trying to get closer so I can hear her better. "Understand what?"

"Him."

She's full of painkillers. It's just the drugs talking.

She winces, grasping my hand with amazing strength, as if to anchor herself in the here and now. I turn to call a nurse, but she grips my hand harder still. "Maybe someday you'll even ... forgive him."

Not a chance in hell.

The pillow seems to swallow her head as she tips her chin up to gaze at the plain white ceiling. "We all have a past. Some people just can't let go of it."

I say nothing, but she goes on.

"Ross ... there's something you should know. Your father had plans. He wanted to go to college, make something of himself. But then, well, I told him I was pregnant with you and he gave that all up to take care of us."

So he had to go to work instead of school. Big deal. And that's my fault how, exactly? I can't tell her I'll forgive him. How can I? I'll never feel anything but anger from him. Anger delivered without cause or reason. I'm just a kid, barely sixteen. What have I ever done to deserve the harsh words, the quick criticisms? What *has my mom done, for that matter? She's as kind a soul as anyone on the planet. She's the only family I have. My grandparents all passed away long ago. There's one uncle in Florida, my mom's brother who is a globe-trekking nature photographer, but there's never been more than the occasional postcard from him and even those have tapered off over the years. I'll get through this. I'll survive. But forgive? Not in a million years.*

She reaches for a piece of paper on her bedside table. I hand it to her, but she pushes it back at me.

"Those are your ancestors," she says. "I thought you might want to know about them some day."

I unfold the paper. Towards the bottom, I recognize my grandfather and grandmother's names, my mom's parents, but there are many other lines branching upward and long ago dates underneath them. My father's side of the family tree only goes back four generations. I fold it back up and put it in my pocket.

The machines beside the bed hum, the red numbers on the displays fluctuating at random intervals. I pat her forearm lightly. It's all I can do. She's too frail to hug.

Tears choke my throat. I've held them off for so long, trying to be brave, to believe she'll kick cancer's ass, but I'm finally coming to the same terrifying realization that she has. She's going to leave me. Go off to a better place. "Mom, I —"

Shoes squeak in the corridor. A growly voice rumbles from the doorway. "Time for you to go home, boy. Let your mother rest. Nothing you can do for her."

I want to tell him what an insensitive bastard he is, but I can't, not in front of her. Leaning in close, I whisper to her, "I love you, Mom. More than anything. I always will."

13

HERE & NOW

Berwick, Scotland — 2013

D R. NEHRU'S WORDS DART around my head like fluttering moths. "It took a few tests to determine the precise cause of her condition, but we did an MRI and we're now certain it's a case of Cerebral Venous Thrombosis, or CVT. Basically, that means she —"

"She has a blood clot in her brain," I say.

I have been directed to take a seat in a quiet hallway. Judging by the machinery visible through one open doorway, this wing is where they keep the more serious cases.

"Yes." The doctor slides her glasses to the tip of her nose and peers over them at me. There's something consoling in her look and I gather there are more details to come — not necessarily good ones. "Unfortunately, the occlusion, meaning the —"

"Blockage." I have a PhD in Biology, for Pete's sake. I'm not going to let her go on talking to me like a fifth grader from backwoods Appalachia.

"Yes, the occlusion is in her sinuses. It has created some complications, primarily vasogenic edema. We're trying to get it under control, but there's already some intracranial pressure."

It's like someone has kicked me in the gut with a steel-toed boot. Claire's brain is swelling. I thunk the back of my head against the wall. How could I have left her alone this morning? I should have taken her to a doctor right away. Maybe they would have caught this sooner, prevented the worst?

Drawing a clipboard from underneath her arm, Dr. Nehru clicks her pen and scribbles a few words at the top of the paper. "Can you tell me what symptoms she's had recently, even as much as a week or two before this? Anything at all."

"She woke up this morning with a killer headache, but she has those sometimes."

"Any difficulties with motor control or vision problems?"

"No."

"Did she seem light-sensitive?"

"Yeah, I guess so." I don't mention the shot of Glenfiddich.

"Nausea?"

I nod. "She threw up a couple times. Said she felt better after that and just wanted to sleep."

"This was all this morning, correct? Anything prior to that?"

I think hard. "A slight earache a few days ago."

"Ah, that helps." She writes furiously, flips the page over and writes some more. "Sometimes the initial symptoms are very vague."

"So ... is this like a stroke, then?"

"You could call it that, but stroke is a very broad term."

"But how? How does a woman who's not even thirty have a stroke?"

"They can stem from a variety of causes: infection, medication, genetic disorders. It's not uncommon for women in her condition, but it is quite rare in the first trimester."

Trimester?

Tucking my head down, I clamp both hands over my stomach.

Dr. Nehru must sense my shock, because she stops writing. "I'm sorry. You didn't know?"

Three months ago, Claire had quit taking the pill and switched to other contraceptives. We were both in agreement that we wanted to start a family sooner, rather than later. Too many couples in their thirties, even forties, that we'd known were trying for their first and had a difficult time conceiving. Claire had said she'd wanted to have kids while she was still young, so she could keep up with them and later enjoy her grandkids before she had to resort to a walker. It made sense to me, although I did enjoy the thought of having her to myself for a year or so before we had to trade feeding duties for a colicky infant.

"No, I didn't. Actually, I don't think she knew." Or had she? She'd been unusually quiet on the way back from the Orkneys. No, she wouldn't have had the one shot of Glenfiddich if she'd even suspected she was pregnant. Claire isn't reckless that way.

I hear the click of a pen again and feel Dr. Nehru's reassuring hand on my shoulder.

"Mr. Sinclair," she begins, "I know this complicates her situation, but we're going to give her the best care possible. First and foremost, we have to find a way to relieve the pressure on her brain."

"Is the baby at risk?"

She withdraws her hand. "The fetus is six weeks, at most. It's at a very delicate stage. If the pregnancy was further along and the baby was in distress of any kind, we could do a C-section, but obviously it's far too early for that. Right now, we need to make sure your wife has every chance of survival."

The words ricochet around in my head like a steel ball in a pinball machine. *Chance of survival ...*

"You mean ... she could die?" From a headache. A headache

brought on by a tiny blockage in a blood vessel. Just like that.

"Survival in these cases runs about 90%, so chances are good she'll pull through. However, the more time that passes, the lower those chances are. Every day matters."

I nod to let her know I understand. I can far from accept what's happening, though. Only last night we had laughed till the early hours of the morning with the locals at The Finch and the Frog in Aberbeg. On the walk home, we'd talked of our trip, how wonderful it had been, and then of our future plans: the vegetable garden, Claire buying out the dental practice, me getting tenure, whether to repaint the kitchen cabinets and gut the 1950's bathrooms or save our money for a new house.

Our perfectly laid out future is dissolving like a sand castle being washed away by the tide.

Laying the clipboard on the floor, the doctor sits next to me.

"We'll have to administer medication to reduce the edema and minimize the possibility of brain damage. If that's not effective, then we may have to perform surgery. Of course, that increases the risk to the fetus, so we'll try to avoid it at all costs. I'll keep you informed at every step. Meanwhile, are there relatives you'd like to call? I know you're a long way from home, but if she has family, they might want to be here with her."

Her implication hits me brutally hard. Suddenly, all those things like tenure and decrepit old cabinets don't matter. All I want is to know that Claire's going to be okay — and hopefully our baby.

"Her mom had surgery recently. I don't think her parents can travel yet. But I'll call her brother." Lacing my fingers together, I exhale the breath I've been holding for what seems like minutes. "Can I see her first?"

She rises and gives me her hand. "Of course you can. Come with me."

SERENE. THAT'S THE BEST way to describe her. Snow White in her hundred years sleep. Her head rests on a pillow of crisp white linen. A sheet and a thin blanket are tucked tight around her, swaddling her like an infant. Both arms lie atop the blanket, the tubes and wires attached to her snaking back toward their respective devices.

I kiss her cheek. It's surprisingly warm. Then again, what had I expected? She's still very much alive. Just not awake. Not completely here.

The rustle of Dr. Nehru's scrubs whisper from the doorway where she lingers. She rattles off a few more facts about Claire's condition and her prognosis. I may have nodded, mumbled okay — I honestly don't remember. All I can think of is how much I miss Claire's mischievous eyes, the way she crinkles her nose when joking, the bubbly excitement in her voice over the smallest of things, like when her favorite song comes on the radio and she'll start singing at the top of her lungs. She's a terrible singer, but I'd give anything to hear her off-key warbling at this moment. Anything.

For almost an hour I sit beside her in a stupor, sure I'll awaken from this nightmare at any moment to find myself back in bed at Dermot's, my arm wrapped around my sleeping wife. I stroke her bangs from her forehead, touch my fingertips to her lips, then at last curl my hand around hers, waiting for her to squeeze back, to let me know she's still with me.

Finally, I tug my phone from my front pocket, thumb through the contacts, find her brother Parker and hit 'Send'.

"Parker? It's me, Ross."

"Ross! How the hell are you? Lucky you. You caught me before bed. It was a looong day in court, but we nailed the greedy suckers. They're going to lose *everything*." He laughs, taking delight in someone else's downfall. "Bet you two are having the time of your lives. Hey, put Claire on the phone, will you?"

"I can't. I ... You ..." My mind goes momentarily blank. The hope that this is only a bad dream vanishes with the reality of having to say her condition aloud.

"Ross, what is it? Is something wrong with Claire?" His voice abruptly turns from cheerful to accusatory. Four years older than Claire, Parker had always been protective of her. We get along well enough, but I've always gotten the vibe from him that I'm not quite good enough for his little sister.

My eyes wander to the medical paraphernalia surrounding Claire: the monitors, the IV drip, the hospital bed with its chrome railing, the long rectangular box on the wall behind her bed that emits a blue fluorescent glow at all hours.

This is real. It *is* happening. I have to deal with it. And I can't do it alone.

"Parker, you need to get on the next flight here."

14

HERE & NOW

Berwick, Scotland — 2013

DAYS FLOAT BY IN a cottony haze. My thoughts churn as slowly as if I've just awoken from an anesthetic cloud. I've never felt as completely drained of energy and will and feeling as I do now.

Every night I sit in the chair tucked in a corner of the hospital room, watching Claire's chest expand and fall, expand and fall, the muted TV flickering on the wall above me. I haven't slept more than two hours straight since they admitted her. I'd even forgotten to eat most days, only pushing food in my mouth and swallowing tasteless bites when Parker insisted. It's my job to watch over her. But with every day that passes without improvement in Claire's condition, my hope dies a little more.

The door handle clicks and I startle awake. Parker strides in, somber but fresh-faced. He'd arrived less than twelve hours after I phoned him. The guy may be a snob, but he's a good brother to Claire. We've taken to exchanging shifts, but I seldom leave the hospital, afraid of being too far away if she wakes up. I want to be the first one she sees when she opens her eyes, so she'll know I love her too much to leave her.

"Hey," Parker says, coming toward me. He tugs on the cord of the blinds and sunlight invades. "You look like something the cat vomited up."

"And a bonny frickin' morning to you, too." I yank the blanket over my face and slouch further down in my chair. By now, I have a permanent kink in my back and neck from sleeping in weird positions. By contrast, Parker has moved quarters from my bed at Dermot's B&B to a posher hotel just a few blocks away, where he makes sure he gets his eight hours of sleep every night.

The problem with being here all the time is that I startle at every little sound, thinking the doctor is coming in with breaking news or that Claire is stirring. But neither ever happens. Claire never opens her eyes. The doctors never have anything new to say. Maybe if I follow his lead, get some real rest, I won't be such a wreck. As it is, I can't even think straight. I inch the blanket lower, letting the light in slowly until my eyes adjust.

Parker cuffs me on the shoulder so hard my chair tips. "Ross, you look like hell. Really. Do yourself a favor. Go back to your own room. Take a shower, get some sleep, sit down to a real meal, and then go for a refreshing walk. I'll call you if anything happens, okay?"

Too damn tired to argue, I pull on my jacket and head for the door. "If she so much as twitches —"

"I will, Ross. I will. Now go."

I steal one last look at Claire. It's been seven, no eight days since I left her that morning, thinking she just needed to sleep off a migraine. I'd wrestled guilt and raged in silent anger, but in time I learned those were useless emotions to harbor. Dermot had swung by on the second day with a stack of books. 'Something to pass the time,' he'd said. Only yesterday had I pulled the first book off the pile. It was a leather bound collection of Alfred, Lord Tennyson's work, the letters on the outside formed in swirls of gilt. The first page I opened was this:

Half the night I waste in sighs,
Half in dreams I sorrow after
The delight of early skies;
In a wakeful doze I sorrow
For the hand, the lips, the eyes,
For the meeting of the morrow,
The delight of happy laughter,
The delight of low replies.

It's the simplest things you miss when someone's no longer there.

I HIT THE CLOCK ON the nightstand three times before I realize it's my phone ringing and not the alarm going off. By the time I find my phone in the pocket of the jeans I'd left in a heap on the floor, it has gone to voicemail. I slump back on the bed and take a few moments to sweep the cobwebs from my brain.

For the first time in a week, I'd slept in a real bed. My head had hit the pillow at 9 p.m. and I'd slumbered hard for twelve glorious hours. I'm still exhausted, though. Yesterday evening, I talked to Claire's mom for over an hour, giving her every detail I could recall and then repeating myself at least twice. Betsy is a sweet lady, but medical jargon is over her head. She and Glenn would have come with Parker to be with their daughter, but Betsy is still recovering from a broken hip. She can barely get up from a chair by herself, let alone tolerate an eight-hour plane ride.

I hit the #3 on speed dial: Parker's number now.

"Hey, Ross," he says, way too cheerily.

"You called?"

"No, must've been someone else. So you're finally awake, huh?"

"Sort of. Sorry. I can't remember the last time I slept like that. I'll be there in thirty or forty minutes. I just need to grab a shower and something to —"

"Why don't you rest a few more hours? Nothing's changed here. They showed me to a couch last night and gave me a pillow and blanket. Not exactly the Hilton, but I'm fresh as a field full of daisies."

I pause. I don't like being away from her. Then again, the sleep deprivation is frying my gray matter. And worrying about her while I stare intently, willing her to sit up with a dreamy yawn and a stretch her slim, toned arms isn't exactly doing much good.

"Ross, it's all good. Really. I've got my Netbook here and am getting all sorts of work done without the usual office distractions. Come around noon. We'll have lunch and then we can swap shifts. Sound good?"

"Yeah, sure. I'll be there at noon. And call me if —"

"You know I will. See you then."

I flop back onto the bed. Sleep calls. But instead of giving in to the Sandman, I put my glasses on and check my messages. It's from Reverend Murray. He sounds flustered, hurried.

"Mr. Sinclair? Oh dear. I'm never sure what to say to these machines. I'll try. You see, I would have called sooner, but I misplaced your number. Terrible habit of mine, stuffing notes into my pocket and forgetting all about them. Sincere apologies. I do hope you haven't already returned to the States. I made an interesting discovery. Thought you might like to take a look at these documents. So, if you're still here, I'll be at the kirk for the next two hours or so. Do come by, but if I've missed you ..."

He rattles off a sixty second apology. Might as well have taken that time to explain what was so important. With everything that's happened with Claire, piecing together a seven hundred year old gap in my family tree doesn't seem so important anymore. I'm so messed up that I'm not even sure what the date is. My phone tells me it's July 19th. I feel like that should mean something, but I don't know what.

I dial him back, but it rings and rings, no answer. Who in this day and age doesn't have voicemail? Then again, I'm the one who can't download an app for my not-so-smart phone. I consider ignoring his plea, but I have three hours to kill before going back to the hospital. As long as I'm in Scotland, I figure I might as well get the information from him. Unfortunately, I'd had the rental car company come and take our vehicle away while I was at Claire's bedside. A quick ride on Dermot's bike in the fresh air will be good for me.

I drag my weary body into the shower, towel off and throw on the least smelly of my clothes, sniff-testing my shirts like I used to do in college when I was too poor to feed quarters into the washing machine. Dermot is nowhere to be found, but he's left some croissants and a few pieces of fruit on the serving table in the dining room. I scribble him a note, letting him know I've borrowed his bike, but will have it back by noon. I've yet to see him use it anyway, so it's not like he's going to miss it.

With a croissant tucked in my jacket pocket, I head out the door to the back shed, which he hasn't bothered locking. Crime must not be much of a concern in Aberbeg.

A minute later I'm flying down the road, my open jacket flaring in the wind, while Aberbeg's morning rush hour traffic buzzes past me — all six cars. I pedal like I'm being hunted down by assassins on motorcycles. The faster I get this over with, the sooner I can get back to Claire. Parker won't care if I'm an hour early.

Less than two miles down the road my quads are on fire and my lungs feel like they're about to burst. I ease up on my pace. At some point, I realize I've forgotten my wallet. No big deal. I'm not going to need it.

My thoughts keep drifting to Claire. Although I'd been scared to death the first couple of days, I remained hopeful. Yet day after day sitting in that hospital room has left me with too much time to think. Too much time to worry. To wonder how long this could go on. If we'd been at home, I could have gone on about my daily life — or at least had friends around me. Here, the solitude only intensifies all my negative thoughts.

Parker isn't the greatest company. He's a total guy's guy. To him, it's okay to whoop it up at the sports bar with a client, but cry at a funeral? Never. I'm not even sure he has tear ducts. Plus, if he talks anymore about which team is going to the Super Bowl this year, I just might have to shock him with the defibrillators. Sure, he's playing the dutiful brother, but he can be a jerk. It isn't like I can open up to him and cry on his shoulder while he's doing business on his smartphone. I haven't even told him about her pregnancy. If I did, he'd probably say something insensitive, like, 'I guess it wasn't meant to be, pal.'

Tears rush to my eyes. Their wetness skims my cheek. Soon, it's a cascade. The road blurs before me. Head down, I pedal harder, as if I can keep my grief at bay through sheer physical exertion.

A strange sound fills the air, like the throaty rumbling of a beast. Then I hear the bellow of a horn and look up to see I've wandered into the middle of the road. Before me is a narrow bridge spanning a small stream. And blasting across it is a full-sized lorry, its grill aimed squarely at me.

I should've veered left, but instinctively I go the other way, thinking *he* is on the wrong side of the road. A wall of hot air blasts into me first. I jerk the handlebars sideways, but not soon enough.

The truck's front bumper clips my back wheel, catapulting me from the bike. I skid on my side across the asphalt, pebbles scraping skin raw, and tumble, tumble, tumble down an endless grassy hillside.

PART II

A shadow flits before me,
Not thou, but like to thee:
Ah Christ, that it were possible
For one short hour to see
The souls we loved, that they might tell us
What and where they be.

From Alfred, Lord Tennyson's *Maud*

15

LONG, LONG AGO

Northern England — 1333

A MOSAIC OF GREEN SPRAWLS overhead. Dapples of sunlight break through in shifting patches. Carefully, I turn my head to the left, then the right to take in my surroundings.

I exhale in relief. I can still see. That's a plus. My neck isn't broken, either. I'm not so sure about the rest of me, though. I have that stunned feeling that follows you when you're flattened in a game of touch football and the air gets knocked out of you.

Where the hell is my bike? Dermot's bike, I mean. If it's banged up, I'll have to replace it with a new one and this trip has already bankrupted me.

Something heavy thumps on the ground behind my head. *Oh, crud.*

Steamy breath warms the crown of my head. There's a loud snort, spraying my hair with snot. Teeth click and grind together. They'd hunted the wolves to extinction in Scotland centuries ago, hadn't they?

Metal jangles and a soft nicker follows. I tilt my head back to see a velvety brown muzzle hovering over me. Lips nibble at my hair. I might have squealed like a girl. Might have. But whatever sound I make it's enough to make it take a step back. 'It' turns out to be a horse, thank God. Then again, one strategically placed stomp of its hoof and my skull will be split open like a watermelon struck by a hammer.

"Hey there, buddy," I say. The horse, a bay, flicks its ears at me. "Niiiice horse." I tuck an arm beneath me and try to roll over, but every bone in my body screams at me to just lie there. So I do.

Well, things could be worse. Maybe.

The horse meanders in my vicinity, happily munching on sprigs of undergrowth, its tail swishing at flies. The smell of earth and pine fills my nose. Apparently, I've tumbled into a small glen. I hadn't noticed all the trees when I was riding past, but then I hadn't actually been paying attention.

There's something weird about this place, though. Why would anyone turn their horse loose to graze in a wooded ravine, fully saddled and bridled? It must have gotten loose, wandered from its paddock through an unlocked gate. Or thrown its rider. Either way, I have no intention of borrowing it to get back to Claire. The last time I rode a horse was at my friend's uncle's farm when I was eight. A few hours later I'd broken out in hives. My throat nearly swelled shut. After that, I admired horses only from a distance — or in movies.

Finally, I bite the bullet and force myself to sit up. My body is already recovering from the fall, but there are going to be some wicked bruises. No bike in sight. Maybe it got tangled in the brush higher up on the slope? Or maybe it's still there on the road, an unattended gift for any thief who happens by? My glasses aren't anywhere near, either. Holding on to a sapling, I start to stand, but the blood drains from my head too quickly. The ground tilts. Trees spin around me. I sink back to my haunches and grip my knees to steady myself.

Now I remember. Claire isn't waiting for me at the B&B. She's in the hospital. An embolism has ruptured in her brain. She's in a coma. They had talked about doing a craniectomy to relieve the pressure, but there are risks. Even if it works, she might already be brain damaged. She could wake up and not know me. Or she might never wake up at all. She could die on the operating table. They'd told me all these things to prepare me for the worst.

I should have never left the hospital. I should have just grabbed a blanket and gone to sleep on a lobby couch. Should be there waiting for her right now. God, I want to puke, but there's nothing in my gut. I didn't eat this morning. Last night, either.

After the lightheadedness and nausea pass, I notice something really bizarre: I'm not wearing the clothes I'd left the house in that morning. Instead of my comfortable old jeans, broken-in Adidas and a button-up shirt, I have on some kind of baggy brown leggings, worn boots and a belted, oversized smock made of coarse, itchy material. *What the hell?* I'd say this is the result of a drinking binge and a blackout, but I rarely touch the stuff. Why would someone steal my clothes and dress me like *this?* I don't get it. The thought is making my skin crawl.

I stretch my hands out before me to inspect a spattering of dark flecks on my sleeves. There are raised rings of red around both wrists, almost like burn scars. The flecks, though, they aren't mud. It's dried blood, but … I'm not bleeding.

Now I'm really freaking out. This isn't right. Oh man, after all these years of telling myself I'm not crazy, it turns out I *am* schizophrenic after all. I cradle my head in my hands as if to keep my brains from exploding.

Get a grip, Ross, I tell myself. *Get. A. Grip.*

I take in a few deep breaths, trying to remember the meditation

Claire once tried to teach me, but all I can concentrate on is the frenzied pace of my heart. Claire was always the sensible one, the one who calmed my panic, but she isn't here right now. Okay, okay, maybe schizophrenia isn't so bad. They have medication for that kind of thing, right? When I get back to Ohio, I can call my old roommate Marc from the Psychology Department. He'll get me set up. Not illegally, of course. But then, what university will hire me if I —

A twig snaps. I jerk my head up and scan among the tree trunks. The horse has looked up, too. Maybe someone has driven by the abandoned bike, stopped, and is coming to see if I've been hurt. *Hallelujah!*

I listen harder, but all I can hear is the neurotic piping of a finch nearby as it clings to a pine cone. I rise to my feet, more slowly this time, and move toward a clearer spot. When I reach it, I'm struck by the view before me: a steep-sided tranquil glen, as green as the greenest green I've ever seen. How had I not noticed this from the roadway? From what I remember, I'd been bicycling through an area that was all open ground covered in grass. Where are the sheep and cattle? The little white-washed cottages and stone barns? Where is the fricking motorway? Maybe I've hit my head and been wandering for hours? Or days, considering how hungry I am. I run both hands over my skull, probing for lumps. None.

Phone, you monkey brains. Use your cell phone.

"Oh, right," I say to myself. A quick pat around my hips and chest reveals I have no pockets. *What the …?* Okay, forget the cell phone. It must have fallen out by the road — wherever that is. I survey the ground nearby. Nothing.

This day is not going well. With luck, I might get a humorous story out of it. I just hope I can laugh about it later. Right now, I want to punch something. Or have a mental breakdown.

A tuft of brownish-gray springs from behind a tree a hundred feet away and darts down the slope, dodging about the trunks erratically. Longer-legged than any rabbit I know, I assume it to be a wild hare and marvel at its speed. As it bounds across the stream at the bottom of the hill, a fox chases after it and leaps across to the other bank, its white-tipped tail whipping behind it. The hare dives into a clump of bushes, then reappears further uphill. But the fox's line of sight has been broken and it falters just long enough in its stride for the hare to break away.

Wherever I am, I need to find a road so I can flag down a motorist. I'll worry about explaining the weird garb later. As for the blood, I could blame it on a nosebleed. As far as I can see, there's no bridge across the glen, no country road wending beside the stream. If I climb to the top of the hill, I might be able to see something. If not a road, then a house, a pub, a cow path, anything that screams 'Civilization!'

The urge to lie down swoops over me. Why do I feel like I've just run a marathon? Every muscle aches fiercely. I can't remember the last time I was this tired.

One look toward the top of the hill convinces me I don't have enough energy to make it there before sunset. Better to go with gravity, on down to the stream, have a drink there. If I follow the water, I shouldn't get totally lost. It will keep me from going in circles, at any rate.

With the first step, my foot catches on a root, causing me to stumble. I regain my balance and glance at the ground behind me. A glint of dulled silver catches my eye. I bend closer. There, half-concealed beneath a fallen pine branch, lies a sword. Crouching, I pull the branch away. That's when I know I've lost my mind.

The sword … I've seen it before. I've held it in my childhood. It's mine.

The blade is straight and plain, forged for the purpose of killing. The hilt is wrapped in leather that, although worn, has been softened with tallow to keep it from cracking. The pommel is gilt, adorned with twining ruby-eyed serpents, and the cross-guard is shaped like a crescent moon.

Hesitantly, I run a finger over the length of the blade from base to tip. When I turn my hand over, a smudge of crimson stains my fingertip. I bring my hand to my nose and inhale ...

The smell of iron and blood.

It has been used. Recently.

16

LONG, LONG AGO

Northern England — 1333

K NEELING BY THE STREAM, I cup my hands and drink. Long and deep, handful after handful. For awhile, it will fool my empty stomach. Sitting back, I catch my reflection in a clear puddle next to the stream. I lean in closer, rub at my chin and cheeks. Stubble scratches my palm. I've started to grow a beard. I'd tried once when I turned twenty, but the growth had come in so sparse that I vowed never to try again. This is thicker, though. A sure sign of maturity. My nose and forehead are ruddy from the sun's rays and my hair brassier than I've ever seen it.

At first I'd assumed I had only been unconscious for minutes or perhaps hours. Now, I'm sure it's been days and I wonder if Claire's brother notified the police when I didn't return his calls. Even if they sent a search party after me, they probably aren't going to find me in the middle of this wilderness.

For a long while I crouch by the stream, trying to keep a lid on the panic that's building inside me. Any moment now, I could explode like a warm can of soda that's been dropped on concrete. The longer I sit there, intermittently closing my eyes, then opening them, then closing them again, the more that sense of panic subsides. Exhaustion takes over.

Grasping the hilt of the sword and using it to brace myself, I stand, my knees wobbling, arms shaking. I desperately want to sleep so I can recharge, but that'll have to wait until later. Right now, I need a way to get back to Claire, make sure she's going to be okay. I put my head down and follow the flow of water.

Flakes of stone crunch beneath my boots. Unable to lift my feet, I inadvertently kick a stone into the stream. I hear a small splash and a low whinny and look up to see my horse-friend trotting toward me from fifty feet away. It's gaining speed. *Holy crap!*

Knowing I'm not quick enough to dodge it, I drop the sword, throw my hands in front of me and wave them frantically.

"Whoooaaa, there! Whoa!" I have no idea if that's the right command, but what else am I supposed to do?

Nostrils flaring, it tosses its head, swings sideways, and slams its front hooves into the stream, dousing me in a cold shower. After the shock wears off, I wipe the water from my face and push my hair back. I can now see from this angle that 'it' is a 'he'.

He takes a step closer and nudges me in the chest with his muzzle.

"Get. Lost." I tap him twice between the eyes with the heel of my hand. Quickly I wipe my hand on my shirt. "I'll probably end up with welts the size of marbles, just for that."

With an indignant snort, he nudges me again. Insistently. Plucking up the sword, I sidestep him and begin along the stream. If I ignore him like a lost puppy, eventually he'll find something more interesting. But the steady clip-clop of hooves follows me, his snotty breath hot on my neck.

"Look," — I spin around — "you're *really* intruding on my personal space, you son of a —"

That's when I see the scabbard strapped to his saddle, the serpent design on it matching the sword in my hand. I reach out, let my fingers wander over the intricate scrolls. A noise makes me jerk my hand away. The distant pounding of hooves rolls through the glen.

Plunging down the steep hillside toward the stream are three riders wearing clothes as ridiculous as mine. They look like they're fresh from the Renaissance Fair. Or a *Lord of the Rings* convention. Maybe they're extras in a movie? Or … hell, I don't know. This day is making less and less sense all the time. Might as well just go along with it. They might be a little weird-looking (I mean, who am I to talk?), but at least they'll be able to get me back to the bed and breakfast.

I tuck the sword in my belt, grab the reins of my equine companion, and wait, mustering the most dignified expression I can manage.

'Pardon me, gentlemen,' I'll say, not even daring to attempt a Scottish accent, *'but could you perhaps direct me to the village of Aberbeg? I seem to have wandered astray.'*

As the ground levels out, they turn their mounts and head in my direction, picking up speed. The closer they come, though, the less friendly — and more intimidating — they look. They're all decked out in very authentic-looking chain mail, complete with helmets and weaponry. Two have their swords drawn and the other is gripping a spear. The two in back have studded round shields strapped to their arms, but the man in the lead is carrying a larger shield, painted with three white stars on a field of blue.

Relief gives way to apprehension, then quickly erupts into panic. I grapple for the stirrup, attempt to shove my foot in. The horse dances sideways at my sudden movements and I slip, smacking my jaw against the saddle. I go down, my knees slamming into sharp rocks.

They thunder nearer, weapons raised. Bearing down on me like the Four Horsemen of the Apocalypse.

So I do what seems sensible. To me. I point my sword at them and scramble under the horse's belly. Which is not necessarily a smart thing to do, when you really think about it.

Lo and behold, they part. Then … they encircle me.

I wag my sword at one and then another, hoping they'll get the message. As I do so, I notice something odd: my shoulder doesn't hurt. The fatigue is gone and in its place, a surge of manly strength courses through every muscle. The burst of excitement has also sparked a rush of adrenalin. Feeling emboldened, I creep from beneath the horse's belly, thankful he hasn't stomped on me, but keep my back to his ribcage for protection — which is a bit idiotic when you consider that I'm surrounded by three armed men who look far more experienced with their weapons than I am with mine.

The man in front of me eases his horse in close and aims his spear at my chest. "Drop your weapon."

He's in his fifties, maybe, but he's broad-shouldered and strong-limbed. If he hurls that thing, I'll be skewered where I stand.

"You dispatched with the last one, Keith," says the man to his right. "This one's mine." His brogue is the thickest I've heard since setting foot in Scotland. I can barely understand him, although my ears are becoming better attuned each day. Yet, some of their words seem only vaguely familiar: more archaic than vernacular, and almost foreign to me. I can barely piece together their meaning by context.

"Like bloody hell I'll hand him over to you, Malcolm," the older one says, still aiming his spear at me. "You'd probably beat him for information, collect his ransom and deliver a corpse to them. I say we just make quick work of it and be on our way."

Malcolm eyes me with eyes that are as dark as they are merciless.

Unruly black hair, bronzed at the ends by the sun, tumble from beneath the edges of his helmet. Despite his boldness, a quick glance around tells me he's the youngest of the bunch — and the one I stand the least chance against. A smirk flashes across his clean shaven face as he relaxes in his saddle. "On second thought, aye, he's yours. One less Englishman to —"

"Englishman?" I blurt out. "Oh no, no. I'm certainly *not* English."

I hope … pray this little admission will save me, because I'm sure at this moment that I've been waylaid by thugs on horseback. I've heard there are modern Scots clamoring for independence even in the twenty-first century. They even have their own parliament now — although to me that's kind of like Texas having its own president. I'm more than baffled that they'd carry their political leanings as far as assault on any Englishman. If I can convince them I'm an American citizen … Or maybe that's just as bad? I should really watch more BBC News when I get home.

Footsteps sound behind me. I turn my head to see that the one who led them down the hill is studying me intensely. Not in an altogether unfriendly way, but not like he's going to suddenly embrace me in brotherly love, either. Or is he? I can't tell from the odd look on his face.

Movement stirs at the edge of my vision. The dark-haired man, Malcolm, has dropped from his saddle and is swinging his sword side to side.

I throw my sword at his feet in surrender. It isn't like I'm going to win this fight, anyway. But it's the man now behind me who swoops in, tucks his own sword back into its scabbard and plucks up my abandoned blade. He inspects the hilt closely. Just as he straightens, Malcolm rushes at me.

"Malcolm, no!" the man holding my sword shouts. He's the one they seem to be looking to for direction. "Leave him. He's not one of them. Who do you think is responsible for the dead Englishman we just found?"

Malcolm glares at him. "*Him?* This spineless milksop?"

"Whose blood do you think he's wearing? Certainly not his own. There's barely a scratch on him."

With a mocking bow, Malcolm concedes. "As you wish, my lord."

"Something about you ..." Their leader circles me to stand between me and Malcolm. "Tell us your name."

"Ross Lyndon Sinclair," I mumble.

A look of recognition sweeps over his face. Flinging his arms wide, he comes at me. I shrink back against the horse until there's no retreat. He clenches my shoulders, yanks me to him and kisses me on both cheeks. "What's wrong with you, man? You should have told us sooner. Keith and Malcolm would have run you through if I had let them." He looks me over, head to toe, then thrusts me aside to peer over his shoulder. "Malcolm, why didn't you say anything?"

"I wasn't sure, my lord," Malcolm says, not convincingly. "He looks ... different."

"Right you are, Malcolm." Wearing a grin of amusement, the leader tweaks my scraggly beard. "You look dreadful. Like you've been in a shipwreck. I barely recognize you. Can't say imprisonment agreed with you. At any rate, we're overjoyed to have you back with us, Sir Roslin. Delighted!"

Imprisonment? Sir Roslin? Or is he saying Rosalind? What the Sam Hell is he talking about?

Keith dismounts and thumps me on the arm hard enough to send me reeling sideways. "By God, it *is* him. They've nearly starved him. Looks like he's been dragged behind a horse all the way from London, as well." He's older than the other two by a good two decades, judging by his white hair. "I say we take him back to camp and feed him a side of beef. Fatten him up."

"Thank you, but ..." How do you politely decline an animal carcass when three weapon-wielding Scots are offering to feed you? "But you see, I need to get back to Aberbeg. I was just —"

"Aber-what?" Keith says.

"Aberbeg, a quaint little village a few miles north of Berwick," I tell him. "I left there just this morning, or at least I thought it was this morning. Apparently, I've been lost for awhile. I was riding toward Berwick when a lorry came at me and ran me off the road and I ... I ... must have hit my head. And then ..."

Three befuddled faces stare back at me. Clearly, I'm speaking Swahili to them. "You know — Berwick, England?"

"Berwick is in Scotland, lad," Keith says. "Although it may not be much longer, if we don't get back there soon. You haven't heard?"

"Heard what?"

More looks are exchanged. Now I'm confused. I get the sense that they're convinced I've been hiding under a rock lately.

The leader grips my arm. "Roslin, do you know who I am?"

I'm about to correct him on my name, but there are more important things to get straightened out right now — like why three grown men are pretending to be medieval knights. "I'm sorry, but I haven't a clue."

His brows fold together with concern. "Sir Archibald Douglas — Guardian of the Realm."

If it's supposed to be a joke, I don't find it funny. The Archibald Douglas he's speaking of has been dead for close to seven hundred years. A huff of laughter escapes me. "Is that some title bestowed on you by the Society for Creative Anachronisms?"

A quizzical look passes over his face, but he quickly erases it. "No, you wouldn't know of my appointment. When you were taken prisoner the same time as Sir Andrew Moray last year, the honor fell to me. No word of a ransom request was ever sent for you. We all reckoned you were dead. You can understand why we are so surprised to find you here."

"Yeah, sure," I say, although this is all more than a bit far-fetched. "And where is 'here', exactly?"

"Northumberland," Archibald says. "Just north of Rothbury Forest. Headed toward the Cheviot Hills. Barring any unexpected encounters, we can be at camp in a few hours and then back at Lintalee by tomorrow evening." His hand falls away from my arm, but his eyes linger on my face. "You'll have to tell us later how you escaped."

Play along, Ross, I tell myself. *These guys have sharp, pointy objects and aren't afraid to use them.*

"To be truthful, I don't know. There seems to be a lot I don't remember right now." I'm not sure where Lintalee is, but that's the least of my concerns. I do know the other places he mentioned are in northern England. How long have I been wandering around, anyway?

"Understandable," Archibald says. "Meanwhile, you've obviously suffered a hard fall. I'll send word on to your father to meet us at Lintalee."

"Are you certain that fetching his father is the best idea, my lord?" Malcolm has returned to his horse, although he hasn't stopped glaring at me the whole time. "The last time someone mentioned his name to Sir Henry, he wasn't exactly overjoyed."

Archibald glances at my sword, then hands it to me. "The man should know his heir is alive and ... well."

His voice falls off at the last word. They doubt my mental capacities. Whoever these men are, they're thoroughly convinced *they* are from the fourteenth century and I'm the crazy one. That or they're damn fine actors.

Whatever is going on, I'm glad they've claimed me as friend, rather than foe. For now, I'll go along with them. But at the first sign of modern society, I'll slip off to find a telephone, get someone to give me a lift back to the B&B at Aberbeg, then alert the authorities that there are some whack-jobs traipsing around the forest pretending to be 'the king's men'.

I slide the sword into its scabbard, jam my foot in the stirrup and haul my aching body into the saddle. By tonight, I'll have a head to toe rash, but I have to get out of here somehow. After a quick mental review of how to steer a horse — pull back for the brakes and a gentle kick to the flanks to accelerate — I make small talk.

"So how is …" — Dang it! What is Robert the Bruce's son's name? I venture a guess — "King David these days?"

"Well enough," Archibald says. "A shame, though, he understands so little of what is going on."

"Why is that?"

"He's still very much a boy. Only nine." Archibald mounts, then brings his horse close to mine. "You don't remember him either, do you?"

"It's all very foggy still. I have a horrendous headache. But I'm starting to remember a few things. Like that the Englishman and I fought. He struck me … I stumbled, bashed my head on a rock. But I managed to run him through before I blacked out for awhile." Wonderful. I'm now a fantastic liar, just like them. But if it keeps me safe long enough to get back to Claire, fine. Meanwhile, I need to keep these nuthouse escapees occupied. "But tell me more of David. And Berwick."

"Hmm, well, you were at David's coronation. And his wedding to the Princess Joan a few years ago. So was the young Edward of England, for that matter. I tell you, Roslin, this King Edward is a fiercer adversary than his father ever was. At his direction, Berwick is under siege. If I can't raise a large enough force to relieve the city, it will fall to him and his minion, Balliol."

Balliol? *John* Balliol? No, that's not right. John Balliol was King of Scots before Robert the Bruce, albeit a very short reign. Maybe he had a son? Was it Edward Balliol? I'd only briefly read over the history of the time during my genealogy research, mainly on Wikipedia. Meanwhile, I run through the various Edwards in my head. Edward I, also known as Longshanks, Hammer of the Scots, died about 1308. Edward II, married to Isabella of France, who invaded England with her lover Sir Roger Mortimer and put her son on the throne. Ah, Archibald would be talking about Edward III then, victor of Crecy and Agincourt. And Halidon Hill …

Halidon Hill, just outside Berwick, against the Scots. But what was the date of that battle?

I give myself a mental slap. It doesn't matter. This is 2013. These guys are just reenactors. Grown men pretending to be something they aren't.

"Um, Archibald." I have to restrain myself from calling the guy Archie, but it's time to drop the pretenses and cut to the truth. "Look, you're all very good at this. I'm especially impressed by the way you barreled down the hill, flailing your weapons like you were ready to gut me. You guys are Oscar material. But the thing is, I *really* need to get back to Aberbeg. My wife's there and I'm afraid she isn't well. If I don't —"

"Your wife is at Blacklaw where you left her three years ago." With a kick, Malcolm brings his mount abreast of mine. His upper lip twitches in a half-snarl. "And I assure you, she's not ill."

I blink in confusion. "I don't know where this Blacklaw is, but I'm sure I've never even been there."

Malcolm casts a dubious look at Archibald. His hand hovers over the hilt of his sword, but Archibald jabs a finger.

"Leave be, Malcolm," Archibald warns.

"He's not right in the head, my lord. Never was. Not even before he left for Spain with your brother. How do you know he hasn't joined in league with Balliol? Don't you think it suspicious that there was never any request for ransom? Nothing. Not that his father would have paid it, but we all assumed him dead. And now he suddenly appears before us with the tale of a fight with his captors and a blow to the head that's conveniently robbed him of his memory?" In one swift motion, Malcolm draws his blade and thrusts the point at my ribs.

Instinctively, I suck my torso back. My balance shifts. I grapple for the edge of the saddle, clamping my knees. The ground swirls around me. A glint of silver catches my eye and I turn my face away, gripping with all my strength to keep from falling.

Metal clangs against metal. I jerk my head around to see Archibald's sword leveled at Malcolm's throat.

"God help me, Malcolm Forbes, but if you hadn't already proven your value on this campaign, I'd cut you down on this very spot for your insolence."

With a growl of frustration, Malcolm slams his sword into its sheath.

Forbes? Now *that* is a strange coincidence.

17

LONG, LONG AGO

Anglo-Scottish Border — 1333

W E RIDE THROUGH THE wooded glen in awkward silence — Malcolm casting black looks over his shoulder at me and me hoping like hell I won't get thrown by my horse. Somehow, I manage to remember enough of how to ride to stay upright. The horse seems content to follow Malcolm's mount, but I don't overlook the fact that Archibald is tucked in behind me like a mole on my backside, with Keith — I learned his full name was Sir William Keith — on my right.

We see no more English — not that I'm worried about it, in fact, I would welcome the sight of any sane person, but these Scots seem particularly averse to such an encounter. Patchy woodland gives way to broad, swelling hills, painted in strokes of emerald and buff. There's no sight of a motorway, not even so much as a single lane road rutted with parallel tire tracks. Only the occasional drover's trail wends from hilltop to hilltop. A large flock of sheep dots a far hillside. To the west, wispy clouds of cotton white are chased by thickening banks of gray. Thunder rolls in the distance and its rumble vibrates through the air. The wind kicks up ahead of the storm, its force flattening the grasses as far as the eye can see.

"Do you suppose," I say, trying my best to appeal to their good senses, "there's a pub somewhere we could take shelter in before this storm drenches us? A round of ale on me — or whiskey, if you prefer." I realize I've forgotten my wallet, but paying for drinks will be forgotten in the mass drunkenness that's sure to follow. The police will be on their way to arrest them for kidnapping as soon as I can slip aside to put in a call.

Yanking on his reins, Malcolm halts his mount and shoves an open palm at me. "Quiet," he growls, then indicates the sheep flock.

At first I can't understand why I'm supposed to be looking at sheep. Then I see the flock lifting off the hillside, heads high, running in a tightening group toward a peak to the north.

Keith nods in that direction. "An English detachment."

A line of riders crowns a distant hill and begins to descend. By the time the last of them brings up the rear, I count close to two dozen. Several times our number.

"Twenty-two," I say. "The one out front is carrying a white shield with a red chevron."

Malcolm narrows his eyes beneath hooded brows. "How can you tell from this distance?"

I shrug. How can they not? From here, the shield is still small, but distinct. "I don't know how. I just can."

That's when I realize that my vision is crisp and clear. Odd and yet … amazing. I glance down at my horse's mane. Every strand is distinct, the shading a rich blend of reddish brown. I can even see the little hairs that fringe the inside of Archibald's horse's ears, as the animal flicks them sideways, then forward.

"You're lying," Malcolm says. "Next, you'll direct us straight into an ambush."

By then, Archibald has seen the same thing I have. "No, he's right. Whoever they are, they're not Scots. My guess is that they're looking for him." Glancing at me, he tugs at his reins to turn back. "We can't take any chances. We will have to take the long way around and cross the river twice, but we'll make it back to camp by nightfall if we hurry."

We retreat behind a hill while the English riders speed away to the east. Once they've been gone awhile and no more are seen, we turn west and ride hard. A shiver ripples from my neck to my tailbone and I realize what it is I'm feeling: fear.

Wherever we're headed, we aren't getting any closer to Aberbeg.

IT'S NEAR DUSK WHEN we come upon the camp Archibald had spoken of. That's the moment I admit I'm not in the 21st century anymore — and it frightens the hell out of me. I pull back on the reins and let Keith and Archibald pass.

"No," I say to myself, "this can't be."

Hundreds, if not thousands, of medieval Scots are milling about. There are too many, their clothing and weapons too authentic, for this to be some reenactment gathering. I've been to enough medieval fairs in my time to recognize machine-stitched garments and anachronistic armor. I see none of that. Besides, at the reenactments you'll always see the occasional person wearing glasses or sneaking in a text on their smartphones; there's nothing of the sort here. No video cameras rolling, no electrical cords snaking between the tents, no generators sputtering and belching out gas fumes, no hint of a car or paved road for miles.

Twists of smoke rise from small fires, over which hang spits and small pots. Low conversation hums in pockets, but my ears aren't attuned to the words and accents, so I can't make heads or tails of

IN THE TIME OF KINGS

any of it.

Slumping in my saddle, I grip its edge. My back aches and my thighs are chafed. My stomach roars for food and yet the last thing I want to do is eat, let alone spend the night here. More than anything, I want to go home, with Claire hale and whole, but right now I'd settle for quaint little Aberbeg in 2013. "When I get back, Claire, you're never going to believe this."

"Clare?" Malcolm approaches me and tugs the straps loose on his arm plates. "Which 'Clare' do you speak of — and what will you say to him? Will you tell him how many we are?"

I blink in confusion. Eventually it dawns on me that he thinks I'm talking about someone with the last name of Clare, someone who's probably English.

"A woman named Claire," I say. "Just someone I know."

"Ah, a woman." He stands before me, one eyebrow cocked. "My sister will hardly be pleased to know you're uttering another woman's name, telling her your secrets."

His sister? As if it isn't bad enough to have landed here in the wrong time, they assume I'm Roslin Sinclair and I know everything they're talking about. "Your pardon, but you're going to have to remind me. Your sister is …?"

Smirking, he shakes his head. "Your wife these past five years. The wife you've barely seen."

Oh, *that* wife.

"Yes, well, I've been in Spain, apparently. And England — or at least so they tell me. But I don't remember anything. Not the last few years, not my wedding, or where I'm from, or —"

"I don't believe you for a moment." Malcolm flashes a snarl just as Keith approaches. "You're a liar, a traitor and a heretic."

"Roslin," Keith calls. "This way. You can share my quarters tonight. Meanwhile, we'll find you something to eat — that is, if this lot hasn't devoured every last cow in Northumberland."

"Beans," I say, eager to grab at a chance to escape Malcolm's company. "I smelled beans."

"I'm sure we can manage that. And a bannock or two, if you don't mind stale and not having any ale to wash it down with."

"If I were you," Malcolm says to Keith, "I'd not close my eyes with that impious Judas in my presence."

"There was a time, Malcolm, when one could have said the same of you." With that, Keith slaps me on the back and guides me through camp.

"What was that about?" I ask him. "The part about Malcolm being a traitor?"

"He and his father were some of the last to swear allegiance to our good King Robert. Loyalties in Scotland shift all too often. It takes time for people to learn to trust you. Don't let it bother you, lad. Prove yourself, that's all you have to do."

Prove what? I wonder. But I'm not about to ask, because I don't want to know.

Food, I can see, is going to be a problem. During my teens, I'd sworn off meat and become a zealous vegetarian. After my dog Ivanhoe died, I'd been pining for a pet, but was always too afraid to ask my parents for another dog. Then one day while doing my paper route, I nearly ran my bike into a young chicken on the road. Afraid it would cause an accident, I picked it up and carried it home. To my surprise, my dad helped me build a small wire pen behind the garage. He called it a pullet and said it could lay eggs for us. And it did, for almost two years. When the eggs became few and far between, he cursed at it and called it useless, but to me it didn't matter. I'd grown quite attached to Florence. Then she disappeared. My dad said she must have escaped, but the latch was closed. Someone, I knew, had taken her. Later that month, after a meal of fried chicken, my dad told me the truth: he'd had her butchered by a friend at work and the supper we'd just enjoyed, well ...

Ever since then, the smell of animal flesh cooking has turned my stomach. I tell people it's a matter of making healthy eating choices, but they wouldn't understand that here.

Everyone turns to stare at us as we pass. Am I that obvious? Until I can figure out how to fit in better, I'll have to hang back and keep quiet. Even a harmless comment could be misconstrued, as I've already learned by Malcolm's reaction. To think he's my brother-in-law doesn't fill me with confidence. I need an ally, someone who can help me learn what I should already know.

Archibald seems fond of me, but he's too busy to hold my hand. Keith will have to do. He shows me to his tent, gives me a clean shirt and offers me a single blanket, saying it's all he can spare. Then he brings me a small meal of burnt beans and stale, coarse bread. I duck inside the tent, having grown weary of the stares and whispers.

After scooping out the last of the beans with my fingers, I push my bowl aside and wash the lumps sticking in my throat down with a swig of tepid water from a flask. Keith is already sound asleep, snoring. I'll get no rest tonight. My nerves are too frayed.

All I can do is lie here and think about Claire and wonder when, if ever, I'll see her again … or if I'll ever know the child she's carrying.

18

LONG, LONG AGO

Anglo-Scottish Border — 1333

"ROSLIN!"

Sitting up, I fling a hand out and grapple at the blankets to search for Claire. The glimmer of a chest plate yanks me back to reality. No, I'm not in Aberbeg, lounging at Dermot's B&B. Damn it. I had really hoped this nightmare would be over with by now.

A wizened face, framed by a full white beard, appears at the tent opening. Full cheeks press upward into a smile. At least this face is friendly. I glance around to see that Keith has left and already rolled his blanket up. Judging by the pale light, it's early morning. Instinctively, I look around for my glasses, but then I realize I don't need them anymore.

"By God, man! You are alive after all." He stoops to enter, then crouches before me. "Don't worry, they told me about your memory. That can happen when a man takes a blow to the head. My brother Kenneth — older than me by a few years, you never knew him —

once fell from his horse while out hunting deer with my father and me. He didn't awaken for three days and when he did … he had fits, was very confused, jumbled his words up." The man waves his hands in the air, then taps on his forehead with scarred knuckles. "He was never the same. My father sent him to the abbey to live. He wandered away in a snowstorm the next year and died. Or so we assume. We never found him." His mouth slips into a frown of melancholy. With a spark of warmth then, his gray eyes light up. "But you … you look well. It will all come back in time. Until it does, I'm here to help."

My neck is stiff and my back sore from sleeping on the hard ground. I stretch my arms, arch my back and roll my head side to side, but every little movement just signals more aches. "I'm sorry. You are …?"

He laughs and sticks out his hand. His grip is bearishly strong. "Duncan of Abernathy. Your father and I fought together many times: Methven, Bannockburn, Byland Moor. It's a miracle we both survived. Named me your godfather for saving his skin more than once. My wife Evelyn took you to her breast and raised you as her own. Shame about your mother. Your father never remarried, he was so heartbroken. He's a fine knight," — he leans in and winks — "if not a bit tough-hided and stony. He means well, though."

Great, the man sounds just like *my* dad. "Thank you, Duncan. But please, don't go far. I'm afraid I'll never remember anything. I feel so … lost." Digging my hands through my hair, I rest my head on my knees. The day has barely begun and already I feel worn out and defeated. Like I've been flogged and beaten brain dead.

Duncan's touch upon my back is surprisingly gentle. "I've spoken to Lord Archibald. He's agreed that once we get back to Lintalee, I can escort you to Blacklaw Castle."

"Why there? What's at Blacklaw?"

"It's your home, lad. Your wife's there. Your father, too — unless he comes to Lintalee, in which case you'll get to see him sooner."

My gut tells me that meeting him isn't something to look forward to. I look up. This Duncan of Abernathy may be big in body, but his eyes are gentle, sympathetic. "Do I want to see him? It doesn't sound like he's very fond of me."

"I doubt he's fond of anyone — even me sometimes, as hard as that might be to believe." Duncan inclines his head toward the opening. "Up with you, now. We'll be moving on within the hour."

ARCHIBALD'S ARMY IS SURPRISINGLY nimble for so many. The men have barely risen and they're already dismantling tents and securing packs to their saddles. I stuff a bannock in my mouth and nearly gag. It has the consistency of cardboard. Then the bitter taste of mold taints my taste buds. I can only hope that back in Lintalee the fare will be more palatable. Right now a large order of fries and a root beer would hit the spot. Even a heel from a loaf of Wonder Bread with a pat of butter would satisfy me.

I might have marveled at the scenery we passed that day, but I'm growing increasingly homesick. Disbelief has given way to despair. Although the grass is green, the trees have barely leafed out and the constant wind carries a chill.

"Duncan? What year is this?"

He startles at my voice, having nearly fallen asleep in his saddle. He pulls a hand down over his face and tugs at his beard. "Year? 1333. Four years now since our good King Robert died."

"And the month?"

"April, I think. If it hasn't already turned May. One day is like the next when you're living off the back of your horse."

I suppose I shouldn't have expected to land on the exact same day of the year when I fell back in time. I can't even begin to figure out how it happened. All I can do for now is cope and believe that somehow I'll get back to where I belong. Back to 2013. For now, since I don't know how I got here, there isn't much point in thinking about it.

All day long, Duncan rides close to me. Whenever someone stares my way, he glares back and growls a warning. Aside from him, I don't speak to anyone. I'm too afraid of being revealed as the impostor I am. Archibald is somewhere lost in the column, but occasionally I glimpse Keith and Malcolm. Keith seems accepting of my presence, but Malcolm … well, there's a story there I'm not sure I want to know.

"So tell me," I say to Duncan, as we begin our journey on the second day, "what's happening with Berwick."

"Agh. Rather than raze it like he did most of the castles he recaptured, King Robert decided to reinforce it, to serve as a stronghold against invasions from across the border. That may not have been the wisest move after all. We stand to lose it to England, lad. King Edward, being clever, sent Edward Balliol north to launch an attack on the city and gave him more than enough men and arms to do it. Berwick's defenses are strong, but surrounded by such a large and imposing force, they become an island with finite resources. All that Balliol needs to do is bide his time."

That much I had already gathered. "And Balliol wants Scotland's crown for himself?"

"Aye, he does. Although the only Scottish nobles who support him are the ones our good King Robert disinherited when they would not join him. So Balliol appealed to Edward of England."

"Why didn't King Edward just march with him?"

He dips his head and I can tell he's swallowing back a laugh. "You really don't remember a thing, do you? That would have violated the Treaty of Northampton, which he signed with King Robert a few years ago. He's made no secret of the fact that he doesn't wholly agree with the terms of the treaty. Claims that his mother Queen Isabella and her bedmate Sir Roger Mortimer had somehow forced him into signing it."

"Why would they do that?"

He shrugs. "War is expensive. Isabella thought it more profitable in the long term to marry her daughter Joan off to our David. Young Edward is ambitious, though. And confident. He eventually took Mortimer into custody and had him tried and executed for treason. He knows what he wants and won't let anyone stand in his path. Takes after his grandfather that way."

"Longshanks?"

Duncan nods, his eyes on the road ahead.

"But Archibald said something about Edward coming to Berwick. He's on his way now?"

"Likely he's already there." Duncan tosses a look over his shoulder and then sideways. He lowers his voice. "Now that we've raided into England, King Edward claims he has every right to enter Scotland in force. He's been waiting in York for months now for just that reason."

"Why would Archibald venture into England, knowing that would provoke Edward?"

"To draw Balliol away from Berwick."

"And he failed."

"You're a keen one." He grins. "I suppose he reckoned it was worth a try. His brother did it many times, to good effect. But this time the English were willing to sacrifice a few villages for the bigger prize and they stayed put. So it's back to Scotland for us to try to raise more troops. Lord Archibald is convinced our only recourse now is to break through and relieve Berwick."

"Wage battle?"

"How else?"

My stomach sinks. As I gaze ahead to the column of soldiers snaking before us, I see not only Scotland's fate, but my own as well.

Lintalee, Scotland — 1333

IF I EXPECTED THE Guardian of the Realm to keep residence at something resembling Fort Knox, I'm gravely disappointed. The first hint of Lintalee that I see as we ride through the forest south of Jedburgh, Scotland, is a spire of smoke curling above the treetops. An hour later we come upon a sprawling stockade fence and peeking above it is a single watchtower. Lintalee was built for practicality and comfort; certainly not for lasting defense. As deep as it's tucked in the forest, though, it would be hard to find, let alone approach. Our column has been forced to narrow down to two across in order to proceed via the narrow road, slowing our progress considerably.

Already there are several hundred, perhaps as much as a thousand other men, encamped outside its walls. I notice several of what I assume are the nobles filtering in through the outer gate.

Duncan tosses his reins to a groom and tips his head toward the gate. I hand off my horse and follow him. With the first steps, I'm painfully reminded that my muscles aren't accustomed to sitting in a saddle for two days. I marvel at the fact that I haven't broken out in hives. Apparently, not only has my eyesight improved, but my allergy to horses hasn't transferred to this time period, either. Still, I'd take the old imperfect me back in a nanosecond if it meant I could return to the woman I love.

Lintalee is little more than a hunting lodge. From what Duncan told me, Archibald and his brother James 'The Good' Douglas built this place with their own hands, felling trees and splitting the logs that formed the framework for the main hall. Later, several barracks-type buildings were added for housing guests, for stabling horses and for storage. The kitchen, set apart from the other structures, is the only one with stone walls — a precaution to keep the occasional kitchen fire from engulfing everything around it. The rest of the buildings are packed so close together within the confines of the stockade, that one spark to a thatched roof and the whole sprawling complex would go up in flames.

Duncan slaps his riding gloves together, creating a puff of dust. "Are you going to stand there gawping all day, lad?"

Everyone is headed in the same direction, so I tuck my head down and follow. "Is there going to be a meeting of some sort?"

As I come abreast of Duncan, he slings an arm about my shoulder. I involuntarily twitch at the contact. Touching anyone other than my wife makes me uncomfortable. Whenever a hug-fest starts at some occasion like a wedding, I tend to duck away from the touchy-feely gestures. I don't like casual acquaintances invading my personal space.

"Nothing formal, no," he says. "Just food and ale. But I did see the earls of Menteith and Ross … Throw a Douglas and a couple of Stewarts in the lot and there's bound to be some heated discussion. All you need to do is sit and listen, nod your head knowingly and laugh when everyone around you does — if they do at all. Whatever you do, don't stare. Some of these men tend to take that as a challenge."

We step through the broad double doors to the main hall. An empty hearth sits at the far end, the stones surrounding it blackened by years of smoke. Before it is a table atop a dais. Either side of the hall is flanked with a row of tables and benches, already crowding with boisterous nobles scooping up cups and emptying them.

With a hand on my back, Duncan guides me to an open space on a bench to the left. "Don't look so sullen and confused. People are going to ask you what's wrong."

Unfortunately, I don't know if I can do that. I've never felt more out of place in my life. It's been less than a day and already I miss ice cold Coke in a can, denim jeans and cushioned running shoes, cream puffs from Schmidt's in German Village, my cell phone ...

I'd gladly give up all those things to be with Claire, though.

I want to laugh with her again. I want to hold her hand. Kiss her freckled nose. Listen to her sighs. Twine my fingers in her silken blonde hair, smelling of mint and tea tree oil. Lay beside her and gaze at the stars.

Without her, it feels like a part of my soul is missing.

19

LONG, LONG AGO

Lintalee, Scotland — 1333

I'M LUCKY ENOUGH TO go undisturbed for close to an hour at supper before someone strides across the room, stops before me and smacks both palms on the table.

"God's rotten teeth!" The man has hair the color of straw and fair skin which makes the three parallel scars on his neck all the more prominent. "You look incredibly vibrant for someone who's come back from the dead, Sir Roslin."

"Thank you," I mumble. Something about this man screams at me not to trust him. The smile is there on his mouth, but it doesn't reach his eyes.

"Sir Alan." Duncan nods in acknowledgment. "How are matters in Edinburgh?"

"Fine, last I heard." Alan plants his elbow on the table and lowers his voice. "Lord Archibald should have anticipated this after he routed Balliol at Dupplin Moor last year. Did he think the man was going to slink off, tail between his legs, and not return for vengeance? I've spent the last month on horseback, gathering men and spreading the word. If we can get as many as we expect from the north, we'll have numbers that will not only rival Edward's, but exceed them. Time will tell if it's enough, though."

"Archibald expected, as all of us did, that Edward would honor the treaty and not enter the country that his sister now calls home."

"We all know that union was a sham. David and Joan are children. They have no affinity for each other beyond casual friendship." Alan's eyes slide to me. Like me, he must be in his late twenties, but unlike me, he isn't afraid of making himself known here. He's spent a fair amount of the evening circulating from table to table and seems to be regarded with a certain amount of respect, if not importance. I haven't been immune to his suspicious glances, however; so when he first approached, I felt a prickle across my skin. The fake smile is gone now, replaced by a sneer. "Perhaps Roslin here can impart some details from the English perspective. After all, he's spent a year in their company without a word to his father or wife. Sad to say that neither mourned you."

I wait for Duncan to fill him in, but instead my friend bites off a hunk from a goose leg and starts to chew, ignoring my distress.

"I don't remember anything from before a few days ago." I wonder how many times I'll have to repeat this story.

"So Malcolm told me." Alan's fingers curl around my knife and he draws it towards him. With a turn of his wrist, he stabs the tip of the blade into the table top. "But *I* think you do. And Archibald is a fool to trust you. So was Lord James. So was your brother."

With that cryptic statement, he turns and leaves. The moment he's beyond earshot, I lean in close and say to Duncan, "What was that about my brother?"

Duncan gulps down a swig of ale, then drags a forearm across his mouth. For several moments, he stares at his trencher, shredding his meat, as if picking at words and trying to figure out how to phrase his reply. "You and your brother William were at Lord James' side at Teba when the Moors attacked. Lord James and —"

"Wait. My brother's name was William? Older or younger?" Was this the William Sinclair in my family tree? Reverend Murray had said it was a fairly common name.

"Older by two years. Anyway, Lord James and William rode forward in the vanguard. You, however, hesitated. They both died. Your father never quite forgave the fact that it was you who returned to Scotland, not William. When you arrived home at Blacklaw, he called you a coward and a disgrace to the entire Sinclair clan. You Sinclairs are a stubborn, contentious lot."

"How do you know I didn't try to help William and Lord James?"

"Because I was there, Roslin. I saw you hang back. But it was your first battle. You were afraid for your own life. Still ..."

So even he thinks me a coward. Not much I can do about that. A change of subject seems in order. "Who is this Sir Alan? Another brother? Cousin?"

"Not your cousin. The king's, although only distantly so. Being a Stewart, he thinks himself privileged. I've no doubt he spends every moment he can whispering into young David's ear, sowing the seeds of his influence. However, none of that is your concern. I suggest you keep an eye on him. You've far more to worry about from Alan Stewart than the rest of us."

"Why would that be?"

"He was your wife's suitor at one time."

So I already have enemies? I'm liking this place less and less by the minute. "Does this have anything to do with why Malcolm doesn't like me?"

"Everything. Malcolm was fostered in Alan's household. They're closer than blood brothers. As far as Malcolm's concerned, you were a poor catch and Mariota — meaning Malcolm, as well — would have fared better had she married Alan."

Things are beginning to make sense now. Too much sense. And it doesn't bode well for Roslin Sinclair.

I've never been much of a drinker before, but tonight I drink until my nerves ease. I'm not the only one indulging. Everyone is talking more loudly, laughing and smiling, some even break out in song. Their words overlap in an unintelligible buzz as feet stomp and hands clap and tankards are refilled. I eat and drink until my stomach aches and I'm sure one more spoonful of custard will make me hurl.

A serving girl leans over my left shoulder and pours my friend another drink. Her hair hangs in long black tendrils over her back and shoulders, but as she pushes it back and turns toward me, smiling, I glimpse bare white shoulders above deep cleavage. Without warning, Duncan grabs her around the waist and pulls her into his lap, nearly upsetting the bench we share.

She laughs and slaps him playfully across the chest. "None of that, m'lord," she teases, tapping him on his whiskered chin with a fingertip. "You always did presume too much."

"How many times must I propose to you, Jean, before you'll make me a happy man?"

"Fancy me all you like, Duncan of Abernathy, but you already have one foot in the grave. Besides, you never did offer to make me your wife, as I recall. An invitation to bed is not a proposal for marriage."

He fingers the laces at the front of her gown as if to tug them loose. "What will it take, Jean? Let me steal you away from Lintalee. I'll give you a room of your own if —"

"Again," — she jabs her finger at his broad chest — "you presume too much. I like it here and I'm not interested in being your bedmate. Once was enough. You're older than my father. But your friend here ..." She wriggles free of his hold, then squeezes into the space between us. "Perhaps he'd like some company?"

"No, I …" I fight a shiver as her finger trails along my arm from wrist to elbow and back again. She doesn't have the prettiest face I've ever seen, but she's certainly well endowed. I can understand Duncan's attraction to her. The whole scenario makes me think about the study that said consuming more than two alcoholic drinks makes everyone in the room seem better looking and affairs are more likely to happen when people are drunk. Did they really need to invest money in a study that's common knowledge? I gaze into my empty cup, wondering how many more of these I'd have to down before I would lose my inhibitions and lapse into adultery. "I'm sorry, but no."

A pout frames her mouth. Instead of being deterred by my refusal, though, she seems to take it as a challenge. She traces the arch of her foot along my calf, her fingers wandering up my thigh. I draw back, unsure of what to do. I've never had a woman be so forward before. She twists around and slides onto my lap, a suggestive moan escaping her throat. Her bosom is right at my eye level. *Holy sh—*

Duncan clears his throat. "My lord?"

I can't move. Not sure if I should. Should I ignore her? Ask her to stop? Throw her off? If I had joined a fraternity during my college years, I might have some experience in this realm. As it is, I have none. Some women may have thought me cute, in that sad puppy dog kind of way, but they generally didn't throw themselves at me. If they'd even tried, I would have slunk away out of embarrassment.

"My lord?" Duncan says more insistently.

"What is it?" I practically gasp. I'm somewhere between embarrassed panic and involuntary arousal as she arches her back and then rocks forward.

"There." He points to the end of the hall near the doors.

The light is so dim there it takes me a few moments to focus enough to see that it's a woman. A very young woman and a very, *very* beautiful one at that. Golden red hair dangles over one shoulder in a long braid that reaches her hip. Her complexion is fair, but there's a rosy blush to her cheeks that hints of the sun's touch. Something about her sparks a flicker of familiarity in me, a sense of …

Suddenly, I *know* why I'm here, in this place and time. To find her.

Abruptly, I shove Jean to the side with both hands as I stand, landing her in the lap of the man next to me. Wrapping his arms around her, he roars with delight and smothers her neck with kisses. She squeals in protest, but soon she's laughing, too — loudly. Their rollicking captures the attention of everyone within earshot, including the lady near the doors. As she begins to unclasp her riding cloak and turns in our direction, her face goes deathly pale. Her knees wobble, but before she can faint, another woman catches her by the elbow and braces against her.

"Who is that, Duncan? Do I know her?"

"That, my lord, is Mariota … your wife."

20

LONG, LONG AGO

Lintalee, Scotland — 1333

MY MOUTH GOES DRY. I grab my cup, bring it to my lips and tip it up, but the damn thing is empty. So I steal Duncan's and in three big gulps drain it halfway. Had she not seen me, I might have ducked behind the four men standing behind us and sought out some hiding place. But I'm frozen where I am, transfixed.

An eternity passes before she takes the first step toward me. Her movement jars me from my trance and I notice Alan and Malcolm on the other side of the hall, rising from their seats and starting toward her. That alone compels me to go to her before they do.

I reach the end of the table as fast as I can and stop before her. Her breaths are coming in rapid, shallow intakes. Eyes downcast, she stands an arm's reach from me, the short distance as solid as a wall. Her hands still clutch at the edges of her cloak, as though she needs it for a shield.

"Roslin."

Although her voice is only a whisper, I still hear it clearly despite the drunken bellowing and bawdy song. I've heard it before — although I can't recall exactly when — in that silver haze between dream and waking. Heard it as clearly then as I do now.

I drift closer. I'm not quite sure where the courage comes from, but I lift her chin and look into her eyes. They're the color of damp moss in a wooded glen, of fully unfurled leaves in summertime, of a grassy hill after a quenching rain.

For a moment, I lose all awareness, of everything and everyone — until Archibald intrudes on the space between us.

"Lady Mariota?" He plucks up her hand and grazes her knuckles with a kiss. "You look well. To what do we owe the honor of your unexpected arrival?"

"Thank you, my lord." She dips her head. "I came to tell you that Sir Henry …" — she flashes a nervous look at me — "Sir Henry was unable to come at your summons. He fell from his horse and injured his back. But already he is mending. He expects to be back riding before the week is out."

"Unfortunate, but I'm glad it wasn't more serious. Why did he send you, though?"

"I came to visit your wife and sons. She extended the invitation last Christmas. But I wasn't expecting so many …" — she glances shyly about the hall, looking like a doe that's ventured from the cover of the brush — "people. I shall return to Blacklaw first thing in the morning."

"Nonsense. You'll stay as long as you like, unless …" He looks at me, smiling with a secret purpose. "Perhaps after a few days, Roslin and Duncan could escort you back to Blacklaw? They're going there anyhow."

I glance at Mariota, hoping to gauge her reaction, but she avoids meeting my eyes.

"Of course, my lord," she says. I sense, however, that she isn't overly thrilled by the prospect of spending so much time with me.

"Perhaps the lady would be safer here?" I offer. "And surely your wife would enjoy the company?"

"She'll have to make do with just a few days," he replies firmly. "Besides, you won't get much privacy here, not with this boisterous lot. The two of you have been parted for far too long, as it is. Now," — he grabs Mariota's hand and drags her closer to me — "look a little happier, will you? You're the only two in the entire hall who look so morose, like you've both seen ghosts. In your case, Lady Mariota, I suppose it seems you have."

As he makes to pass me, he leans in close and whispers loud enough for Mariota to hear, "I have a spare private room for you. The bed is small, but my guess is you two won't need the extra space."

Mariota's cheeks redden. Her reaction is telling. She and Roslin … me, we haven't been together often, if at all. We are, in effect, strangers. This scenario is becoming more awkward by the second.

I do the only thing I think will help. I offer her a seat beside me, but she declines. Instead, she seeks out Archibald's wife, Beatrice. The stares intensify as she walks from me. Humiliated, I keep my head down as much as possible. When I look for her a short while later, she's already gone.

Drunk, tired, I spend the night alone as rain pounds on the roof overhead and thunder shakes the ground.

WATER DRIPS ONTO MY forehead. I wave an arm and turn my face aside, sputtering as I sit up. "What the — ?"

A thin slat of sunlight pries around the partially closed door's edge. Duncan looms over me, sporting a scowl. He plunks the cup he's been holding over me down on a stool — the only other piece of furniture in the room besides the bed, if one can call it that.

Last night's heavy rain has diminished, although I can still hear the occasional drip-drip from the eaves. A quick scan reassures me there are no leaks in my humble lodging area.

Turns out that Archibald's 'private room' is a storage area off of the main hall, stacked to the ceiling with barrels of ale. A pair of benches have been pushed together and a mat of rushes lain over them to serve as the bed. I might have been grateful for the privacy had some groping, grunting pair of lovers not thought to intrude on my sleep in the middle of the night. They'd stumbled through the door, tearing at each others' clothes. I'd thrown that same cup at them that Archibald had used to awaken me. But instead of going back to sleep, I'd lain there for hours, the hollowness of my solitude eating away at me.

Two days have gone by and there's no hint of a possibility that I will ever get back to Claire, my so-called wife is avoiding me, her brother outright hates me, and his friend would prefer me dead so he can have Mariota. It's not that I want her to myself, but the thought of that snake's hands on her … No woman deserves that.

A wave of vomit pushes up, burning my esophagus. I swallow it back, then swing my legs over the edge of the bench and hang my head between my knees. I can't hold my liquor. Never could, even though my dad could down a six-pack of Michelob like most people guzzle lemonade on a hot summer day.

Duncan pushes my head back to look into my eyes. "Tell me that you went and found her, brought her here, but she woke early."

I scoot from his reach and stand, swaying on weak legs. A bowl of water sits on the barrel closest to the bench. I cup my hands and douse my face over and over, then dry my face on my sleeve. "Why is everyone so adamant that we *get to know* each other?"

"Why are you afraid of doing so?"

"You wouldn't understand if I told you." Besides, I don't want to get into this right now. Just outside the room, a pair of servants gather, one issuing instructions to the other. I step toward the door.

He braces an arm across the door frame, blocking my exit. "Try."

I'm not in the mood for a long conversation, but I did have a lot of time last night to think. There isn't any clear solution to my predicament. For all I know, it's permanent and if that's the case, then I need someone I can talk things through with.

I draw a deep breath and nod. "All right. Close the door."

He pulls it shut, but drags the stool in front of it and plants himself there to make sure I don't have second thoughts.

"First, you can't tell anyone this," I warn. "It'll only make things worse if you do."

I stall long enough that he opens his hands wide in a questioning gesture.

"I'm … I'm not who you think I am." That sounds so cliché, but how else am I supposed to explain it to him? "I'm not Sir Roslin."

He arches an eyebrow at me, then slaps his thigh, laughing. "Lad, I raised you from a weanling. You may have been gone awhile, but you *are* Roslin Sinclair, as sure as I sit here before you."

Pushing the blanket aside, I sit down on the bench. "Okay, um … I know I *look* like him … I may even be him physically, but … How do I put this?" I pull at my hair so hard I can feel my scalp stretching. "My memories are someone else's."

"Perhaps the blow to your head affected more than your memory?"

He starts to get up, but I grab his sleeve. "No, sit. Hear me out. I'm not crazy. I know this sounds insane. Hell, I wouldn't believe me, if I were you. But here goes." I pour it out all at once. "I am *Ross* Sinclair. I was born in 1984. In America, a big country across the western sea. Balfour, Indiana, to be specific. I moved to Ohio at eighteen and later met my childhood sweetheart, Claire Forbes. We were married, came to Scotland on our honeymoon. She suffered a blood clot in her brain, went into a coma ... They don't think she'll make it." I leave out the part about the baby she's carrying. It's too hard to talk about even now. Too raw. "I left her one day just to get away, to recharge. I was hit by a semi truck and ... when I woke up, I was here. Thrown back in time. Or maybe I'm reliving a past life. I'm not really sure."

Duncan gives me a blank stare. Finally, his eyelids flap. "Right. I don't understand you."

I point at him. "See, I said you wouldn't get it. Now you think I'm insane, that I'm just making this stuff up. But you wanted to know why I've been like I have, why I can't remember anything from this life, why I'm not willing to jump in bed with Mariota. I *can't* be unfaithful to Claire. I still love her. Madly."

"Ah! There's another woman. That makes sense." He clamps a hand on my shoulder. "Plenty of men keep a woman on the side, lad. I know the Church frowns on it, but it seems unnatural to me not to ... sow your oats widely, if you expect a few sprouts to grow. Keep your woman — I'll not mention it to Mariota. Still, why not get the business of producing an heir over with? Lie with her only as often as it takes. Just remember, the more sons the better. Daughters can be a boon, too. The Sinclairs are a powerful family. The more connections you can forge through marriages, the better for you."

Exasperated, I smack my palm to my forehead. "You still don't get it, do you? I love Claire. We want to have children of our own someday."

"Your father won't be pleased with you having an army of bastards, but —"

"I'm *married* to Claire."

At that, he wrinkles his brow. "You have two wives? That's bigamy, lad."

"No! I married Claire in 2013. *Ross* married Claire, not *Roslin*. Roslin only has one wife, at least as far as I know."

"So ..." — he glances up at the ceiling and wiggles his fingers, counting under his breath — "in about seven hundred years, you marry this woman named Claire. But Claire's not here? She ... doesn't exist yet?"

Finally, we're getting somewhere. "Yes, yes, that's right."

"Then there really is no Claire. Mariota's your wife. So what, exactly, is the problem?"

He has me there. Tired of going in circles, I slump against the wall. "I need to find a way to get back to Claire, that's all. And if I can't, well ... I need time to accept that, change my thinking, you know?"

"Roslin, I have been both a father and a friend to you since you drew your first breath. I wiped the spittle from your chin when you had no teeth yet. I taught you how to sit on a horse, how to hold a sword, how to use your shield. I was there at the cathedral in Kirkwall when you were wed and by your side at your first battle when a foe tried to end your life. I'm not going to let you down now — or ever. Take all the time you need. Just know that others will expect things of you — Lord Archibald, for one. Your father, more than anyone. He'll be hard on you, once he knows you're back in Scotland — and he's not likely to accept what you're telling me."

"You don't believe me, do you?"

His fingers splay across his kneecaps as he sits back against the door. "I think *you* believe what you're telling me. All that matters to me is that you're alive and back in Scotland where you belong."

"Yeah, well, I'm not so sure I do belong here. I feel completely out of place. And I can't even begin to tell you how weird it is to have a wife I don't know anything about. Especially one who seems less than thrilled to have me back."

"As far as Mariota goes, you should at least keep up appearances. Don't give folk reason to talk. Ever since you returned from Spain, there have been rumors ..."

"Rumors? Of what?"

He glances toward the door, then whispers, "Heresy."

I know enough of medieval thinking to realize that's worse than adultery, thievery and murder all rolled up into one. "Why would they say that?"

"Unlike Lord James, who died in the first clash at Teba, your brother William survived his wounds. It was clear, though, that he would not last the day. He struggled to hold on, waiting for a priest to deliver last rites. We all knew he was going to die at any moment, but there was nothing we could do for his pain. That was when you laid your hands on him and delivered the *Consolamentum*, the Consolation to the dying, so that his soul might be admitted to heaven. It is a Cathar practice." The pause that ensues carries an ominous weight. He knows what he saw, but he's struggling between his beliefs and his love for me. "It was thought the last of the Cathars were defeated almost a hundred years ago at Montsegur. Many say they still exist, though. That they live secretly among us, recruiting to their fold. Some say you are one of them."

More confused than ever, I'm about to ask him more about these Cathars when a knock sounds at the door. My heart jumps. Duncan jerks his head sideways. His hand flies to his side. His fingers curl around the hilt of his sword.

"Who is it?" I say.

"Simon, my lord," comes a squeaky, youthful voice. "Lord Archibald requests your presence in his meeting chamber at once."

"On what business?"

"Something about Berwick, my lord. That's all I know."

I look at Duncan. He tips his head toward the door and mouths the word, 'Go'.

"I'll be there as soon as I'm dressed," I say to the young man outside the door.

"Aye, m'lord," he answers. "Have you seen Sir Alan or Sir

Malcolm this morning? Lord Archibald wishes for them to come, as well."

"No, but if I do, I'll let them know."

Footsteps recede. When all is quiet in the corridor, Duncan narrows his eyes at me. "Probably conspiring, knowing those two. I'd not trust them if I were you, Roslin."

"I'll take your advice on that." I grab my boots from beneath the bench and tug them on. Before I rise to go, I eye Duncan intensely. "Please, you won't tell —"

He holds up the flat of his palm. "Don't worry, lad. I've invested too much in you over the years to put you in danger. If anyone asks, you're the most devout Christian I know and you love your wife with all your heart."

"Thank you, Duncan. If I can ever repay the favor ..."

"I hope to God you never need to."

21

LONG, LONG AGO

Lintalee, Scotland — 1333

I CLOSE THE DOOR to the meeting room behind me. The hinges groan and twenty pairs of eyes scrutinize me, making me feel as obvious as a cat at a dog show. I recognize a few faces from the night before, but their names were forgotten soon after Duncan told me. That's one of the reasons I don't drink: it tends to make me forget things. There are far too many men named James, William, Robert or Thomas, too many earls and knights to keep them straight, that much I remember. Most of the men are seated at a long table, but several are forced to stand along the wall.

Keith glances at me and nods a 'hello'. I squeeze between one of the benches and two dark-bearded men to stand across from him, glad not to have to make eye contact with the two brutes beside me. I'm so intent on keeping my eyes downcast that it takes me a few moments to realize Archibald isn't there yet.

The men talk in small huddles. One on one, I can by now

understand an individual fairly well, but in a group setting like this, my mind struggles to sort out the differences in speech. So I try to focus on the two next to me, but all I can figure out is that they're talking about cattle and the names of towns. It's some time before it comes to me that they're talking about the English towns they've raided and the cattle and other goods they've taken from them.

At length, the door opens and Archibald walks through. Everyone stops talking and rises to their feet. Close on his heels are Alan and Malcolm. Alan graces me with a fake smile, but Malcolm sneers so venomously I notice a few people looking back and forth between us. If I could slip through a crack in the floorboards just then, I would. Between the two men, however, it's Alan I fear. Malcolm makes no secret of his hatred for me. He's all brawn and no brains. Alan is deceptively clever. The kind who'd plant the clues that would pin me for some crime I didn't commit and smile while he offered his condolences for my impending execution.

Archibald has barely taken his place when he begins. "King Edward has crossed the border. As we speak, he may already be at Berwick." He sweeps a hand downward, indicating for everyone to take their seats. "Their supplies have already been sent ahead from Newcastle. Edward was more than prepared for this siege; he has been expecting to launch it for some time."

"How long can Berwick hold out?" the older bearded man beside me asks.

"Months, perhaps. Much will depend on the town's water supply. If that is cut off, if it doesn't rain enough …" His voice fades away. He strokes at his chin, pondering it all. "Berwick has thousands of inhabitants. Sir Alexander Seton knew to begin rationing immediately when Balliol arrived. Indications are that they can still hold out awhile. Knowing King Edward, however, I fear the danger is not in starvation. He may imitate the attack of 1296."

"Why do you say that?" Keith pushes forward. "The town's

defenses have been reinforced greatly since the massacre. They're not as vulnerable as they were then."

Archibald plucks a splinter from the table and examines it as he ponders the question. "The English have already sent engineers to Berwick. They're cutting timbers and building catapults as we speak. Saltpeter was among the shipments to Newcastle."

"Pots?" someone on the far end of the room says. "They'll blow holes in every roof and wall big enough for a man to walk through."

"Aye, pots. They've nearly completed the catapults to launch them." Archibald lets his gaze sweep from face to face. "We've tried diversionary raids — to no avail. Apparently, Edward is willing to let half of England burn before he'll abandon Berwick. He covets the place. And no army of Scotland will thwart his ambitions."

The room erupts with oaths against King Edward's life. A few even suggest disembowelment and castration before decapitating him.

"It's only the beginning," Malcolm says. "He won't stop at Berwick."

Leaning back, Archibald raises both hands until a tense hush settles over the room.

"Perhaps," Alan says calmly, seizing the moment, "we should have attacked Balliol when he first set foot in Scotland, rather than wait until he surrounded Berwick?"

His message is clear, even to me: Archibald's response was too slow and will ultimately cost them.

"We would have been outnumbered three to one," Archibald says, "had we advanced on him two months ago. I've already sent word to every corner of Scotland. If even half answer — and I know they will — we'll outnumber the English handily."

"That could take weeks yet," the man beside me says. I cringe as everyone glances in my direction.

"It will." Archibald scoots his chair back and stands. He's not a tall man, or big, or even loud, but there's a tranquility and thoughtfulness about him that makes others listen to his words, maybe even trust him. I do and I barely know the man. "They'll be amassing east of Edinburgh at Dunbar."

"Close to Blacklaw," Alan says.

"Sir Henry Sinclair will see to it that supplies are kept in order." There's a pause and it takes me a moment to realize that Archibald is waiting for me to look at him. "Sir Roslin, you will carry my instructions to your father. Wait there until it's time to march on Berwick. I'll set up other gathering points, so our numbers are not known to the English, but Dunbar will be our main one. We'll talk soon, Roslin."

I nod, hoping he'll move on to something else. And hoping even more strongly that the next time I go to sleep, I'll wake up in 2013. I can always hope. Although so far hoping hasn't amounted to much.

I LINGER ON THE edge of belonging. Present, but not really a part of the goings-on. An older woman in servant's rags glances at me as she gathers up empty bowls and cups from the tables in the great hall after the noon meal. Her look is one of deference and something else — unworthiness? Not mine, hers. As if she considers herself less deserving of respect. A boy scampers by hugging pitchers of ale. His mannerisms are those of someone who's fearful, who is never sure when the next backhanded correction will come at him. And yet other servants appear content with their duties, competent and eager to please. Then there are the men surrounding me: highborn nobles, lesser knights, and all their squires and pages, and some of the more seasoned warriors who've earned their positions through bloodshed ... What a fascinating lot they all are.

There's a lot to learn from just watching people: who holds sway, who's a follower, who serves who, who's indifferent to personal politics, who has purpose —

Purpose. So far it's other people who seem to know what my purpose here is. I don't have a clue. My plan is simply to fit in long enough to return to where I came from. That was a moment to moment thing at first. Now it's day to day. My spirits are sinking. It's like being thrown into a race, knowing you have to finish, but having no idea how far away the finish line is. I need something to take my mind off this senseless craziness. Or someone — and I know just who to look for.

Later that afternoon, I find Mariota as she's leaving Beatrice's solar. 'Solar', that's a new word for me, or at least a new meaning. I take it to mean the room where women gather to gossip, which is reinforced when they begin to depart in murmuring clumps. Kind of like the faculty lounge at the university whenever there's a rumor flying around of a professor-student fling or a hint from the dean about staff reduction.

A pair of women whispering back and forth fall quiet as they pass me, then ten feet later they sneak a look in my direction and begin to whisper again. I half-wonder if they aren't talking about me. Actually, I *know* they are. I've never been the paranoid type before, but I seem to be the object of a lot of curiosity and conjecture around here.

Mariota hangs back near the doorway, nodding as Lady Beatrice Douglas speaks to her, although her eyes keep flitting to me. Finally, it's Beatrice who turns around and waves to me.

"Sir Roslin," she calls. "Do come in. There's a fire in the hearth still. It will take the chill from your bones after last night's rain."

"Thank you, but … I thought Mariota might like to take a walk outside. I've had so little chance to talk with her."

"Of course," she says. Smiling faintly, Beatrice gives me her hand. It takes me a few seconds to realize I'm supposed to kiss it, but I do. "When you're done, I'd like to steal her back for a few hours.

The boys have missed her sorely. She was such a good nursemaid to them when they were younger. She'll make a wonderful mother to your own children one day soon."

After Beatrice and Mariota exchange a flurry of kisses, I find myself alone with Mariota. I don't know what to say or where to begin. Apparently, neither does she. So I turn and start walking. We make our way through a short corridor which connects to the main hall. Malcolm is there, clutching a tankard like a sailor on furlough after six months at sea. Mariota raises a hand to him. He tips his head in acknowledgment, then eyes me scornfully. If he could shoot lasers with his eyes, I'd be reduced to a pile of smoking ash. I ball my fists defensively, expecting him to get up and storm at us. Thankfully, though, one of the men he's with slaps him on the back and shares a joke, rescuing me.

The outer doors are open and we walk outside into a light mist. It's now the first of May and the day is warming gradually, if not drying out. As we walk slowly, the space between us widens.

"You wished to speak with me?" she says.

"Do I need a reason to be with you?" I say a little too tersely. She flinches. I can't help myself. The hopelessness of my situation is beginning to wear on me. Realizing how snide that sounded, I try another approach. "It's just that ... we haven't been alone yet. I wanted to talk last night, but I couldn't find you. It's like you're avoiding me. Like you're more disappointed than glad to find me here. Are you?"

The pungent smell of hay assaults my nostrils. We're nearing the stables now. I expect to start sneezing and itching, but nothing happens. I inhale more deeply. Until now, I hadn't realized how good that smell actually is.

"Was I what?"

"Avoiding me. Disappointed." I hold out my hand and begin to count on my fingers. "Angry. Indifferent. Shocked. Disbelieving ...

Take your pick."

Mariota puts a hand on my arm to halt me. But it's only to keep me from plowing into a horse's side as a groom leads it from one of the side stalls toward the smith's shed. She starts forward again, but I quickly turn in front of her, blocking her path.

Her mouth twists with unspoken words. Fine creases furrow her forehead. "You're different, somehow."

Tell me about it. Seeing Roslin again may have been hard for her so far, but she has no idea what the past few days have been like for me. "I'm sorry, but I don't remember —"

"I know. They told me. Still ... it's as if I look into your eyes and I see someone else."

"Is that a good or bad thing?" I try to joke, but it falls flat. If anything, I've only confused her. Or put her off even more, if that's even possible. "Look, whoever I was before, I get the feeling I wasn't entirely good to you. That things between us were shaky, at best. Whatever it was I did, or didn't do, I'm sorry. I'd like to start over, if that's okay?"

She blinks at me in confusion. Oh, I've just used a word, 'okay', that won't be invented for several hundred more years. "I mean, can we put the past behind us, please? Maybe later, you can explain things to me and I'll understand how I may have upset you. Until then, I desperately need someone to tell me who's who, what's going on, how I'm supposed to handle things with my father when we get to Blacklaw —"

Her features darken at the mention.

"You don't like Blacklaw? Or is it my father?"

She looks around, as if to avoid meeting my eyes. "It ..." Her gaze drops to the mud at her feet. Her shoes are caked with filth, yet she hasn't complained. "It was supposed to be our home. Yet every day I waited for you, trying to fill the hours. As for Sir Henry ... we haven't much to talk about beyond the weather and the crops. Even then my opinion is seldom valued."

She looks so vulnerable, so wounded. I brush her cheek with my thumb. So, I had abandoned her and left her alone with a disagreeable father-in-law? If I'd done that to Claire, she would have murdered me upon my return. Mariota, instead, has drawn into herself, suffered the solitude. I know what living with a person like that's like. It's worse than being alone. "Would you rather stay here with Beatrice?"

"No!" She looks up suddenly, panic widening her eyes. Something, or someone, has made her change her mind about being in Lintalee since yesterday.

"All right, then." I stroke her hair, trying to reassure her. "We're supposed to leave for Blacklaw tomorrow. I'll try to make up for lost time."

She looks away. "It will take you more than a day to do that."

"Then I'll take as long as is needed." I'm not sure why I've made her those promises, but for now it seems the right thing to do. As long as I'm stuck in the fourteenth century, I might as well make the best of it.

"Now, tell me about my brother William, will you?" I offer her my elbow.

Tentative, she slips a hand around my arm. The yard is crowding with people: soldiers carrying supplies on their shoulders, grooms tending to horses, women scurrying about in small groups with baskets of laundry and food, children trailing at their skirts.

"Perhaps we could speak more privately somewhere?" Her gaze sweeps around the compound. She points. "There, in the granary."

I'm not entirely sure what a granary is, so I let her guide me. We begin toward a building that looks vaguely like a barn.

"He left a son behind," she says.

"William did? How old is he now? And where is he?"

"Four, I believe. He was an infant when you and your brother left. The boy is in Orkney with his mother's family." She guides me in the direction of a wagon piled with sacks of grain. "This way."

A few nobles pass us and raise a hand in greeting; I smile at them, even though I have no idea who they are. Mariota whispers their names to me: John Thomas, Patrick Graham, Robert Gordon, John le Fitzwilliam ... I catch a couple of earls in there, but by the time we reach the granary, I've already forgotten who's who. When she starts to tell me how they're all related, I wave my hands at her.

"One more and my head is going to explode." I press my fingertips to my temples.

Laughter trickles from her throat. She clamps a hand over her mouth, trying to quell it, but it spills out, light as duck down. We're standing between the cart and the granary. A trace of grain dust hangs in the air, despite the dampness from the previous night's rain.

"What's so hilarious?" I ask. It's the first I've seen her let her guard down. I like this side of her.

Finally, she puts a hand on the cart's bed to steady herself as she waits for her laughter to subside. "You always used to complain about keeping straight who held a grudge against whom. You believed most of it was posturing for favors or overblown misunderstanding. You found it aggravating and petty, yet you partook of your share of it yourself. This way, although you may find it frustrating to not be able to remember, everything is new to you. Old grievances are forgotten." Her smile fades away. "If we could all forget, then maybe we could forgive more easily."

The echo of a long-ago voice, my mother's, sounds inside my head:

'Maybe someday you'll even ... forgive him.'

I turn away. No, it's not that easy for me. It's been years since I've spoken to my dad and I still can't forgive him for the way he treated us. Even here, centuries removed, I still get riled up over it. Would it have been that hard for him to tell us he was sorry for the things he'd said? To make it up by showing Mom compassion when she'd needed it most? To have supported my aspirations in some way or maybe just once told me he was proud of me?

Mariota touches my arm. "Roslin, is something troubling you?"

"No. I'm fine." She doesn't need to know. It isn't her problem. Turning back to her, I take her hand, holding it firmly as I try to anchor myself in this place and time. I'm about to ask her about William again when I see someone striding toward us: Alan Stewart.

"Sir Roslin!" he shouts.

Too bad I didn't see him first.

When he reaches us, he steals Mariota's hand from my grip and places a kiss on her knuckles — a tender, lingering kiss. Even as he looks up at her, his hold on her goes on uncomfortably long. Mariota doesn't pull away or even glance away coyly, but meets his gaze with a degree of coldness I didn't know was in her. He tilts his head as he takes her in, his words softening to a husky murmur. "And the lovely Lady Mariota."

Heat flares at the back of my neck and spreads around to my chest. If he hadn't finally let go of her hand, I might have punched him. Then again, who am I kidding? I've never hit anyone in my life. Instead, I bury my feelings. I hate conflict. Hate the yelling. Hate how it never solves anything.

"Good morning, Sir Alan," I say between clenched teeth. I place Mariota's hand on my forearm, trying to make a point. "If you don't mind —"

"Did Lord Archibald tell you?" He grins smugly.

"Tell me what?"

"I am to accompany you to Blacklaw. He was concerned, given your condition, about your ability to oversee the organization of troops and the collection of supplies at Dunbar. He thought I should, perhaps ... how to put this ... replace you in that capacity, for the most part. I'll keep you well informed, though." He gives me a patronizing pat on the upper arm. "In the morning then. We depart an hour after sunrise."

As he strides arrogantly away, I glance at Mariota. Her mouth is set in a firm line, her fingernails digging into my flesh. If it's possible, she looks even less pleased than I am.

Before I can probe for details, Mariota has plucked up the hem of her skirt and begun back toward the great hall.

"Where are you going?" I reach for her, but she's already several steps away.

"I'm late. Lady Beatrice is expecting me."

Somehow, I don't think that's true. Something about Alan unsettles her. Something she isn't willing to share. At least not yet.

22

LONG, LONG AGO

North of Lintalee, Scotland — 1333

THE DAY DAWNS IN rare brilliance. A scattering of sunlight, bright as a welder's torch, falls upon the forest floor surrounding Lintalee as our party heads out. The air is thick with the scent of pine needles being crushed beneath horses' hooves.

The road — if it can be called that, for it's nothing but a beaten dirt path — curves around massive tree trunks and crosses gurgling streams. This is old forest, ancient trees soaring to scrape the heavens. The deeper we go into it, the more the earth below is so scant of light that very little grows underneath. Birds sing unseen from the lacework of branches and small creatures scatter at our passing.

There are two dozen of us, most of them Alan's men. Duncan leads at the front of the group with Alan, while Mariota and I ride side by side in the middle, surrounded by men who wear their armor as comfortably as their own skin. While the armor hasn't proven to be nearly as hot or heavy as I expected, I still find it a far cry from a broken in pair of jeans and a well fitted T-shirt. Even if I'd been able to wear the clothes I'm used to, I wouldn't have. The more I make an effort to fit in here, the fewer stares I'll get.

With every snapped twig, my eyes dart through the undergrowth. I listen intently, my ears keened for the twang of a bowstring. Whenever the wind rushes through the leaves, I glance behind us, thinking it's the rising rumble of hooves from an English ambush party. Duncan has taken pains to warn me of the possibility we could come under attack and instructed me in how to defend the womenfolk if that comes to pass. I figure both my first and final objectives are: don't die — or at least avoid being maimed. I'd signed up for a fencing class during my freshman year of college, but during the first session my impulse whenever my opponent thrust his rapier at me was to roll up in a ball on the floor and cover my head with my hands. I quickly switched to bowling class. Me landing in a century where carrying around a length of steel is commonplace is a joke. I'm more likely to accidentally cut myself than intentionally harm someone else.

I hate to admit it, but when Archibald started to talk to me last night about collecting provisions and the organization of further raids into the north of England to gather cattle and sheep, I was thankful the task had been handed over to Alan. I want no part in planning for a war. I'm about as far from being militarily-minded as a guy can get. I'm a biologist. I'm constantly distracted by the range of flora and fauna around us, reciting genus and species in Latin in my head — *Hyacinthoides non-scripta*, *Pinus sylvestris*, *Martes martes* — whenever I'm not imagining enemy arrows whizzing through the air at my head.

Mariota tugs her hood back. A long braid twists over her shoulder and down her front, the ends of wispy curls escaping at random intervals. Fair skin complements the golden red of her hair and beneath delicately arched brows, her green eyes take in the road ahead. It's the same look Claire gets whenever she's daydreaming. Mariota's gaze sweeps from left to right as the road opens out into a meadow speckled with spring's first wildflowers. Laying the reins across her lap, she lifts her face to the sky, closes her eyes and inhales. Her hands, palms up, drift out to her sides. Silk ribbons trail from her flared sleeves, which are hemmed with gold-embroidered knotwork. Breathtaking. It's like something out of a Waterhouse painting.

A dove coos from behind us, startling her. Her eyes fly wide and she suddenly realizes I'm staring at her.

"What?" I say. "Can't a man admire his wife?"

A blush infusing her snowy skin, she looks away. She grabs the reins again, pinching them hard. That's when I notice her gaze is fixed on something in the meadow. As I peer into the brightness, two shapes part from the far grove of trees.

My heart seizes. For a moment, I stop breathing. Everything around me fades away. All I can see is them, unafraid and un-wavering, as they gaze back at us. There are two of them, just like before.

The majestic stag lifts his head higher, ears perked forward. The nostrils of his black nose flare as he lets out a snort. His antlers are tipped with six prongs on each side. The winter fur is thinning to a sleek reddish brown hide. Behind him, the doe sniffs the air, then goes to stand next to him, making the contrast in size between them more apparent. Her neckline is more elegant, her features more refined than his. She curves her neck around to rub her head against his shoulder.

The edges of time blur. I am back there, with Claire, when we got lost in the Grampian Mountains and stopped by the side of the road. The doe gazes back at me and I swear I can feel her presence — Claire's — surrounding me, filling my heart, coursing through my blood.

Love never dies.

The stag's hide twitches. He steps back, his muscles rigid, ready. The doe's head snaps up, dark eyes wide, ears alert.

The rest of our party has halted. Beside Malcolm, one of the men has an arrow fitted to his bow. The string is taut, his elbow cocked back.

Malcolm jabs a finger at the deer. "Now!"

All I see is the flick of the bowstring and the feathered end of the shaft zipping past his fingers. It hisses across the open meadow and thwacks into the ground where the stag and doe had been standing only seconds ago.

They're already bounding back across the meadow on slender, powerful legs, propelled by fear.

I kick my horse in the flanks and race toward Malcolm. The man who shot the arrow and two others are galloping across the meadow in pursuit.

"Call them off!" My horse's hooves slam into the ground as I jerk back on the reins. It wheels around one full turn before coming to a complete stop. Vertigo rushes over me. I grip the edge of my saddle until the world stops tilting.

"Call them off?" Malcolm's deep laughter rattles in my ears. "That's our supper they're going to bring down."

"They won't catch them." They can't. It's not the deer's time to die. I'm not sure how I know that. I just do.

"I say they will." Arching his back, he pats his stomach. "Ahhh, venison roasted over an open spit ..."

If he keeps this up, I'm going to spew vomit all over him.

"Sir Roslin is right." Alan lays his reins over his mount's withers and dismounts. "Sound the horn and call them back, Malcolm. We don't need to lose any men over an impulsive hunt. We're too close to the border for that sort of folly."

A grumble escapes Malcolm's throat, but he complies. The horn blasts once, twice, and a minute later the three men are cantering back into the clearing.

"Thank you," I say to Alan.

"For being sensible? Save your gratitude for more important things — such as the fact that I've been sent along to carry out a duty that should have been yours, but which you are presently incapable of doing." Contempt bubbles beneath the surface of his words. He uncorks his flask and takes a drink. "We'll stop here to eat, but not long. We need to reach the Teviot before nightfall."

If he's expecting an argument, he won't get one from me. I don't want the duties he's taken over. I don't even want to be here.

"Roslin?"

Behind me stands Mariota, holding out bread and a flask. My stomach rumbles. If there's one shining light in this backwards world, it's her. I climb down from my saddle, glad to be on firm ground again. Beneath the broad boughs of an oak tree, we share our bland meal, barely saying a word. Oddly, I find the silence comfortable, the way it is with an old friend.

A tingle of electricity sparks in my chest and I can sense her eyes upon me. We smile briefly at each other and then look away. Sitting in silence with her, I begin to understand her better. She's not quiet because she's shy or awkward. It's more of a calmness that she exudes. Serenity. And right now, I need that, because so much around me is beyond my control.

A half hour later, we're riding again, the dense growth of the forest having given way to grassy hills.

"I don't like the forest," Mariota says, unprompted. "There are too many places for the English to hide."

"We agree on that. What *do* you like, then?" Anything to steer the talk back to something more lighthearted. I don't need to feed my paranoia. I still remember that English detachment we came upon after Archibald and the others found me.

She thinks a moment. "The sea. From the topmost tower window of Blacklaw, you can see forever across the sea."

"Beautiful, I'm sure." But I'm not talking about a castle perched above the sea. I have a clear picture in my mind — of her, standing at the edge of a very tall cliff, her arms wide, the wind fanning the hair from her face …

A vacuum of shock sucks the air from my lungs with a sudden, terrifying force. *She* is the woman in my dreams. The one I'd seen since childhood. The one I'd known since before I was born.

"Watch it!" Malcolm glares at me as he rides by, a furrow of anger cleaving his brow. "If you are going to stop like that, take your horse off to the side." He jerks an elbow as he guides his mount past us, then adds under his breath, "Stupid bastard."

Mariota darts a curious look at me as she joins her brother. I don't remember doing it, but I must have yanked back on the reins and halted my horse when the revelation hit me like a wrecking ball: that this body I'm inhabiting doesn't belong to me. I'm just borrowing it for the time being. And all those visions I'd had growing up — they're memories.

I hadn't fallen into a wormhole and gotten sucked back in time. I've been *remembering* who I once was. So maybe, just maybe, I can go back — or forward, however you want to look at it. But how?

That still doesn't answer what happened to the real Sir Roslin. Had he died in a scuffle with his captors as they brought him back north? Or was he still here, in this body, unable to speak, waiting for me to leave?

I shake myself, nudge my mount in the flanks and ride on. Malcolm and Mariota are now several horses ahead of me. I'd seen my reflection in the water the day I woke up here and then in a piece of polished metal while at Lintalee. I look a lot like the old me, but not entirely. My face is leaner, my shoulders more muscular, and my hair is more burnished, as if I've spent more time out of doors than my previous academic lifestyle would have leant itself to. Everyone here has accepted me as Sir Roslin without question — even Duncan, who's known me … Sir Roslin, I mean, all his life.

Rain begins to fall, heavily. In minutes, I'm soaked to the bone and shivering. My senses tell me this is real, not a dream. Intensely, miserably real. Still, my logic-driven brain is having a hard time accepting it.

For two more days as we ride on to Blacklaw, I can't stop asking myself, wondering, when this will all end. I'm starting to think I'll never get back to 2013, never see Claire again, never go home.

The worst part is that I'm not sure I want to go back. Not if Claire isn't going to be all right. Not if the baby isn't going to make it.

Might as well be somewhere else. Even here.

MY WORLD HAS MORE than been shaken. It's been flipped upside down, turned inside out and beaten bloody with a spiked iron mallet. Like nothing I ever planned, let alone even imagined.

Before a week ago, I'd been meticulous about plotting out my future, graphing our combined incomes versus long and short-term investments, our retirement savings plan and a college fund for our still-in-negotiations 2.5 children. Claire and I had debated over which school district to purchase our next house in, which was the most reliable car to buy once my 2001 Toyota Camry slurped its last tank of gas, and how much of our money should go to every assignable budget category. She wanted to buy organic, locally grown food and I pushed for bulk packaged foods from Sam's Club. Even though we were often on different ends of the spectrum, our debates were always logical exchanges of intellect and shining examples of compromise.

This is bad. Very bad. Already, I'm starting to think of her in past tense. Not 'we are …', but 'we were …'

I can feel the gaping hole in my heart. And it needs filling.

God, how I miss her spontaneity. I ache for the little surprises she always showered me with that brightened otherwise mundane days. A few weeks ago, when we were up to our ears in the details of wedding plans, she had told me she'd pick me up at lunch to take me for a tux fitting. I'd been avoiding it for weeks. Crawling out of my T-shirt and donning a button-up Oxford for important functions at work has always been absolute torture for me. I tried to convince her I had to work through lunch, that I was behind on grading papers, but she refused to buy into my flimsy excuse and hauled me from the building.

Imagine my surprise when she turned her car into the botanical gardens parking lot and pulled a picnic basket out of the trunk, complete with roasted Cornish game hens, a fancy raspberry vinaigrette pasta salad with little black olives and sun-dried tomatoes, a bottle of sparkling cider and a red checkered tablecloth. What I wouldn't give for another day like that.

But it's slowly sinking in. There's no way to go back. None.

I'm here, in this place. I'll never see her again. Ever. And it hurts like hell.

23

LONG, LONG AGO

Blacklaw Castle, Scotland — 1333

MY FIRST IMPRESSION OF Blacklaw Castle is that it doesn't look like much of a home. More like a prison. I can see why Mariota finds the place so desolate.

Ahead of us, a long narrow road curves around a small bay, before winding its way upward along a finger of land that juts out into the sea. Towering cliffs soar above crashing waves, with only a thin strip of shingle beach edging the shore below. Thousands of sea gulls are perched on tiny ledges in the cliff face. Here and there, fledglings peek from their nests, crying out in hunger to watchful parents. Others glide on crescent wings above the froth-capped ocean, sometimes dipping their heads to dive, dive, dive, into the dark, choppy waters, later emerging with a flopping silver fish in their yellow beaks.

Above the cliffs, almost at the very end of the peninsula, squats the castle. Built more for defense than residence, it imposes on the landscape for miles around. A tall curtain wall maybe fifty feet high throws long shadows across the outer court. Beyond that is a lower wall that spans the width of the land from the sea cliff facing us to the other side, where I assume is another equally sheer drop-off. Two stout towers flank either end of the inner wall and in the middle a semicircular gatehouse projects, complete with drawbridge. The moat between the inner wall and outer yard is a dry one, but steep.

As we round the bay and pass through a small village, I see movement along the wall walk. Archers are scurrying to their positions, bows gripped.

Blacklaw might not be the biggest castle in Scotland, but anyone inside it is certainly well protected from the enemy.

At the head of our party, Alan breaks away, galloping his horse boldly toward the outer gate, helmet tucked beneath his arm. Malcolm is close behind him. Shouts are exchanged. A loud groan issues from an unseen winch as the portcullis slowly lifts. The drawbridge lowers, as gears and chains clank and screech. It hits the far side of the moat with a low thud. Alan and Malcolm ride across, disappearing into the shadowy throat of the gatehouse.

Duncan eases his horse up to mine. "Are you ready?"

"No." I urge my mount forward, eager to settle onto a chair or bed and rest my back after three days in the saddle. "But are we ever really ready for anything?"

Heaven knows I wasn't ready to land here in the fourteenth century. It's a wonder I'm not dead yet.

HIS GAIT IS STIFF as he lumbers across the inner bailey, like he's got an iron rod shoved up the backside of his trousers. His hair bushes out from his head in a wiry brownish gray mop, the ends grazing the tops of his rounded shoulders. A bristly beard, threaded with silver, fans from his cheeks to partway down his chest. He's a man with a substantial frame, his torso as broad and deep as a whiskey barrel, but there's lion-like strength in his movements, however battered his body might be. The man reminds me of Hagrid from Harry Potter — but without the friendly disposition.

So this is Henry Sinclair. He looks less than happy to see his only son again.

I don't know if it's the disdain in his stare, or the fact that my lower back aches, but I go down on one knee before him, my head bowed.

"How did you manage it?" he says.

I raise my eyes, trying to gauge his mood. His brow is clouded with anger and I can tell by his tone that he's accustomed to being feared. "Escape, you mean?"

"Of course I mean your escape, you imbecile!" he bellows.

"Henry." Duncan steps forward. "Been almost a year, has it?"

"More than a year — but still too soon." Henry clasps Duncan's forearm in greeting, as something vaguely resembling a smile plumps his cheeks. "I'll post a guard by the cellar door. Last you were here you drank my stores dry."

"You should tell your serving girls not to refill tankards so readily. I was only accepting the generosity of my host and dear friend."

"A liar and always were. Some things never change."

"You received my message?" Duncan tips his head in my direction, then motions for me to get up. "About him?"

"Aye." Henry studies me. For a moment I'm afraid he'll figure out I'm not his son after all, that I don't belong here. With a brusque jerk, he grabs Duncan by the elbow and pulls him aside. "He still doesn't remember anything? Who brought him north or how he escaped?"

Duncan shakes his head. "Nothing."

"I find it hard to believe he could have managed it without help

— or a stroke of luck. However it happened, he saved me a fortune in ransom. Is he …" — Sir Henry taps his temple — "all right here?"

"Not entirely, if I may say so. He doesn't seem a danger, but he's not quite himself." I detect a faint wink directed at me. "I suggest you give him time."

"We don't have time, Duncan. You bloody well know that. Balliol has been harassing Berwick for weeks and now Edward has joined him. We need every able-bodied man we can muster."

"Let me work with him, Henry. He won't be a bother to you that way."

Henry lets out a loud 'humph'. "Do what you will, although based on everything he's done so far," — his eyes slide to me — "I'm not expecting much."

Yeah, some things never change. I may be used to a father's derision, but it still stings.

24

LONG, LONG AGO

<u>Blacklaw Castle, Scotland — 1333</u>

F OR A WEEK I see very little of Sir Henry or Alan. They're holed up in the meeting room making plans for the movement of supplies and men. On the one occasion Henry did include me, he was annoyed by my questions. So I stopped asking them and sat in the window instead, gazing out at the sea, which only irritated him further.

Couriers come and go on lathered mounts, bearing letters from all across Scotland. A few nobles and chieftains arrive, but most have already gone on to Dunbar or are on their way to Berwick. Some of them seem to remember me, but they regard me warily; it's Henry they ask to speak with.

I'm immeasurably relieved when I hear Alan is supposed to leave for Dunbar in the morning. I've barely seen Mariota since we got here. We have separate rooms and while it's strange to me that a husband and wife reside apart, no one here seems to consider it unusual. While I try to circulate out in the open as much as I can, however uncomfortable it may be for me, Mariota stays hidden away most of the time. I can tell it's not me she's avoiding, but Alan. The communal supper in the great hall is the only time she will stay in the same room as him for more than a minute.

Today, supper is a special occasion. The Abbot of Melrose is visiting. Everyone's a nervous wreck. The floors have been scrubbed, the hearths swept clean, and the beddings all washed. The cooks began preparing days ago. It reminds me of the time the Nobel Prize winner came to our university to give a talk. The custodians waxed the tiles and cleaned windows in wings where he was never going to step foot.

The abbot sits at the head table next to Sir Henry, looking very righteous. So far I've avoided any exchanges more in depth than a polite 'hello'. I'm afraid he'll quiz me on church rituals or the differences between Cistercian and Benedictine monks. Maybe I've grown more paranoid in the time since I found myself here, but I'm sure he keeps looking at me. He's probably heard things: that Sir Henry's son is mad, that he's suspected of treason, or that he used witchcraft to defeat his six captors and flee to freedom.

While I'm preoccupied with whether or not the Abbot of Melrose is passing judgment on me, Mariota glares contemptuously at Alan on the other side of the hall from where we're seated, not so much in challenge, but as if she's trying to send a message: Keep your distance. He's a master at masking his reactions toward her, barely even acknowledging her presence. Her spoon clacks against the table as she lays it down to grab her knife. She attacks her meat, slicing it into ribbons.

I've been sawing away at my slab of meat for ten minutes, letting little chunks fall into my lap and then brushing them to the floor. Without a convenient supply of packaged nuts at hand, my body has been craving protein so badly I almost consider shoving some of the meat in my mouth and swallowing. Almost.

"Tell me why you don't like him," I say aside to her. Looking around to make sure no one's watching, I slide the last piece of mutton from my trencher into my hand at the table's edge, then lower it. Hungry jaws snap at my fingers, pinching the tips. "Watch it, you greedy bitch!" I growl, peeking under the table. Lips pull back in a grin of submission before the deerhound slinks away with her prize. Two nosy pups instantly take her place at my knee. I scratch one of the furry beasts on top of the head, grateful to have made a few friends, at least.

One eyebrow arched as if I've just insulted her, Mariota plunks her knife down. "Your pardon?"

"Alan Stewart," I whisper, darting glances left and right. "I know when you were both young, it was presumed the two of you would marry. What did he do to — ?"

"Nothing. Why do you ask?"

"I'm not blind, Mariota." I point at my eyes like a petulant child. "I see the way you look at him. You *hate* him, don't you? And yet if I weren't here, he'd scoop you up and carry you away on a white horse, kicking and screaming. What went on between the two of you? What don't you want to tell me?"

She stares at her food, mouth firmly closed, her delicate nostrils flaring with sharply drawn breaths. Several seconds pass before she lifts her chin and speaks. "As I said, there is nothing to tell, husband. We were childhood friends. He finds it hard to move on. I do not." Her shoulders twitch in an unconvincing shrug. "That is all. Nothing more."

She's a worse liar than I am. Maybe this isn't the time or place. She'll tell me when she's ready. Eventually, I'll tell her about me. If I ever think she'll believe me.

Setting my cup down, I reach for the bowl of cherries to my right. The hair on my neck prickles. Three seats down, Malcolm is leaning on his elbows, glowering at me.

Wonderful. I may be getting rid of Alan and the abbot soon, but I'll still have that oaf hovering around. Not to mention Sir Henry.

Decision made. Tomorrow I'll ask Duncan for sword fighting lessons. Can't say I'm looking forward to getting the tar beat out of me, but if it gets me out if here for awhile, I'm all for it.

I raise my cup to Duncan. He returns the gesture, the froth of his ale spilling over the rim as he thrusts it in the air, his belly quaking with laughter.

DUNCAN MARCHES OUT THE door of my chambers with conviction. I'm less enthusiastic, but better to take a few lumps from a well meaning friend than get skewered by an Englishman in my first — and possibly last — skirmish. I tap the pommel of my sword with the heel of my hand, grab my shield by its hanging strap and follow him.

Today I'm sore as hell. Getting out of bed was painful enough, but going down the stairs …? The only reason I make it to the bottom is gravity. I swear every muscle in my body has been battered beyond repair and every tendon shredded from my bones. I have so many bruises it's a wonder I haven't bled to death internally.

For three weeks now we've been repeating this cruel routine. Up before dawn, out the gate on horse, then a mile down the road to a trail through the woods. There in a clearing, Duncan abuses me, liberally. And I let him. Then in the evenings we do it again. For the first several days, he wouldn't even let me lift a sword. Instead, he made me tear down a stone wall and rebuild it fifty feet away. When I was done, he made me move it back. For variety, I got to run to the top of a *very* tall hill. When I stopped breathing so hard after a week and told him it wasn't that bad — I was being facetious — he gave me a sack of stones to carry and told me to do it again. He has no sense of humor. The son of a —

"Are you coming, Roslin?" Duncan pivots at the bottom of the stairway, tapping his thumb against his hip.

Morning sun glints above the eastern wall, temporarily blinding me. I blink away the glare, put my head down, and begin down the last few stairs outside the great hall. A rhythmic thumping, emanating from somewhere near the stables, echoes from wall to wall. I stop dead with one foot on the step below and one on the step above it.

He rolls his eyes. "Forget something again?"

Before I can dash away in panic, an unwelcome voice hails me from the far side of the bailey.

"Roslin!" A knight in full chainmail hands his sword and shield to a nearby squire and flips his visor up. I cringe inwardly as Alan parts from the circle of men gathered around him and his sparring partner, Malcolm, and comes toward us. "Impeccable timing. I've just beaten your brother-in-law. He was on his knees only a minute ago, pleading mercy like a little girl."

Malcolm is standing sideways to us, head down, his wide shoulders heaving with each labored breath. He looks unsteady on his feet, ragged, defeated. If Malcolm had been alive in the twenty-first century, he'd have been a gym rat, bulked up even more on steroids, grunting at the barbells several hours a day and downing protein shakes by the gallon. He might not be quick on his feet, but the man is brutishly strong. If Alan beat him, it was on skill and quickness.

Alan's teeth gleam beneath a clean-shaven upper lip. Sweat is beading on his forehead, dripping down his neck. He turns his palms outward and lifts his arms. "Care to have your turn at me?"

"Thanks," I say, "but not today."

Not ever, I hope. If he'd given Malcolm the Hulk a pummeling, I don't even want to think what he'll do to me.

I step to go around him, but he blocks me. "I hear you killed your English captors to gain your freedom. Is that right?"

My heart speeds up. Instinct tells me to keep quiet, let his taunt pass and go on my way. I'll learn how to fight on my own terms, in my own time, not like this.

Alan, however, isn't about to let it go. He reaches out, flicks his fingertips over the sleeve of my chainmail. "Come, Roslin. You're prepared. The rest of these men would love to see how it's done." He flings his hand wide, indicating the onlookers. There are at least two dozen fully clad and armed knights.

"I told you," I say lowly, "not now."

Grinning, Alan cocks an eyebrow. "Why not now?"

"Aren't you supposed to be at Dunbar?"

He breaks into a full smile. "You're avoiding the question."

"And you're avoiding mine."

"Very well, then. I'll answer you. I returned to give a full report to your father and request more supplies. Our numbers have increased by more than two thousand this week alone." He yanks a leather glove off, pushes the sweat from his brow, and slides the glove back on. "Now you. Why not now?"

"Leave him be, Alan."

I spin around at the booming tenor. Standing at the top of the steps to the great hall is Sir Henry. For once, I'm thankful to see him.

"Your pardon, my lord." Alan ducks his head in a symbolic bow. "We were simply making good use of our spare time. An idle soldier is an unprepared one."

"I won't argue that point." Descending the stairs, Henry grunts each time he unbends a knee. With only a single tunic on over his leggings, the spread of his paunch is more apparent than usual. On level ground, his stride evens out. He stops two steps away and extends a hand out toward Alan. "But if you'll loan me your sword, I'll be the one to test my son, see how far he's come since I taught him how to fight."

That isn't true. Duncan was the one to teach Roslin how to

fight, practically raised him. Still, Henry had survived decades of battles, including Bannockburn. Old or not, he's experienced. I barely know how to parry.

"We were on our way into the village, my lord," Duncan says in a vain attempt to rescue me.

"It can wait." Gruffly, Henry hooks a hand beneath my armpit and drags me into the middle of the bailey.

Someone lays a sword in his hand. Alan's squire is pulling a padded jerkin over Henry's head and strapping a shield to his arm. Then the same squire lifts the shield from my grip, guides my arm through the straps and tightens them.

I swallow back a volcano of vomit and close my eyes, trying to summon the spirit of Errol Flynn and imagine myself as Robin Hood. But when I open my eyes again, the only thing I'm aware of is the sensation that my knees have turned to water and are going to buckle beneath me at any moment.

Henry taps the flat of his blade against my shield to get my attention. "You look like death already." He lumbers back several steps and raises his shield to just below eye level. "Go on. Strike the first blow."

I don't move. Just stare at him as his face clouds over in frustration, a storm of anger and aggression brewing behind his gray eyes. He wags his sword at me tauntingly. "What's the matter with you, boy? Forget everything you were taught?"

For a moment, I am ten years old again.

My dad wallops me in the upper arm with the back of his leather baseball glove. So hard I'm sure I'll have a bruise there.

"What's the matter, boy? Forget everything already?" he says in a mocking tone.

I rest the bat against my knees and rub at the place where he smacked me. It's throbbing. I can feel a lump forming. If another kid on the playground had hit me like that, I'd have tattled on him to the teacher. But he's my dad. Who am I going to tell?

"Pick up the bat now, will you? And quit looking like you're going to cry." He turns around and stomps back to the mound, muttering as he goes. "Good Lord, at this rate, you won't even make bat boy."

I don't remind him that Little League was his idea, not mine. I wanted to join the Young Scientists' Club that Mrs. Harnish advises. They're at the planetarium in Ft. Wayne today, looking at constellations and moon rocks. It's probably air conditioned there. I'm here, roasting in the sun, standing on a patch of dirt that makes me cough every time a dust devil blows across the infield, while my dad pelts me with fastballs and yells at me for not paying attention.

I hoist the bat onto my shoulder, bend forward and squint into blinding white sunlight. I hear the ball slam into the chain link cage behind me. It rolls to my feet, so I pick it up and lob it back to him.

"That was a strike," he says. "One more and we're done. I'm not going to waste my time if you won't even try to hit the ball."

"I didn't see it. The sun's right behind you."

"I didn't see it," he mimics in a sing-song voice. "Christ, boy, do you think the major leaguers tell their managers that? No, they get fired, lose everything they own because they don't have a job anymore, and then they end up robbing convenience stores and going to jail."

I fail to see how me not being good at baseball will land me in jail, but somehow it makes sense to him.

"Now cock the damn bat like I showed you," he says, repeatedly tossing the ball in a little arc, catching it in his mitt and

rolling it back to his right hand, "*and swing when the ball comes across the plate. Don't just stand there like a zombie, for crying out loud.*"

A cloud scuttles across the sun and for a moment I can see everything clearly. He pounds the ball into the pocket of his mitt, eyes me sideways, spits at the ground. He might look more intimidating if it weren't for that donut of fat hanging over his belt. He steps out wide, brings his other knee up as his right arm cranks back, then snaps forward.

A blur of white hurtles toward me. Suddenly, I'm fixated on the crosshatching of red stitches as the ball spins on its axis. There's a brand name stamped on its surface in big swirling script, but it's marred by gouges where Ivanhoe's teeth have punctured the leather during numerous sessions of fetch.

It occurs to me a moment too late that the ball is coming straight for my head. The sound it makes when it impacts with my skull is a muffled thud, like someone whacking at a watermelon with a rubber mallet.

I'm on my back now, looking up at the sky. I see stars, but not the kind in the planetarium, fixed pinpoints on a dome of black, or even the night sky, twinkling far away. It's daytime. The stars are big, very big, flashing and colliding in a kaleidoscope of color. Gradually, they begin to fade. But instead of blue sky and sunlight, I see him, standing over me, looking very unhappy.

And my head hurts like holy hell.

"*Get up,*" *he says.* "*You're not bleeding.*"

The world is spinning around me wildly. I try to lift my head, but the edges of my vision start to go black. My head hits the dirt again. I wait for the feeling to pass, blink hard, but I'm still too dizzy. "*I can't.*"

"*Then just lie there.*" *He picks up the bat, pounds it against home plate once and kicks a clod of dirt at me, just as I close my eyes. It strikes me in the cheek. "I've given up on you. You always were a lost cause."*

25

LONG, LONG AGO

Blacklaw Castle, Scotland — 1333

"GET UP. YOU'RE NOT bleeding."

The toe of a boot strikes me in the cheek, hard. I open my eyes to see Sir Henry above me, hands on hips.

"Should have given you up to the priests when your mother died, lost cause that you are. Little good you are to me." He spits at the ground, inches from my face, grunts, and stomps away.

Duncan blocks my view, his hand outstretched. Clasping his forearm, I sit up and slide the shield from my arm. There's a lump near my temple the size of a golf ball. "What the hell just happened?"

All around us, men are laughing, prodding each other with elbows.

"The truth?" He glances over his shoulder. Sir Henry, his weapon sheathed, is striding toward the armory, Malcolm and Alan at his side. "You stood there like a dolt. Didn't even draw your blade. So he hit you with the pommel of his sword."

I draw my knees up, bury my head in my hands.

Duncan sinks to his haunches before me, his joints cracking. "Could you at least not make my job impossible? I taught you before when you were a foul-mouthed stripling, I'll teach you again, wilted flower that you are. Now," — he gives me his hand again, helps me to my feet — "let's take it easy, shall we? How to defend yourself would be a good place to start."

"I'm only wasting your time."

"What irritates me is not your lack of skill, Roslin," he snaps. "It's your lack of a spine."

I look down at my boots. He's right. Retreating into my shell like a turtle is my only line of defense. The problem is I don't know how to change that. It's hardwired into my brain.

The clanging of metal rings like a discordant pealing of bells. Several circles of mock fighting have reformed. My hands are shaking. My stomach has been turned inside out. I don't belong in this world, not by a long shot. But if I don't become a part of it, it's going to get nothing but harder for me.

The crowd in the bailey is thinning. I look toward the stables, expecting to see Duncan, but he's not there. Then I see him — heading back toward the door to the great hall. I dart around a group of men who shake their heads at me and I'm followed by a wave of guffaws and mumbled insults.

That isn't the worst of it. A cold whisper brushes over the back of my neck. I glance up at the east tower. There, framed in shadow, is Mariota, a hand braced to either side of the window in which she stands. I can't read her face from here, but I know what she's thinking — that she could have done far better for a husband.

More than having disgraced Sir Henry, it mortifies me that she saw it all. I turn away, a familiar cloak of shame surrounding me.

This world is different. Turning the other cheek, proclaiming myself a pacifist — that doesn't cut it here. It matters what she thinks of me. More than I'd like to admit.

I catch up with Duncan just as he reaches the top step to the hall. "Teach me how to fight, Duncan."

"I have been trying, day after day. So far not with any measure of success," he says with his back to me. Several moments lapse, before he turns around. He too is disappointed in me, and it tears at my soul. "For weeks now, I have dragged you to the woods before half the castle has risen for the day, done all I can to make you stronger, quicker, more persistent ... taught you how to balance your weapon, how much weight to put behind each blow, how to watch your opponent's eyes and stance, where a man's weaknesses are — and at the first opportunity to prove yourself," — he stoops his head and lowers his voice — "against a half-lame old man, you don't even try to defend yourself. Why?"

How can I explain childhood trauma to a medieval warrior? I can't. Besides, it doesn't matter anymore. The old tactics aren't going to work here. What am I going to do — run away? Tempting, but I'd have to leave Mariota ... and Duncan. I couldn't do that. They're the only ones who make this ordeal bearable.

"Your problem" — he jabs a thick finger at my sternum — "is that you don't know what you're fighting for. You get up every day and go through the exercises because it's easier than turning me away or risking your father's wrath. Call it what you will. It's cowardice when done for those reasons. *Nothing* matters to you. You're simply biding your time. But for what? As I see it, you're sure to die in the end — because you won't so much as raise your sword in your own defense." A pair of young women descend the steps, passing curious glances at us. Duncan nods resolutely. "You're right, Roslin. You are wasting my time. I have better things to do. I could go back home until I'm needed. I could train men more willing and capable than you. I could rest my weary bones and dull my troubles in ale — even that would be a better use of my time."

The weight of his words burrows into the deepest hollow of my gut. I've chosen to be invisible, while waiting for my problems to magically disappear. I begged Duncan for lessons only to pass the time and partake of his company. I did it to avoid Sir Henry's disagreeable manner. And to have an excuse not to spend time with Mariota, no matter how much she intrigues me. Because even now, I still hope that I'll wake up back in the time and place I came from and that Claire and the baby will be all right.

How much longer can I live in denial like this? Until I meet my fate at Halidon Hill? Why not just throw myself from the sea cliff right now?

No. I won't. Because I want to live. And maybe someday, know what it is to love again.

His body twists as he turns to go, but I grab his arm. "Teach me, Duncan. Teach me how to fight, so that I can live. I won't waste that chance. I swear to you."

Lifting his face to the sky, he mutters something about 'God' and 'a promise'. Then he looks down his nose at me. For the first time I notice there's a distinct crook in it, like it's been broken more than once.

He snorts at me. "Very well. We'll go to the sheep meadow today, out beyond the mill. There's an old tithe barn there that will shield us from view."

Minutes later, we're standing before the stables. A groom tromps out, leading two saddled horses. When we pass beyond the outer gate and are on the road to the village, I clear my throat. "Just how long would it take you to teach someone how to really fight, the way you do. From scratch?"

Duncan wrinkles his furry brow at me. "From scratch?"

Right. Another anachronism. "I mean from the beginning. Someone with no experience."

He sets his gaze ahead, sighs. "Years."

"Is it too late for me to join the priesthood then?"

"It is if your name is Sinclair."

We ride in silence awhile longer as we go through the village. It's no more than a few single story houses, a mill by the creek and a tiny church that couldn't hold more than thirty people. When we reach the far side and are nearing a pasture where sheep are grazing idly, Duncan finally speaks again. "You're his only son now, you realize that? He may not live to see William's boy grown. You're all he has."

"Yeah, I know. But why does he have to be so hard on me?"

"Maybe that's the only way he knows how to prepare you?"

"That hardly makes it right."

"Somehow I don't think begging you would work very well, either."

At the edge of a grove of trees, Duncan dismounts and unstraps his shield from the saddle. As I pull my sword from its scabbard, he instructs me to set it aside. Then he unties another sack hanging from the saddle and takes out two blunted wooden swords.

"Here." He tosses one to me, grinning. "I'll take it easy on you today, but I can't promise you won't get a few bruises."

I test the wooden sword with a few swipes and square up.

Duncan fits his arm into the straps of his shield, then pauses, a far off look in his eyes, like he's remembering something. "He was a different man before your mother died. It changed him, hardened him."

"If you say so." It comes out harsher than I intend, but it's already said. I have a difficult time imagining Henry being anything but bitter and resentful. I heft my shield, brace myself for the first blow. This time, I'll watch, be prepared. And I'll remind myself *why* I'm doing this.

"He loved her, deeply. He does you, as well. He'd give his life for you, whether you think it or not."

"I find that hard to believe."

"Believe it. Every day you spent in Beaumont's captivity drove him deeper into despair."

I lower my shield. Beaumont? Why does that name sound so familiar? "Who exactly is this Beaumont, besides being an Englishman?"

"Henry de Beaumont, Lord of Liddesdale and self-proclaimed Earl of Buchan. One of the Disinherited."

"The who?"

"The Disinherited. A few years before the Battle of Bannockburn, Beaumont married Alice Comyn, niece and heir to the former Earl of Buchan. The Comyns, along with the Balliols, were never friends of the Bruces. When King Robert came to power, he declared the lands of all those who still fought for England as forfeit — they are the 'Disinherited'. And so when the old Earl of Buchan died, Beaumont was denied the earldom, an affront which he has never forgotten. The man is a greedy opportunist. He served Edward II, but turned on him when it became advantageous for him to do so. After helping Isabella and Mortimer bring the younger Edward to the throne of England, he then betrayed Mortimer. He's the one who helped bring Balliol back from France and convinced him he could avoid violating the Treaty of Northampton by simply sailing up the coast and depositing an army on Scottish soil, instead of crossing the border with them on foot. A scheming rogue, if there ever was one. For now, he stands behind Edward III. For now. But I reckon he'll do whatever it takes to gain back the inheritance he feels he's been denied for far too long."

Before I can absorb everything he's said, he flails his weapon at me, sideways, then down, sideways, down. Gentle blows, slow and methodical. Sideways. Down. Sideways ... I block each one, as we lapse into a monotonous rhythm. In time, I learn to let my body react to the motion, my innate defenses taking over.

"Now strike on the offensive," he instructs.

I feint to the left, then flick my sword crossways. It glances off the top rim of his shield with an unimpressive click.

"Harder. Put your whole strength into it. And come at me faster. You're giving me too much time to prepare in between."

Three times, I punch my training sword at his chest, but it's as if he knows my moves before I make them.

"More force! Faster! Don't think so hard. And stop looking where you're going to hit next."

Now I'm just flailing at him like an angry toddler whacking away at a piñata. I'm frustrated. But determined.

"Your mother was an ugly whore," he mutters.

"What did you say?" I lower my weapon slightly. He seizes the opportunity and swings his blade backhanded. My reflexes are barely sharp enough to ward off the blow.

"Your mother was a whore, Sinclair. Stood like a bitch in heat for every rutting lad who could sniff her out. She birthed you in a latrine, hoping to lose you down the drain hole. If not for a vigilant servant, you would have drowned in the moat."

"Oh, stop. You're making all this up." Besides, the mother he's talking about wasn't *my* mother.

"Am I? What if I told you she could pleasure a man the whole night long?" A hint of a wink dances across his brow. "I know. I had her."

"Does your wife know that?" I joke.

"She died three years ago." A sadness creeps across his face, but he shrugs it away. "I do not pretend to be a saint, by any measure. Nor was your mother."

Neither was my *real* mother. She loved a man who couldn't love her back and wasted her life in the effort. But there was good in her. There was. "Ah, now that you have wrong, my friend. She was a good woman."

"Good, aye. Good for one thing. But good to you? Hardly. She left you, remember?"

She did. And left me with that miserable bastard.

Rage surges inside me, the pressure mounting until my will to contain it is a wall neither high enough nor strong enough. I strike at him — forward, backward, down, up, down, back, spin, thrust. He parries each blow deftly. The collision of dense wood reverberates up my arm, rattling bone and sinew. My hand begins to cramp and I grip the hilt tighter, swing harder, faster. Inch by inch, foot by foot, he yields ground.

His breathing grows more ragged. He leaps backward and stumbles over a root. He throws his sword arm wide to regain his balance. His concentration broken, I attack again, my blade swiping horizontally.

But instead of blocking my blow with his shield or parrying, he ducks behind a tree. My wooden sword whacks against the tree trunk so hard it splinters with a crack.

The next thing I know, I'm holding a jagged piece of wood. The blisters in my palm are beginning to burn.

Duncan slaps me on the arm. "Now that is how you fight! Remember that."

Laughing, he marches over to the fence where his horse is tied and takes a long swig from his flask. Two little boys, maybe four and six, peek beneath his horse's belly from the other side of the fence, watching with fascination and awe.

"You did make all that up about my mother," I say, joining him, "didn't you?"

His laughter falls away. "Aye, I did. Your mother was an angel who graced the earth with her presence for far too short a time. 'Tis no wonder your father loved her so. But the next time someone comes at you with a weapon, think of her, think of Mariota. Think what would happen if your attacker sought to kill you so he could violate them. Tap into that fury. Use it to survive. Use it to keep them safe. Fight for them."

26

LONG, LONG AGO

<u>York, England — Late 1332</u>

*W*ith every inhaled breath, the sackcloth over my head flattens against my dry, cracked lips, chafing them raw. I would sell my soul for a drink of water right now, if only a sip to moisten my mouth.

Between the darkness and the coarse threads of burlap, I cannot make out the faces surrounding me, although their whiny English accents assault my ears. The taste of smoke is on my tongue. It scratches at my throat and a cough shoves upward from the depths of my chest. Eyes watering, my ribs convulse as I hack up sputum. When the tide of coughing passes, I sit back, the heels of my boots digging into my buttocks. That's when I sense the heat of a fire warming my back, almost singeing the hairs on my neck.

I dare not move. I cannot. My hands and feet are bound.

As the minutes plod by, my skin grows hotter, until I can

imagine my flesh melting from my bones. The air inside my lungs is burning now. Around me, the murmurs rise in volume, their tone shifting from one of secrecy and contemplative debate to intense argument.

I am the object of their disagreement.

Two men on either side hook me beneath my armpits and haul me forward, my knees scraping over frozen rocky ground. A flake of stone tears at the cloth of my leggings. As they continue to drag me, I can feel flesh peeling from bone. I'm shoved onto my side, blood oozing from my kneecaps, smears of it wetting my shins. Snow melts against my cheek.

"He came unarmed and unescorted, as bid," a voice says.

Gruff hands grab behind my back at my wrists. The cold metal of a knife slides between them, sawing at the ropes until the threads fray and finally the pressure breaks. Slowly, I pull my arms to my chest, cramped muscles resisting. Next, they release my feet, long since grown numb from the tightness of the binding. The cloth is ripped from my head, but I keep my eyes closed.

"Look at me, Scot."

I comply. Shapes and edges come into focus in the wavering firelight. A man is crouching before me, chainmail covered by a brightly colored surcoat. I know the emblem on his chest. I was told to look for it. A gold lion on a field of blue with fleur-de-lis. It's him.

"York's a long way from Annan now, isn't it?" The cloud of his breath hangs suspended in the cold December air. Henry de Beaumont extends his hand to the side. Someone lays a roll of parchment into his open palm. "Pitiful bad luck for you, Sinclair, meeting up with Balliol just as your own people chased him from Scotland. Good luck for me that he had the presence of mind to bring you along as he ran for his life.

"Now," he says, an exultant smile on his mouth, "let us see how complicit your father is."

He tilts the roll to catch the light and inspect the seal. Satisfied it is what he's been expecting, he breaks it and unrolls the letter. As his pupils scan the contents, the smugness fades from his countenance, his mood quickly replaced by annoyance.

"Damn him to hell if he thinks he can bargain with me." Rising to his feet, he spits at the ground in front of me. A moment later he circles behind me. "He wants Liddesdale, does he? Well, he's not going to get that now, is he? Not now that I have you. I'd say matters have shifted entirely to my favor. Perhaps you'll be a little more compliant than your father proved to be, the covetous bastard."

He slides his blade from his scabbard. Its point pricks the small of my back. I flinch, but hold back a gasp. Sweat springs from my temple, trickles down my cheek and neck.

"Kill me now," I tell him over my shoulder. "I won't —"

"Shut up!"

His gloved fist slams against the side of my head, toppling me. Again, my world goes black.

27

LONG, LONG AGO

Blacklaw Castle, Scotland — 1333

COLD SWEAT DRENCHES MY body. I press a hand against my chest. Inside, my heart is beating at a frenetic pace. I'm hyperventilating, so I force myself to draw air deeper into my lungs.

It was so real, so vivid. But was it a memory — or merely a dream?

Pale moonlight casts a silvery glow, barely enough to see by. It'll be hours yet before the rest of Blacklaw's residents are up. Kicking my blanket onto the floor, I swing my feet over the edge of the bed. My whole head hurts, like someone has rammed a railroad spike into the top of my skull, shattering the bone. I cradle my head in my hands as I try to recall the details of the dream: my thirst, the darkness, the December cold, the bindings, the men around the fire ... the blow of Beaumont's fist. I had been sent to Annan to deliver a message to Balliol and ended up there with Beaumont, somewhere outside of York.

No, it had happened. It really happened. But how is it that I remember that night with such stark clarity when everything else from this life is hidden to me?

Cool night air drifts from the open window, encircling me in tranquility. My breathing deepens; my heart rate slows. Sir Henry had been conspiring with Beaumont. But ... was he still? Why would he even consider it to begin with?

The edges of my vision blacken as I stand. A rush of lightheadedness washes over me and I grapple blindly for the bedpost. Moments pass before the blood returns to my head. This is how it was when I was a kid and had the visions. Sometimes they came to me in the hazy hours of half-sleep just before dawn; sometimes during times of full wakefulness, but usually when I was alone. They always took a few minutes to recover from, for my awareness and body control to return to normal. This time is no exception.

I push away from the bed, but my knees are rubbery. I stagger, stumble, and throw a hand against the wall to steady myself. The floor tips beneath me. I sink down, my hand trailing over rough stone, until my knees hit the floor. There I wait for the world to stop spinning, while golden sunlight banishes the silver light of the moon.

BENDING OVER A BASIN, Sir Henry brings cupped hands to his face. Water trickles between his fingers and down to his elbows, wetting the wide sleeves of his nightshirt. He dips his hands again and then pauses, having caught sight of me.

"What is it?" He wipes his hands across the front of his shirt and stalks toward me.

"My lord, I'm sorry." An older servant with lopsided shoulders brushes past me and stoops low in a bow to Henry. "I told him you had not yet risen and that he should return to his quarters to await your summons."

Ignoring the servant, I stride into the room. It's on the topmost floor of the main tower, just above the meeting room where Henry conducts his business. Even though it's one of the bigger rooms in the castle, there's little more here than the bare necessities: a bed wide enough for only one, a small table with a basin and a cup, two unadorned chests, and a bench.

Henry wheels around. Color flares at his neckline. He shakes a fist at me. "What do you —?!"

"I remember," I say.

His fist sinks to his side. "Leave us, Alfred." With a wave of his hand, he banishes the servant. "Remember what?"

"That I was at Annan to meet with Balliol."

Turning away, he walks to the hearth and braces a hand above the mantel. "How much more do you recall?"

"That I carried a letter from you. Balliol was to deliver it to Henry de Beaumont. But I was taken captive and sent to Beaumont in York. He read the letter. Your response angered him. Greatly." I pause to let him speak, but he says nothing so I go on. "You were bargaining your loyalty for land."

His shoulders heave in a shrug. "And ...?"

His nonchalance surprises me. I'd expected more: anger, denial, name calling. Instead, he reacts as if I've just given him a weather report. "That's all."

Slowly, he turns around, tilting his head in thought. I realize he's weighing how damaging that amount of information is and what I intend to do with it. His bare feet drag over the floor planks as he approaches me. The urge to bolt from the room nearly overcomes me, but I force myself to remain where I am.

He stops midway. "You assumed I was giving secrets to the English? Information that would aid Balliol's cause and in the end benefit me with some lofty title and a swath of land rich enough to reward me and my heirs for eternity?"

"Were you?" I say bluntly.

"If I was, what do you think your part in it was?"

"I told you, I don't remem—"

"How convenient that you recall some things and not others. Let me refresh your memory, then." He goes to the bed and sits on the edge, his fingers splayed across broad thighs. His nightshirt falls to just below his kneecaps. On the inside of his right calf is a puckered scar about four inches long that forms a gouge in his flesh. I wonder how many other permanent reminders he bears of all the battles he's fought in. His bed, I notice, is already made and beside him, his clothes have been neatly laid out. "After you returned from Spain, I was approached by an agent of Henry de Beaumont. I didn't know who he was at first, though. He was merely a traveler who happened by here. I offered him food and lodging. Somewhere between tankards of ale, it came out that Blacklaw was not my possession, but my daughter-in-law's." He raises his eyes, deeply set and hooded by thick brows feathered with gray. Something behind his pupils hints of self-pity.

"You see, Roslin, I was a poor knight, always living off the generosity of distant relatives and a few dear friends like Duncan. My father had fallen into debt and left me with little more than a rusty suit of armor and a warhorse with very few useful years left. When the Disinherited were stripped of their lands, I saw an opportunity. I vowed to fight for my king, in the hopes that he would one day reward me. Every year I fought, battle after battle, hoping to win his attention. And I did. But King Robert was very frugal in distributing those forfeited lands. Eventually, I was given a castle in the Orkneys in dire need of repair, and a few paltry holdings to the north, but it was not enough to keep from debt. If anything, I was worse off than before, trying to maintain my estates. Even marrying you to the only daughter of a respectable landowner did very little to keep the moneylenders at bay."

I'm not buying it so far. People are always desperate to explain why they've done bad things. Sir Henry is no different. He's justifying his actions. And rambling in the process. The longer he goes on, the more pissed I'm getting. "What does any of this have to do with why I ended up as Beaumont's prisoner?"

"You always were impatient with my stories," he mumbles. Grabbing the leggings from the pile beside him, he shoves his feet into the toes and stands to pull them up. Then he doffs his nightshirt and replaces it with a dark blue tunic. "A man will say things over ale that he would otherwise never divulge. The guest — Beaumont's agent — somehow surmised that I was resentful of King Robert's parsimony, even though I was not. He then began to talk of the rumors of Edward Balliol's return and how he might lay claim to the throne of Scotland now that our good king was dead — *if* Balliol had enough support from within our borders. So I asked him what he meant by that."

"What *did* he mean?"

For a minute Henry doesn't answer. He's too busy digging through the chest at the foot of the bed, cursing under his breath. Finally, he pulls out a belt and fastens it around his waist. "That there would be land and wealth for those who supported Balliol's claim to the crown." As he walks across the shaft of sunlight on the far side of the room, he readjusts his spreading middle over his belt and gazes out the window. "The man returned on three other occasions. There were other discussions. Other promises. I was tempted. Sorely tempted. If Balliol succeeded, I stood to be one of the richest men in Scotland. So I made my decision. When I told you about it, you were angry with me. And rightly so. Because of you, I couldn't go through with it. But then Beaumont made one last offer. I never believed he or Balliol would follow through on any of their promises, so I made a counter request, Liddesdale — Beaumont's own lordship — knowing he would refuse me. I was supposed to meet with Balliol, but you volunteered to go in my stead."

"I was captured. I spent a year in ..." In prison? A dungeon? Another missing piece. For all I knew, I had been a privileged guest of Beaumont's as he tried to win me over.

"You were supposed to be gone by the time they came to get Balliol."

"I don't understand."

"Your arrival at the house where Balliol was staying and the assault on the town that night led by Lord Archibald — they weren't a coincidence, Roslin. You wanted me to prove I was done bargaining with Beaumont. It was you who proposed the plan for Balliol's capture. Your mission was to make certain he was there, in that house. You were supposed to be gone from there long before the assault. But Archibald's men came too early. Balliol escaped — and took you with him."

"Because he believed I had led Lord Archibald to them?"

"You did."

"What about a ransom? I assume that's why they took me."

"Humph. An astronomical amount. Beaumont knew I couldn't pay it. I dared not ask Lord Archibald for help. If he had found out about my past dialogue with Beaumont ..." His gaze skipped toward the ceiling and then to the floor before returning to me. "So you see why all exchanges about the ransom had to be done in secret? There was nothing more I could do."

"Why didn't you try to negotiate a lower amount?"

"I did. He said 'no'."

"So why then was I headed north under guard, if not as an exchange? If you couldn't raise the ransom, then ..." There are so many holes in his story. What is it that he isn't telling me? "Were you going to give them information?"

"What information could I possibly have given them that they could not have easily learned themselves? That Scotland is ill-prepared to defend Berwick? I'm disappointed you think so little of me, Roslin."

As he hobbles out the door, I can see how his shoulders slope downward to the right, how he holds one arm closer to his chest, and the way he drags a foot when he walks. The years have hardened his character; the battles have exacted their toll on his body. After so many brushes with death, so many sacrifices all in the name of Scotland, how can I even think he would turn against his brethren?

28

LONG, LONG AGO

Blacklaw Castle, Scotland — 1333

"PENNYROYAL."

The leaves of the plant still pinched between my fingers, I look up to see Mariota smiling at me. She stands at the opening in the hedge, wearing a simple gown of pale blue with a plain white smock of some sort over top. She floats between the neat garden beds, bending her head one way, then another. Abruptly, she halts, stoops over and plucks a weed from between the rows. Satisfaction lights her face and she returns her attention to me. "The one you're holding is pennyroyal. That is, if you were curious to know."

Pennyroyal, I think. *Mentha pulegium.*

"I am." I wander toward her, careful not to intrude into the well-tended beds. The herb garden, bordered by a low hedge, is tucked into the southwest corner of the inner bailey, well shielded from the northern winds of winter and the persistent breeze from the sea. The soil has been worked over with a hoe and the faint scent of manure, used to fertilize, has been renewed by a recent rain shower. "What are all these used for?"

"Many are used by the cook to season the food. Some have medicinal purposes. Others are grown for their aroma: to strew in the floor rushes or on beddings, or to place in little cloth sacks and tuck into our chests of clothes." She breaks a stem from a spiky grayish-leaved plant and draws it across her upper lip, inhaling. Her mouth curves upward in delight. She extends the stem to me.

I don't have to smell it to know what it is, but I do. It reminds me of Claire's favorite soap. "Lavender." Of the mint family Lamiaceae, genus *Lavendula*, species indeterminate.

"Yes!" she remarks in surprise. "How did you —?"

I point to another plant. "Marjoram." Then another and another. Latin names flow through my mind, but I avoid those. They wouldn't mean anything to her. Plants and animals won't be classified for centuries yet. "Rosemary, tansy, feverfew, spearmint, basil, valerian … But you already know all these."

"When …?" She blinks at me. "When did you learn all the names? Such things never held interest for you before."

"In England, maybe? I don't remember. I just *know* them, somehow." As in years of studying and teaching them to others. I can identify most of the native trees in my area by the color and texture of their winter bark alone.

She tilts her head at me, puzzled by my newfound knowledge. "You have changed so much."

"For the better, I hope."

"To me, yes, I think so. But others … others have noticed things."

A sentry pacing on the wall walk nearest us pauses, watching as if we're doing something of interest. Most likely he's bored. I would be if I were him. I raise a hand to him, a friendly 'hello', but he resumes pacing. "Oh. Who?"

Flattening a palm against her abdomen, Mariota turns away. Her head dips slightly. "The Abbot of Melrose has questioned some of your ... habits."

"Such as?"

"He noticed you feeding your meat to the dogs at supper when he was here."

"Is that all? I've done it since I was a child. The loyalty of a dog is worth twice that of any man I ever knew." I drift closer to her, so near I could wrap my arms around her. "You like dogs, don't you?"

She doesn't answer me. Her shoulders are tensed, her hand still pressed to her middle, as if she's holding something back. "Be careful, Roslin."

"Careful of what?" I lean my head close. Her hair smells of spices. Cloves, I think.

She begins to turn back toward me and gasps, startled to see me so close. Her hand flies to her throat. I catch her wrist and pull her to me.

"Careful of what?" I say lowly. "I don't understand."

The gardener shuffles through the gate nearest us and comes our way, his tools piled in a little hand drawn cart. Mariota shakes her head at me vigorously. The terrified look in her eyes tells me I need to know. That this is serious.

I put my mouth to her ear. "Come to my room tonight. Tell me then."

Then I kiss her on the forehead, bow, and saunter away. When I reach the gate, I dare a glance over my shoulder.

The gardener is stooped over, cutting blooms from the yarrow and tucking them into a basket at his hip. But Mariota's fingers are laced together, knuckles touching her whispering lips, as if in prayer.

THE DOOR CLICKS SHUT behind her. I stand moored in place, arms leaden at my sides. A trio of candles flickers on a table by the wall, their golden light too dim to reach into the shadowy corners of the room. All I can see before me are a high four-poster bed … and Mariota.

I've been waiting for her all day, pacing a rut in the floor, my mind a maelstrom of fear. Yet my worries melt away at the sight of Mariota. Her red hair is unbound, falling past her shoulders and over the curve of her breasts in a twisting cascade of flame. Instead of a modest high-waisted gown, she wears a clinging white shift, the cloth so thin it's nearly transparent.

I shouldn't be looking at her. I shouldn't, shouldn't.

She takes a step nearer, and I avert my eyes. If this is only a dream — or a memory — why am I so afraid to be near her, speak to her … even just *look* at her? What's wrong with simply appreciating a beautiful woman?

Ah. So that's it. This is what guilt feels like. As much as I want to get back to Claire, as much as I hope and pray she's all right, I can't help but wonder what Mariota looks like beneath her clothes. How she would feel underneath me. God, do I ever wonder.

Here, there is no Claire. Only Mariota. And I am here. Now. With her.

The whisper of skirts draws my attention. Slowly, I raise my eyes. Mariota is a mere arm's length away. So close, so available. So *mine*, if I want her. I don't even need to ask. All I have to do is lead her to the bed, lay her down and do as I wish. As my wife in this time, she has a role to fulfill. There are certain … expectations.

"What does the Abbot of Melrose say about me?" I blurt out. Anything to distract myself from her nearness. But it doesn't work.

With each breath she inhales, her flesh pushes against the gossamer shift, revealing the fullness of her breasts, the shadow between them inviting my touch. The heat in my body is rising, blood gathering in certain places.

I don't even realize I'm staring at her *there* until she lifts my chin with her finger and forces me to look into her eyes. It's the first time I've seen her this closely, taken her in this completely. It's impossible to look away now. She's undeniably beautiful, in a sublime way. Hair the color of copper, falling from her crown in a river of golden fire. I pluck a lock from where it twines against the long curve of her neck, twist it around my finger. Her skin is soft, white as first-fallen January snow. Her lips part slightly, awaiting mine. I turn my head to kiss her, my eyes drifting shut.

Her breath is a whispered promise, in which doubt yields to possibility and restraint gives way to passion. To be present, to live in the here and now, is to abandon control. To trust in tomorrow.

First, I must let go of yesterday. When I do, this moment becomes something more.

The beginning of our forever.

The touch of her lips is like a white hot spark to dry tinder. Electricity zings through my body: sudden, frightening, and glorious all at once. A moment becomes an eternity.

'I will always love you.'

'Forever.'

'And ever ...'

Heaven flies from my grasp. I pull back. My heart is banging inside my chest.

Mariota's breath comes in rapid gasps. Her hand drifts to her mouth, covering it.

I clutch her hand, pull it away, wanting so badly to kiss her again, to silence the shame clawing at my conscience.

No. No, I can't go there. I can't forsake Claire just because it feels right in this moment. Forever means forever.

I force myself to take a step back. But that's not far enough, not safe. I take several more.

As if I had struck her, she stumbles backward, throwing out a hand to catch herself against the bedpost. Confusion clouds her face.

"Who are you?" Tears brim in her eyes and she blinks them back as she sinks to the bed. "And why are you doing this? Why torment me so?"

In three steps, I'm before her, kneeling. I touch her, just above her knee, and a tremor ripples through her. It rips at my heart to have thrust her away, but I'm torn. I miss Claire and yet ... yet there's something about Mariota that draws me to her, something deep inside my soul.

"Tell me about that day," I say, "when we became husband and wife."

Her fingers flutter nervously over the blanket on which she sits. She swallows, bunches the cloth in both fists. "It was cold, January. I had no sooner stepped off the ship, than I was taken to the great kirk in Orkney —"

"St. Magnus Cathedral in Kirkwall?"

Her eyes narrow. "You remember?"

"Just the place, not the day. Go on."

"There is not much to tell. The bishop held a box containing the bones of St. Rognvald. I kissed the holy relics, but you would not." She arches an eyebrow at me and then continues. "I was fourteen; you, twenty-two. It was a ... a formal ceremony, but brief. Hardly anyone was there."

I had hoped details would jog my memory, but it's all a blank. "Tell me more."

"The next day you left to join James Douglas, who was tasked to carry our king's heart to the Holy Land. You fought at Teba, some say bravely ... others claim you were a coward. Within the year, you returned to Scotland, but ... even when I came south to Blacklaw to join you, you would not visit my bed. Again and again you quarreled with your father. Then you were captured and taken to England. Do you remember that?"

"No, I don't." Half a minute passes before I remember why I asked her here to begin with, "Tell me, what ... what does the Abbot of Melrose say about me?"

"He questions your faith. Many do. There were rumors that while in Spain you had converted, become one of the Cathars." She lays her hand over mine then. "Are you?"

"Am I what?"

"A Cathar — and if not a Perfect, then a Credente."

Again with the Cathars. I'd never questioned Duncan much about them, but he, too, had mentioned them. "I'd answer you if I knew what they were."

"Cathars believe our souls are reborn seven times before they finally ascend. As you know, that goes against the teachings of the Church." I don't know, but I'm not about to admit my ignorance of Church matters. "When the abbot was here, you refused the meat. In the time I have known you, I have not seen any pass your lips." Her gaze drops to her lap. "Cathars do not eat meat."

That explains the stares and whispers. Apparently, in the Middle Ages being a vegetarian amounts to heresy. "The night the abbot was here, I wasn't hungry, really."

"Then you live on bread and water. Cathars renounce the world."

I feel like I'm being unjustly judged, convicted on rumor alone. "You seem to know a lot about these Cathars. How is that?"

"I know what I need to. I also know that in order to obtain purification, Cathars believe they must abstain from pleasures of the flesh." Her voice takes on a plaintive tone. "Why have you never shared my bed?"

What am I supposed to tell her — that I already have a wife and I come from almost seven hundred years in the future?

As to why Roslin Sinclair had kept from her ... Maybe what

she's saying is true? I draw my hand from her leg, rest on my haunches. "There's so much I don't remember. I wish I did."

"Yet you're here with me now and still you will barely look at me, as if you do not want to be tempted. I was young when we married, yes, but I'm more than old enough for childbearing now." She looks at me a long time before speaking again, her gaze cutting to my soul. "Are you one of them?"

Clasping my head in my hands, I sigh. "No, I'm not *one of them.*" Then I fold forward, my forehead touching the worn planks of the floor. I just want to get back to Claire, see that she's well, and take her home. I want this to end.

Yet I want to be here. Completely. Where I am now, it's like being trapped between heaven and hell and I hate it.

Mariota slides to the floor to sit beside me, her slender fingers stroking my hair. "Who *are* you?"

It's all too much to deal with. I don't know what I should tell her, if anything at all. Hell, I'm beginning to doubt myself. I roll over to look up at her. Her concern is genuine. Stretching out, I lay my head in her lap. This is weird and yet … comforting. I need someone to tell my secret to. Someone who will believe me. If I don't confide in someone soon, my skull is going to implode.

"If I share the truth with you, Mariota, you must swear on your life not to tell anyone."

"That is a grave oath to make without knowing what that truth is."

"Then maybe you aren't ready to hear it yet? I can't tell you if you can't promise me."

"Is there danger in knowing?"

Given what they do to non-believers here, yes.

I sit up and frame her face in my hands. "No, I won't tell you. Not yet. In the end, it may not matter anyway. We need to get to know each other first." Closing my eyes, I lean forward, touch my forehead to hers. "Whether or not you trust me will make all the difference. Until then ..."

With a sigh, she puts her head on my shoulder. Her breath, warm and moist, caresses my throat. All resistance, all anger is gone from her body. I slide an arm around her back and pull her closer. Her hand moves across my thigh, fingers curving lightly around the inside. I lean back against the bed, watching her, thinking I should tell her to stop and yet wanting her to go one step further, past that irretrievable point. If this is a dream, why not let it play out, take its natural course? What red-blooded man hasn't had one of 'those' dreams?

"If they believe you are a Cathar," she says softly, a tremor of fear in her voice, "they will kill you — and it will not be a quick death. First they will torture you, make you name others. Then once you confess, they will burn you alive."

Lovely. That's one way to douse my rising desire. "They have no proof."

"They don't need proof to claim you are one." She slides a leg over mine. "But you could give them proof that you are not. Irrefutable proof."

"How?"

"Prove you have not forsaken desires of the flesh." Turning to face me, she straddles my hips and sits back. Her fingers skitter over the laces on her chemise. With agonizing slowness, she tugs them free, revealing a deep cleavage. She inhales, then rolls her shoulders back, shrugging her garment off. Even though the light is dim, the candles wavering on the table behind her, I can make out the pale curving outline of her breasts.

I draw back as much as I can, but that's hard to do with her weight, however slight, pinning me to the floor. "And just how would we 'prove' that? I don't think they're going to take our word for it."

She bites her lip, then bends forward to offer a kiss. Her lips brush mine, teasing. "If we make a child, they will know."

Oh, God. If she shifts forward a few inches, she'll know had badly I want to do that.

"Up, Mariota." My palm cupping her jaw, I guide her face back from mine. "To bed."

She rolls back, her glance darting nervously to my face and then down as she moves from me. I get to my feet, offering her a hand, but she stands on her own, her arms now limp and awkward at her sides, as though she doesn't know what to do next.

Of course she doesn't. She's a virgin.

The light from this angle is different, even more revealing. Her eyes still downcast, she raises a hand and touches the opening of her chemise.

I grab her hand to stop her. "That honor will be mine, when I choose to take it."

Perplexed, she blinks at me. I peel back the covers for her. Hesitating, she slides beneath them, her back to me.

I open the chest at the foot of the bed, remove two blankets and place one on the floor.

"Good night, Mariota."

Slowly, she turns a questioning face to me.

"You don't trust me yet," I say. "Until you do, and until I can give up that which I left behind —"

"You love someone else."

I do ... *did*.

I snap the remaining blanket out and toss it over my shoulders as I lie down. How do you go on loving someone you may never see again? Someone who might already be dead? Can you grieve, not knowing, and simply pick up and go on to give your love to someone else?

All I know is that with every day that goes by, it's Claire who passes further into memory and Mariota who becomes more and more real, more and more a part of me.

29

LONG, LONG AGO

Blacklaw Castle, Scotland — 1333

T HE FIRST SHARDS OF the sun's rays span above the horizon, far out over the sea. Here and there, the sky is broken by high dusky clouds of purple etched in silver, drifting lazily northward, promising the splendor of a brilliant morning. The stones on which I sit, tucked away in a crenel along the northern battlements, are damp from the nightlong drizzle. It's here that I come to think when I can't sleep — which of late is almost every night.

Closing my eyes, I let my chin drift to my chest. Salty air fills my lungs, the tang of it barely sharp enough to keep me awake. Mariota hasn't come to my room since that night, over a week ago, nor have I gone to hers. I can't allow myself to be tempted, even though what I feel for her is so strong it seems like I'm denying a part of myself by keeping from her.

"Who is she?" Mariota says.

My head snaps up. I throw a hand out to catch myself, even

though the crenel is deep enough that I'm in no danger of falling. "What?"

She's standing not ten feet from me, the scuffed toes of her slippers peeking out beneath the hem of a light green gown that has seen many wearings. Her hair is loosely gathered at the nape of her neck, loose strands teased away by the breeze. She, too, looks as though she hasn't slept much. Step by step, she drifts closer, like one would approach a wounded and frightened animal. "There is someone you care very much about. Someone you love."

I stretch my legs out, glancing back out over the sea to avoid her gaze. "Why do you think that?"

"I am a woman, Roslin. Not a fool."

I blow out a loud breath. There's no longer any sense in keeping my secrets from her.

"Her name is Claire." It pains me to say her name out loud. I haven't spoken of her to anyone except Duncan since I arrived here. I'm sure he doesn't believe me. Carefully, I dare to look at Mariota. "But it doesn't matter. She's no threat to you."

"How so?"

"She's gone. I'll never see her again." Not because Claire had died, because in truth I would never know the outcome of her condition. Finally, I understand. When the truck ran me off the road outside Aberbeg, it was *me* who had died that day.

And I had ended up here, reliving a past life, but with the memories of my future life completely intact.

It's the only explanation there is. The only possibility.

If Reverend Murray is to be believed, my days here are numbered. Yet … what if I don't return to 2013? What if I did die the day I was run off the bridge and it's some other life that awaits me after this one?

My head hurts just thinking about all the 'what ifs'.

Mariota stops beside where my shield rests against the wall. With light fingertips, she traces its edge. "Are you *certain* you will never see her again?"

I turn her words over in my mind, trying to gauge the purpose behind them. There is no jealousy in her question, that much I can tell. "Am I certain? No. But ..."

That's the problem: I'm not certain of anything. Things would be so much easier if I would only choose a path.

I have to let go of my other life. Give up the hope of ever going back. I have to live this life. However short it might be.

Next thing I know, I'm standing an arm's reach from Mariota. I touch her shoulder.

She's not a dream or a memory. She's real, she's here. I reach out again to draw her to me —

"Ah, there you are!" Duncan waves an arm at me from the inner bailey below. With his other hand, he shakes a spear in the air. I've graduated from wooden swords to real ones. Lately, he's been teaching me not only how to wield other weapons — axe, spear, mace — but how to defend myself against them.

Moving toward the edge of the wall walk, I raise my hand to let him know I'm coming. Then I return to Mariota. "I'll be back in a few hours. Sir Henry wants to see me then to go over supply lists. Perhaps later ..."

She steps near, nestles her head against my chest. I wrap my arms around her lightly and rest my chin on the top of her head.

"I'll always be here," she says, "waiting for you."

I sense, though, that she's tired of waiting. And I've grown tired of hoping that my life will go back to being the way it once was. Because I can't keep wishing for what might never be. What I want, what I need, it's right here in front of me.

IN THE TIME OF KINGS

THE SUN IS ALMOST at its zenith and I'm gripped with a sudden panic. I urge my horse into a gallop over the bridge. "Sir Henry's going to be mad as hell. I was supposed to be back an hour ago."

"I'll tell him it was my fault," Duncan says from behind me, although I can barely hear him above the clatter of hooves. "He'll fume awhile, I'll suggest a tankard of ale and after a few gulps all will be forgiven."

"For you, maybe." Everything I do seems to provoke Sir Henry. At any rate, I hate being late. I always used to set my watch ten minutes fast to make sure I showed up places on time. Time is relative here, but still if you tell someone to meet you in the morning and it's well past noon when they arrive ... I deliver a sharp kick to my mount's flanks and Duncan's grousing fades away behind me.

Two months ago, it was a struggle to stay in the saddle for more than a few hours. Now it's as second nature to me as commuting down I-71 once was every morning in my Camry. I can read my horse by the direction of his ears or the arch of his neck, guide him with my thighs and a lean of my body. Duncan has a hard time keeping up with me. He won't admit it, but on a good day I could beat him at swords now, too.

The portcullis is open. At first I assume they saw us coming, but then I notice some horses being led away by grooms and several men standing around the bailey who I recognize as Alan's men. I slide from my saddle and lead my horse to a watering trough. I don't worry about him wandering off. He'll drink his fill and then wait until someone comes to get him. I know him that well by now. I place my helmet, weapons and shield beside the trough.

My gut tightens. Alan's here, somewhere. His presence, whether expected or not, always concerns me. I scan the bailey. Some of the men are already heading to the hall, but there's no sign of him. Unconcerned, Duncan ambles toward the kitchen. There's a kitchen maid who's gained his attention of late, so it figures that he'd go there and leave me to Henry.

When I hear a woman's voice, at first I think it must be coming from the kitchen. Then I hear it again. It's Mariota. She's standing with her back to me, just inside the doorway from the east tower to the wall walk. I can't hear what she's saying, but her pitch hints at agitation. I hurry in that direction.

I race up the stairs of the tower, treading as lightly as I can. Then I hear a man's voice reply to hers. It's Alan. I slow my steps, steady my breathing.

"Blacklaw should have been ours, Mariota," he says. "You would have been so much happier with me. We were always meant to be together. *Always.*"

"We were young then, Alan," she says.

"And in love."

I stop dead. Moments crawl by in silence. I should either leave or let myself be known, yet I can do neither. I want to hear what she'll say back. I need to know.

From somewhere in the bailey, Malcolm calls for me. Did he see me enter the tower? I say nothing, pressing myself closer to the inner column of the stairway.

Still, she hasn't answered him. Finally, she murmurs something and then ... she winces. Or is it a moan? I fly up the stairs three at a time until the back of Alan's surcoat comes into view. Mariota's back is to the wall, his body pressed to hers. He's gripping her arms, his mouth seeking hers.

I snag the back of his surcoat and yank hard, slamming him against the opposite wall. He flails a hand out. One foot slips on the smoothed edge of a stair and he tumbles back, landing several steps below.

Before I can get to him he's already on his feet again. Anger blazes in his eyes. Suddenly, I wish I hadn't left my sword in the bailey. I'd gore the bastard.

As if reading my mind, Alan reaches for his blade.

"No!" Mariota screams. "Alan, stop!"

I wheel around to her. "Why? Did I interrupt? Why not let him run me through? Does your conscience trouble you?"

She's nothing but a silhouette against the light from the open door above. Her face is concealed in shadow.

Then, Malcolm's voice calls out more clearly from the bottom of the stairs. "Sir Roslin? Are you there? Sir Henry has called a meeting — at once."

"I hear you," I answer.

"The time has come," Alan says behind me. As I turn to him, he releases his hilt. A gloating smirk tips his mouth. "We are to leave for Berwick today."

With that, he goes, leaving me alone with Mariota. She trails a hand over the stones of the outer wall to steady herself as she descends. Her other hand is pressed to her lower ribs as she tries to control her breathing. She's almost past me when I grab her wrist and pull her to me. I don't want to leave her.

"I'm sorry," I tell her. "I shouldn't have —"

"Say nothing, Roslin." With a light twist of her arm, she frees herself from my hold. "My heart is yours. It will always be so."

For several minutes I remain there, alone and adrift, listening to hurried footsteps on the cobbles outside and the faraway cry of seabirds.

WE'RE AFFORDED BUT A few hours to make final preparations and assemble in the open stretch of grassland beyond the outer wall. Several hundred men have already gathered there, packs stuffed full with the barest of necessities, carts piled high with supplies and spare weapons. A column of thousands is marching off into the distance. Whatever I may think of Alan, the man has made a great show of organizing all of this. His correspondences to Sir Henry were detailed and frequent, complete with the name of every lord and chieftain promising men and weapons, the date of their arrival and the breakdown of their numbers into foot soldiers, cavalry, and archers — although I know it's in that last respect that England will show their strength and so be our undoing.

There's a curse in knowing what is to come. I'd rather *not* know. It robs me of hope and hope is a precious thing.

As I take my place in the column beside Sir Henry and we head south, I twist in my saddle to look back. A skeleton of sentries is posted on the wall, but I see no one else.

She's not there.

My heart is yours. It will always be so.

Small consolation, considering that I won't be coming back.

Sir Henry and I ride side by side in silence for hours. I'm thankful he hasn't spoken yet; it would be impossible to answer him about anything without sounding like I want to snap his head off — or anyone's, for that matter. I'm mad as hell at myself for a lot of things. For not being more clear with Alan to keep his distance from Mariota. For keeping her at a distance myself.

If I hurt right now, it's my own damn fault.

Every time I glance at Henry, his jaw is clenched tightly, like he's holding back words. Sooner or later, he'll open his mouth and I'll have to deal with whatever he's brewing beneath that gruff exterior.

"I suppose you've heard," he finally spits out.

I flick the ends of my reins at a fly and give him a questioning glance. The less I say the better.

"The Abbot of Melrose has levied accusations of heresy," he says.

"Mine or yours?"

"Don't be flippant, Roslin. This is a grave matter."

I clamp my teeth shut and inhale deeply through my nose. There are so many things I could say, the least of all how ridiculous this is. I don't eat meat. So what? How can that be a crime?

"Does he have proof?" I say, sure he doesn't. Short of me standing up in public and mocking God or the Church, how could they prove anything?

"They don't need evidence. Just enough witnesses to speak against you."

I don't need to wonder who he's talking about. Alan could probably conjure witnesses by the dozens and they'd be sure to distort mere rumors into fantastical lies.

"What's going to happen, then? A trial? Excommunication, maybe?"

He snorts loudly. "Excommunication would be a kindness. Death by fire is more likely. It's your good fortune there's a war to be fought right now, or else you'd be on your way to Edinburgh to stand trial. I'll speak to Lord Archibald, arrange a delay. But once matters are settled in Berwick, there's little I can do to stop the course of events. If you prove yourself there, however, it's possible they may be lenient."

"Lenient how?"

Maybe instead of burning me at the stake, they'll take pity and grant me a quicker death by lopping my head off.

"Penance, perhaps? A pilgrimage? I know very little about such things." He falls quiet, his eyes set squarely on the road ahead, but I can see something's still eating at him.

"I had so much hope for you on the day of your birth, Roslin," he finally says. "Since then, you have done nothing but bring shame upon the Sinclair name. Berwick is your chance to return honor to the family. Do not disappoint me again."

Wow. How am I supposed to reply to that? Short of single-handedly saving the town, there aren't enough hoops I could jump through to change his mind. So I'm not even going to try, let alone argue with the grumpy old goat.

Berwick, Scotland — 1333

"THEY ARE MANY," LORD Archibald proclaims, grinning faintly. "But we are more."

I'm not so sure I share his optimistic outlook. The journey from Blacklaw Castle had taken the remainder of yesterday and almost all of today. Some of the supply wagons would be trickling in for another day, with more reinforcements yet to come. But the flood of so many Scottish forces all in one day must have stirred some concern on the part of Edward III and Balliol. From where we stand on a hill well beyond Berwick, it appears impressive to me: the gathering of forces before an epic battle on which hinges the course of history.

Sir Henry squints against the brightness of a setting sun, emphasizing every wrinkle and fold in his face. "How does the town fare, my lord?"

Several other nobles have convened on the hill with us: Menteith, Atholl, Keith, Moray … It's taken a lot of tutoring from Mariota and Duncan, but I've learned their names and histories. Knowing family politics and personal alliances is critical in this era. Without that knowledge, I could unwittingly offend a lot of people and I've already done that without even trying. The crisis we're facing, however, seems to have erased a lot of those lines. Scotland is only just now learning how to stand as one against a common enemy. It took years for the Bruce to make them see the value of solidarity.

Archibald gazes eastward across the valley to the town. "The English have smashed the water conduits. Even if Berwick has enough food to last weeks more, without water ..." He lifts his eyes to the sky. No possibility of rain. Not even a wispy white cloud gracing the horizon.

I hear a 'thump' and shoot a look toward the northern wall. A dark object hurtles through the sky in a low arc. As it sinks in its trajectory, every man there falls silent. It crashes through the roof of a house barely visible over the top of the wall, crumpling the framework on the side nearest us. We can't hear the screams, but we know innocent people have been hurt, if not killed.

It's all I can do not to bend over, grab my knees and vomit. Finally, I say to Duncan beside me, "What was that?"

"A stone launched by a trebuchet. But that isn't the worst of it."

"Oh. What is?"

He slaps my back. "The severed heads."

Gulping, I close my mouth. Suddenly, all the weeks I spent preparing with Duncan don't seem to amount to much. Futile, in fact. It's hard to remember humanity's potential for kindness when so much senseless cruelty exists.

In the days following, we wait and watch from a safe distance while the atrocities continue. Messengers shuttle back and forth, to no avail. Neither side will yield. They will have all or nothing.

Amazing how little things have changed in seven centuries.

30

LONG, LONG AGO

<u>Berwick, Scotland — 1333</u>

I WAKE TO THE SCENT of ashes. I should be used to this by now, I tell myself. There are always campfires burning. Food must be cooked. But it's a different smell. More acrid. And not just wood smoke. It reminds me of the grassfire in the field outside of Balfour when I was a kid, the summer of the drought.

I emerge from my tent and follow the flow of traffic on foot to the ridgeline. A stiff wind blows from the west, making it hard to hear what others are saying. Day has barely broken, but it's not the sun's light blazing strongest.

The roofs of Berwick are burning.

Archibald pushes his way through the crowd to take in the sight. The River Tweed is choked with English ships. The points of more masts can be seen further downstream, toward the sea. Ladders have been thrown up against the town's walls. Men are amassed at the breeches. The fighting is furious.

"What happened?" Archibald says.

Close at his shoulder, Alan gives an account. "The English sailed upriver in the middle of the night, surrounding the town to the east and south. Edward dispatched his men from the ships along the riverbank, while his archers took aim at the walls. Seton was expecting such an assault. Faggots soaked in tar were set to be dropped onto the assailants, but as you can see, the wind wreaked its havoc. Flaming ashes blew back into the town, setting it alight." He points to the tower at the town's gate. There, a white cloth has been flung over the wall. "Seton will beg for a truce. If we move quickly, my lord, we can attack their remaining forces to the north. It will cause confusion. Give us a temporary advantage."

Arms crossed, Archibald peers intently at Berwick.

"My lord?" Alan urges impatiently. "You must decide — and soon."

"No. Let Seton negotiate. We will choose our course then."

"But —"

"Has the Earl of Ross arrived with his Highlanders yet?"

Swallowing, Alan shakes his head. "No, my lord."

"And you said there are another thousand due to arrive from Strathbogie and Mar in the next few days?"

"Tomorrow, perhaps."

"Good. We wait then. A truce will buy us time. Haste would cost us dearly."

I can see the disappointment in the men's faces. Many do not agree. They're impatient to get this over with, yet fearful that their resolve to defeat the English will be compromised by diplomacy. They want to fight, not volley words.

They'll all have their chance. Just not today.

FIFTEEN DAYS. THAT'S THE length of the truce agreed to by Alexander Seton and King Edward of England. Ross has arrived with his Highlanders, as well as the others, but upon hearing that battle is not imminent, they're more riled up than relieved.

With each day that slogs by, the mood becomes more sullen, tempers sharper. Yet beneath the edginess, there's an undercurrent of camaraderie unlike anything I've ever experienced. Then again, I've always been a geek, a bit of an outcast, rather than a team player.

In the evenings, we gather around the cooking fires and the men share stories, mostly of battle, but sometimes about fishing adventures in tiny coracles on storm-tossed seas, or forays into blowing snow to gather lost sheep from treacherous mountain landscapes. The lines between noble and commoner become blurred at these times, the connections deeper.

I gaze into the bubbling waters of a cooking pot, watching the steam rise and swirl across the faces of those standing around, bowls in hand. To my right, there's a small commotion, but I don't pay any heed until I hear her voice.

"Roslin?"

I blink in disbelief at Mariota. Both joy and anger surge in my chest.

I grab her hand and haul her into the closest tent. "What are you doing here? As soon as Malcolm finds out — or Henry or Archibald for that matter — they'll send you back. You know that?"

"I had to come."

"*You* didn't have to. I did." I'm trying to be forceful with her, but it's beyond hard. "Now leave. It's too dangerous for you here."

"No. Not yet." She burrows against my chest. "I needed to see you again."

How can I be angry with her? The sound of her breathing fills my ears, surrounds me, calms me. It would've been better if she had stayed away. It was hard enough to leave her at Blacklaw. But ... I needed this, too.

When I was first dropped into this world, I was sure it was only a dream. But day after day I woke up, still in the fourteenth century, running from an enemy I did not claim. I have been cold, starving and exhausted to the bone. Yet I have survived this far and in that triumph, in many ways, I feel more alive in this world than I had in my own.

Until now, my only goal had been to get through each day, so I could get back to where I had come from. But how? When? I don't even know how I got here. Or maybe …

It's as if someone launched a kick to my gut. The realization sucks every last drop of denial out of me.

I *am* Roslin Sinclair — and I can never go back.

This is my life now. She is my reason for living it.

My fingers wind through the hair loosely gathered at the back of her neck. I tilt her head, bring her trembling mouth to mine, and press a kiss upon her plump lips, then another and another, until finally her mouth parts.

In that moment, my world changes.

Mariota returns my kisses with an urgent passion. Her hands slide around my neck, her hold on me decidedly possessive. Blood thunders through my veins, propelled by a racing heart. I steal a much needed breath between kisses and look deep into her eyes.

"Roslin," she whispers breathily, "there is something I need to tell you."

I love the sound of my name on her lips. I touch a finger to her mouth, trace around its edges. "Mariota, I —"

"Sir Roslin?" Malcolm pulls back the tent flap. The heat in his gaze flares, then dampens as his eyes flick from Mariota to me and back again. "Mariota, you should not be here."

So I've told her.

"Sir Roslin, Lord Archibald requests your presence."

I break away from Mariota. "What is so important it can't wait five bloody minutes?!"

He pushes the tent flap wider. Firelight spills around his hulking form, casting his face in wavering shadow. "Edward has reached an agreement with the citizens of Berwick."

I nod. "I'll be right behind you."

A few moments pass before he lets the flap fall shut. In the now dimmed light, I turn to Mariota and wrap her in my arms.

"There's something I need to tell you first," I breathe. "Something that will make sense of everything I've said or done until now. But you have to believe that I'm in my right mind and what I say is true. I have no reason to lie."

She turns her face to mine, her fingertips exploring my jawline, my cheek, my forehead as if she means to impress the memory of my features upon her touch for eternity. "I already know."

"You can't possibly —"

"You believe in their teachings, don't you? You believe, as the Cathars do, that another life awaits you."

"Something like that, yes." I press my hand against the back of hers, then bestow a kiss in her palm. "But I'm not done living this life, Mariota. Whatever this agreement is concerning Berwick, it won't last. It won't solve anything. There will be a battle. I'm afraid I may not sur—"

She clamps a hand over my mouth. "Do not say it. Do not even *think* it."

I draw her hand down. "Mariota, Mariota … Listen to me. There will be a battle. The bloodiest one Scotland has ever seen. Far more lives will be lost than at Bannockburn and it might not turn out in our favor this time." I couch the truth in that statement. 'Might' is a boldfaced lie.

Shaking her head at me, she retreats, crosses her arms. "No one knows the future."

"*I* know. Believe me."

"*How* do you know?"

"Because I come from the future. I have lived another life, seven hundred years from now."

With a scoff, she whirls away. Why had I insisted on telling her? Why now? I should have kept it to myself. No one has ever believed me.

"Roslin?" someone calls from outside.

"What?!" I bellow.

"Sir Roslin?" It's Duncan. "Lord Archibald —"

"I know," I say tersely.

I pop my head out and tell him to wait for me. When I look back at Mariota, her countenance is such a storm of emotions I can't read it. Is it confusion, fear, disbelief? I've certainly shattered any hope she might have clung to.

"Go," she says softly. "You must not keep Lord Archibald waiting. When you are done here, I will be at Blacklaw, waiting for you."

I kiss her once more on the forehead and murmur, "I love you, Mariota." Then I part from her and step outside.

A hand clamps my upper arm in an iron grip and spins me around. Just inches from my face, Malcolm's eyes blaze with contempt. "I swear, if you have brought shame upon her, I will see that you pay for it — dearly."

Before I have a chance to tell him I'd never do that and never had, he storms away. I have no idea why he'd even think it.

31

LONG, LONG AGO

Berwick, Scotland — 1333

I'VE NEVER SEEN ARCHIBALD'S face so grim. His shoulders are rolled forward, his elbows on the table where maps are scattered about. He holds his head in his hands, not even looking up to see who's there. Several enter the cramped tent after Duncan and me, some seething with anger, some cautious, others appearing concerned, but none of them looking hopeful.

Menteith and Atholl congregate in the corner opposite Archibald, quietly discussing something. Finally, Menteith clears his throat and speaks the question everyone else is avoiding. "Will Berwick surrender — or will you wage battle?"

"It may come to the latter," Archibald says, his voice strained with fatigue. Slowly, he lowers his hands, looks up. Bloodshot eyes gaze blankly ahead. Several moments pass before his chest heaves with an inhaled breath. When he lets it out, his shoulders relax. "There is one hope left. One small, small hope."

Glances are exchanged. There is no hope. I know that. Everyone does.

Alan shoves his way between two men to stand at the table's edge. "And what is that?"

Only he would be so bold. It has become abundantly clear that he wants to be the next Guardian. He's made no secret of his disdain for how Archibald has handled this every step of the way. Unwilling to risk the wrath of Archibald's supporters, he's stopped short of outright criticism so far.

Archibald scoots his chair back and half stands, his palms braced on the table's surface. He scans the maps, draws one toward him and peruses it for a good half a minute before answering Alan. "We can relieve Berwick."

"How?" Alan plants his hands on the table, too, his stance defiant. "How can we relieve Berwick? It's not possible. Whatever route we choose, they'll swoop down from that lofty hill and cleave us in two."

"Not the whole army, Alan." His tone is almost chiding, as one would correct an infant. "Two hundred men. The number required by the terms to constitute a relief."

"What then? You think they'll just turn and leave, slink off to England?"

"No, but Berwick won't be forced to surrender."

"So the siege will continue indefinitely," Menteith remarks. "You're only buying time, my lord."

Archibald slams his palm down. "If time is all we can get, we'll take it!"

"But to what end?" Menteith continues calmly, trying to counter Archibald's desperation. "There are only two outcomes: Berwick surrenders and we withdraw. Or we fight and leave the fate of Berwick to God."

Atholl speaks. "How do we relieve Berwick with two hundred

men, my lord? How do we gain access to it?"

"The bridge here." Archibald points to a faded slash on the map. "We can use the existing framework for men to climb across carrying supplies on their backs. Once across, the town's walls are accessible. This must of course be done under cover of darkness ..."

"I'll do it," I hear myself say. What do I have to lose? I'm supposed to die on the day of the battle, not before. If we're successful in relieving the town, I reason to myself, then maybe history can be changed? Even though I might never be able to return to the twenty-first century, if there is no battle, maybe I won't die that day after all? By now everyone's looking at me — everyone except Sir Henry. It doesn't matter what he thinks, though. I have to do this. I have to try to take charge of my fate. Otherwise, I might as well lead the charge on Halidon Hill bare-chested and with a bull's-eye painted on my forehead. "I'll take part in the relief. Just tell me what to do."

"Thank you, Roslin." Archibald slowly lowers himself back into his chair. "Sir William Keith will lead the mission. He knows Tweedmouth and the bridge well."

Keith nods in acceptance.

"I'll go," Sir Henry says.

I don't look at him just then. I'm still in shock as much that I've volunteered, as he has. It's done then. We're both fools. I'll scramble across the broken remains of an old bridge, in the dark, carrying whatever is supposed to constitute relief, while the English lob stones and arrows at us. Brilliant.

Archibald conveys details to Keith, but nothing registers in my brain from that point on. I'm now wholly, stupidly, irrevocably involved. I remain unmoving as men begin to leave the tent. It isn't until I hear my father's voice that my trance is shattered.

"Suicide," he utters from behind me, his mouth inches from my ear. "But if there's going to be any chance of my only son getting through the night alive, I'll do my best to make sure of it."

I don't respond, don't turn around as he walks away. What am I supposed to say? Thank you for not letting me kill myself? Or — you're stupid for risking your life alongside mine?

The truth is, I don't know how this is going to turn out, if it will even have any impact on whether or not the Battle of Halidon Hill occurs at all.

One way or another, chances are good I'm going to die in the service of Scotland.

Keith is the last to exit. He waits at the flap, holding it aside for me. In a daze, I move toward him. He holds out his arm. I clasp it in brotherhood.

I realize that I've come to care as much as Keith or any of the others about what's happening outside Berwick's walls and within them. It shouldn't be happening. Men should never believe they can take someone else's lands or possessions through force. And yet it's gone on since mankind began.

What I'm about to do, I do not for myself, but for children not yet born. For posterity. For the hope of peace.

What a selfish, cowardly life I've led until now.

A MILLION STARS GLITTER above. I crane my neck to take it all in, feeling at that moment very insignificant, yet somehow connected to every event that has ever occurred through time and every person who has ever lived. I'm thinking of Claire and wondering if she's pulled through or ... or ... No, I can't go there. I'll never know. But these stars, they make me think of her. We had walked beneath these very same stars, laughing and holding hands, the night before the blood clot changed everything. The last time I saw her she was comatose in a hospital bed. I understand now what it must be like to have a loved one disappear without a trace and to never know what became of them. It means hanging at the cusp of grief, while being taunted by hope. There's guilt in letting go and moving on.

Yet I have. Being here has made that easier. My one regret since arriving has been in keeping Mariota away. So much time wasted. I should have lived these last two months to their fullest, uninhibited, unafraid.

There are so many things — in this life and my future one — that I should have done. Like standing up to my dad. Telling my mom I loved her more often. Spending more moments enjoying life and less working my tail off.

Too late for all that now.

I roll over onto my side and stare down the line of men waiting with me. We're lying in the grass on the crest of a hill, overlooking the shambles of a village. In packs slung over our backs, we carry sacks of grain, dried meat, fresh fruits and vegetables, and sheaves of arrows. My pack is stuffed with leeks and turnips, but Duncan's has several small bags of salt. It will be a help, but still, it all seems so insignificant. Like trying to wipe out hunger on the continent of Africa with one airplane drop of vitamin-enriched protein bars.

The smell of smoke lingers in the air. Earlier that day, Archibald sent men into the village of Tweedmouth ahead of us, and — as the English watched from the opposite bank across the River Tweed — the town was sacked. With fire spreading from rooftop to rooftop, Archibald made a show of retreating; yet still Edward did not move from his spot.

Keith scoots along behind us on his hands and knees, whispering last minute instructions. As the first man in line creeps down the hill crouch-backed, no one makes a sound. The longer we go without being discovered, the better our chances at crossing the bridge and reaching Berwick.

We lurch forward in groups of four or five. Ours is one of the last. With me are my father, Duncan and two men I've never met:

a slight-framed man named Adam who left his farm near Aberdeen to come and join in the fight, and a boy of seventeen named Christian with platinum blond hair. I have to remind myself that in this age, Christian is hardly a boy. He has more battle scars than most people I used to know had tattoos.

Doors of houses gape open as we descend into the village and make our way along a narrow alley, climbing over charred timbers, scattered heaps of straw and trampled midden heaps. We dash across a main thoroughfare and even though it stretches emptily, the remnants of life are everywhere. The inhabitants had abandoned their homes and businesses at the first sign of Scots this morning, leaving behind all their belongings. They must have known the moment Balliol encamped outside of Berwick that this busy port village would eventually become the object of a Scottish raid — and yet they had remained, going about their everyday activities. Plucked fowl dangle by their feet from the window of a butcher's shop, the meat growing rancid in the thick summer air. Feral cats feast on overturned baskets of fish. The gates of sheep and pigpens hang open, their herds driven back to the Scottish camp to feed the men.

Somewhere a lamb, trapped in the ruins, bleats. I slow, keening my ears, and finally see it, its pink nose pressed between the bars of a wooden fence that has been pushed over. The small building next to it is still on fire. Adam sees it, too. He glances at me, shrugs in pity and goes on. A gap opens up between us and I dart after him, the lamb forgotten.

Suddenly, a hen bursts from atop a barrel, startling me. Duncan plows into me, nearly knocking me flat, then mutters a curse and shoves me forward. The alley narrows even further. In its middle runs a gutter of sewage. I have no choice but to walk through it, muck and filth sucking at the soles of my boots.

A hundred yards later, the alley jags around a corner and opens up into a wider street. I can see further ahead now. At the end of the street, the River Tweed writhes lazily like a bloated snake. The men are moving more quickly, twisting back and forth as they wind their way around broken down carts and toppled market stalls.

Wisps of smoke drift through the night air. Sparks crackle in a clump of thatch at roof's edge of the building next to us. The smell of ash claws at my throat. I swallow, but a cough tears free so hard I nearly gag. A calloused hand clamps over my mouth. I stiffen.

"Hush!" my father growls. He grabs my elbow and jerks me onward. Toward the river.

We creep past the last building onto a sandy beach. That morning, the beach had been littered with boats, but as Archibald and Keith descended with their hundreds, the villagers had run here and rowed out into the mouth of the Tweed and along the shore, away from the mayhem. I had watched them from a distance, their oars dipping in frantic rhythm while the town went up in flames.

Across the water, the shore climbs sharply upward, the base of Berwick's walls meeting with a steep, rocky hill. Occasionally, a face peeks between the crenels, watching. I wonder if they see us, know we're coming to help. I hope to God they don't start shooting at us.

A pair of ducks paddle upriver — two black silhouettes bobbing on a sea of silver. I follow their course and see, to my left, the bridge we are to cross. Or what's left of a bridge, actually.

"Oh my God." I crouch next to Duncan. A shiver spreads from my chest, quickly engulfing my entire body in tremors. "We're supposed to cross that ... bridge, climb that hill ... and somehow get inside Berwick?"

"You were the first to volunteer," Duncan says, "were you not?"

"Yeah, I guess."

"And you were expecting what?"

I have no answer. At least nothing that won't sound entirely idiotic. Everything had looked different from so far away. But up close, I can see the gaps in the planks of the bridge. Some of the stones that make up the piers have been jarred loose, too. I'm not sure how two hundred of us are supposed to get across the river, up the hill and over the walls unassaulted. Sounds like a death wish to me.

Then I noticed the ropes coiled over the shoulders of those in the fore. Hope zings inside my chest. A dozen men are already scaling the framework of the bridge underneath, securing the ropes wherever they can. Soon, another dozen men scramble up after them, passing along more coils of rope. The rest of us huddle at the base of the first and second piers, hidden from view. While we wait, I scan the hillside on the opposite bank. Every stone stands immutable, every blade of grass unwavering in the still night air.

The ropes are now strung from end to end of the bridge, looped among the timbers that once supported the planks. Every few minutes, one group clambers up the stone pier and begins their way across. Some swing hand over hand most of the way, others sling their legs over to shimmy across. There's no time for rest. Every second is crucial.

Christian is the first in our group to make the climb. He moves nimbly, his limbs wiry but strong. Frozen, Adam stares up at him.

I grip his shoulder. "Go on. I'm right behind you."

He nods, shoves his toe in a foothold and reaches up. I follow him, whispering encouragement whenever he stalls. Behind me, Sir Henry grunts with the strain of heaving his old bones upward. At the top of the pier, I latch on to the rope, dangling awhile as I talk myself into it.

If I let go now, there's sand below me, maybe only fifteen feet down. But then Sir Henry swears as a stone crumbles and his foot slips. He flails a hand out, grabbing the rope from which I hang for support. I bob with the impact, my pack shifting to my side, then quickly recover and grapple for the next handhold. Hand over hand, I work my way across, my palms stinging even through leather gloves.

By the time we reach the third pier, my fingers are cramping and my shoulders burning. I cling to the stones. The ledge on which I stand is barely deep enough for my toes and the balls of my feet. My heels hang over the edge. Far below, dark water laps at the base of the pier. I glance at the far bank. Men are already scaling the hill and the first few have reached the lower wall of the town. I look back to where we started, then ahead to the opposite bank. Not even halfway.

Adam is already twenty feet ahead of me.

"Go, go," my father urges impatiently.

I suppose this would be a bad time to tell him I've reconsidered, that I don't belong here, that I'm more at home with textbooks and microscope slides and rows of students scribbling down my every word. I pull in a breath and inch my way around to the next rope. The gap between Adam and me widens. I grab the rope with two hands and pull myself along. This time, my father stays close.

"For Berwick, son," he says, "and Scotland."

For Berwick and Scotland. Berwick and Scotland, I chant to myself over and over, my grip growing stronger. Adam waits at the next pier for me. He extends a hand, beckoning. Only a few feet to go now. Distant, scattered voices shatter the silence of the night, but I shut them out, focusing on Adam's hand.

And then ... his hand isn't there anymore. His body jerks away and buckles backward, away from the pier, then plummets. I catch the barest flash of an arrow shaft protruding from his chest before the river swallows him whole.

Propelled by fear, I reach above my head and grip a broken timber to pull myself up into the framework.

"Hold tight, Roslin!" my father yells as he begins toward me.

I look into his eyes and recognize the fear there — the fear that we both might not make it through this day.

A force smacks against my right shoulder. At first I feel nothing, then a bolt of pain tears through me. I sense my fingers losing sensation, slipping. Far below, the river gurgles. I lose my grip … and fall.

"Nooo!!!" my father screams.

His voice fades with the rush of air around me. Cold blasts my body. Water rushes into my nose and mouth.

No air, no air. Weight pressing all around me. My ribs tightening.

Darkness, everywhere.

32

LONG, LONG AGO

<u>Berwick, Scotland — 1333</u>

MOMENT BY MOMENT, LIKE rousing from a long sleep, my senses return. The flap of wings begins as a rustle, then rises to a crashing din. Wind beats against my wet clothes. Only the warmth of the sun's rays keeps the chill at bay. Grains of sand coat my tongue, their grit grinding between my clamped teeth. I try to spit them out, but gag instead. A cough wracks my lungs so hard I retch.

Then, a broad hand pushes at my ribs, forcing me onto my back. "I told you I would be behind you."

I open my eyes and blink at the brightness. The first light of dawn shimmers over rippling waves. Water laps soothingly at my legs.

My father kneels over me, concern weighing his features. Beads of water drip from his hairline. "Bloody English archers."

"My arm," I croak. "I can't ... feel ..."

In the distance, a city rises above the shoreline: Berwick. How had we gotten so far from it? I struggle with the question, my mind cluttered with cobwebs. I close my eyes, thinking hard, remembering.

'Clumsy jackass. I told you to hold on.'

Slowly, it comes back to me: we were trying to relieve the town, get supplies to them, crossing the underside of the bridge, when —

"You're going to live." My father grips my left arm and shakes me. There's blood on his hands, yet I see no wounds on him. "You're going to live, damn it. D'you hear me, Roslin?"

I do, but why does he care whether I live or die? And since when did I start thinking of this man as my father?

The sea wind bellows in my ears and snatches the warmth from my body. I gulp for air, but can only manage a small breath.

My father's gruff voice comes to me as if from the end of a very long tunnel. His words are too muffled to make out. I turn my head toward him. That's when I see the feathered shaft sticking out of my shoulder.

THE NEXT THING I'M aware of is that I'm in a tent. Duncan is asleep sitting next to me, his arms crossed, his beard touching his chest. His lips flutter as he snores.

"Where am I?" I say. It takes all my strength just to summon those few words.

Twitching awake, he slaps his cheeks, then smiles. "Back at camp."

"Did they get the supplies into the town?"

"They did." His shoulders slump forward. "Those ahead of us on the bridge all made it across. Some of the men were even able to enter the town. It seems the archer who killed Adam and wounded you was only a sentry. But it didn't take long for others to arrive. Keith ordered everyone back across. Nearly twenty died and as many were wounded."

Every breath I inhale is painful. I glance at my shoulder. Thankfully, I was unconscious when they extracted the arrow. The point had burrowed deep within my flesh, shredding muscle and sinew before hitting bone. The arrowhead had been an armor-piercing pile, its metal tip barely wider than the shaft, rather than a barbed broad head. A smelly poultice had been applied and dressing packed over it, but around the edges of the rags used to soak up the blood, my skin is red and inflamed.

"It's so damn hot in here." Sweat saturates my clothes. I attempt to sit up so I can push back the blankets and cool off, but the moment I lift my head a rush of dizziness sweeps over me. I move my good arm to grab at the blanket's edge, but even that effort drains me.

Despite my struggles, Duncan tugs the blanket tighter. "You've had a fever. Been asleep for over two days."

"How bad is it?"

"If you can fight off the infection, you'll pull through. No telling how well you'll be able to use that arm, but at least you have another one."

He fakes a grin of encouragement, but I'm not entirely sold on his optimism. This is the first time in quite awhile that I wished myself back in the twenty-first century. Treating and closing up a wound like this would be standard emergency room procedure. A day or two in the hospital for observation and then home with a generous dose of painkillers. Here, I'm relegated to leeches and someone trying to interpret the color of my urine.

"The siege?" I mumble. "Did they lift the siege?"

His lip curls. "The bastard said since we didn't get our two hundred men *inside* Berwick, it didn't constitute a proper relief. Lord Archibald argued the point, but to no avail. When King Edward still refused to break the siege, Archibald threatened to fly south and wreak havoc on the north of England." He leans in close, his voice low. "We found out Queen Philippa is at Bamburgh."

"How far is that?"

"Twenty miles, perhaps. But Bamburgh is reputed to be impregnable. It sits on a rock at the sea's edge. Its towers part the clouds. Archibald hasn't the machinery to take it. He knows that."

"He hasn't the time for a proper siege, either," I add.

"Aye, but he went anyway, hoping Edward would chase him." Scoffing, he stares down at empty hands. When he finally speaks again, his voice is husky with grief. "The moment Archibald was out of sight, Edward began building gallows in plain sight of the town's walls."

"They're going to hang the hostages, aren't they?"

"They've already begun. Thomas Seton, Sir Alexander's son, was the first."

A pit of sorrow opens up inside my chest. I hadn't known Thomas Seton or his father, but these men had become like brothers to me. "So what now?"

Shrugging, he pours me a cup of ale. "More negotiations, I reckon. Nothing but empty talk. In the end, we either hand over Berwick — or fight to keep it. We'll know soon enough."

I want to ask him more, but the outcome is already written. The details seem too insignificant to share. As soon as Archibald returns, I'll insist on talking to him, convince him to surrender the town, so he can live to fight another day. But I know him well enough by now to realize that isn't going to be easy to do. Probably impossible. What weight does my word carry?

Even knowing what will happen, I can't change anything. Yet why do I keep trying?

A heavy silence settles between us as I empty my cup. I don't have the energy left to ask anything else. I'm hungry and thirsty, but more than that I need to rest. I close my eyes and let the drink infuse my bloodstream, washing away my worries.

A GOOD NIGHT'S REST has left me feeling slightly more human. My fever has broken, although my shoulder still throbs. I can use my right hand now, but I still can't lift my arm more than halfway.

"Seton has signed a truce with King Edward." My father hands me a bowl of stew as I sit up. "The agreement expires at sunrise on the 20th."

I dip a finger in the steamy liquid. It's warm, but not scalding. I sip at the broth. It tastes of beef, but I force myself to swallow anyway. If I want to regain my strength, I have to eat something and fresh fruits and vegetables are in very limited supply here. "What is today?"

I have to ask. I've lost track. Without a regular schedule, the days blur together. I can't tell what day of the week it is, let alone know the date, especially after losing two whole days slipping in and out of consciousness.

"Today is the 15th of July." He plops down on the stool next to me. Grimacing, he kneads at his knees with gnarled fingers.

One side of the tent has been left open and while the breeze is welcome, the afternoon air is still hot — nothing near as torrid as a July day in the Midwest, but today is abnormally oppressive for summer in Scotland.

"Thank you," I murmur.

"For what?"

"Saving me." I set the bowl down. It seems a useless gesture that Henry saved me, given that I'm going to die soon anyway. I suppose it's the thought that counts. "I know we've had our differences, but —"

"The day you were born, your mother died. She was twenty years younger than me and yet ..." He hangs his head, his words coming haltingly, as if he has to force every syllable out. It's not the

Henry I know — the hardened warrior who regards sentiment as a weakness. "She had just enough energy to push you out. By the time you drew your first breath, she had taken her last. I loved her more than life, more than anything."

I have no idea where this is going or why he's mentioning it now, but I let him go on.

"She had the same hair, same eyes, same nose as you. Even the laugh was the same. Every day I look at you is a reminder of what I lost."

"So that's why you let Duncan and his wife raise me?"

"In a way, aye. But where William was rugged and independent, learning to ride and fight at an early age, you were often ill and read to pass the time. I knew Duncan would teach you how to fight and he did. In time you grew stronger and healthier, but also more defiant. You often voiced your dislike for war, saying we should embrace peace and trade, instead. At one time, you wanted to join the priesthood, but I wouldn't allow it. If I'd had more sons, I might have, but I had only the two of you, so I couldn't. I've worked too hard to gain what little I have. I grew up as one of the lesser Sinclairs of Orkney, fourth son of a fourth son, always overshadowed by my more prominent cousins. When Mariota's father proposed your marriage, I leapt at it. Apparently, he'd had a falling out with Alan Stewart's father. Blacklaw was part of her dowry, so I had to move quickly on the matter before the offer was gone."

His lips twitch with a wry smile. "You argued with me over that, too. Even as beautiful as she was, accepting her meant giving in to me. In the end, you yielded — only because Duncan talked you into it." There are bags beneath his eyes so deep they form creases in his cheeks. Hard years have taken their toll on him, making him appear far older than I know he is. "When William told me he was going to join Lord James Douglas as he carried King Robert's heart to the Holy Land, you decided to go with him. I made you promise to keep each other safe, but you ..." His voice cracks. He blinks away tears, turns his head away to hide them. "You alone returned."

A reminder of his grief twice over by then. But how does blaming me solve anything? "So why did you jump in after me? Why not just let me die?"

Slowly, he turns his head to look at me. "And lose you, too?"

"You were going to let me die in England, anyway," I remind him. "You didn't even try to raise the ransom. Why should I —"

"Do you want to know *why* you were coming north when Archibald found you? There was indeed an exchange to take place. But not for ransom."

"For what then?"

"Me." His joints crack as he rises to leave. "I was going to take your place, so you could have your freedom."

33

LONG, LONG AGO

<u>Berwick, Scotland — 1333</u>

O N THE MORNING OF the 19th, I rise before the sun's light falls upon the western hills. With exquisite slowness, Duncan's page helps to dress me in full armor. It's the first time I've worn it since the day I fell from the bridge. Working the mail hauberk over my head has been a feat unto itself, since I can still barely extend my right arm above shoulder height. I have to bite my tongue to keep from screaming out in agony as I straighten that arm to slip it through the sleeve. Even the lesser weight of the aventail — a hood of mail that extends to the tops of my shoulders — causes discomfort. Finally, the page straps the metal plates on to protect my arms and lower legs. I may not be Iron Man, but I certainly look the part.

Last night, the rain had poured down hard, not relenting until an hour ago. I hadn't slept at all, more for knowing what's to come than because I'd been afraid of being swept away in a flash flood. Looking at the faces around me as I join the others, it's obvious I'm not the only one with that problem.

Yesterday, Lord Archibald returned from his feigned attack on Bamburgh. Nothing had come of it. He'd barely arrived within sight of the great fortress before receiving news of Edward's hanging of young Thomas Seton. In the meantime, our camp had been relocated far to the west, near a village called Duns. The intention was to get ourselves well out of sight. From the top of Halidon Hill, just north of Berwick, Edward can see almost everything. The only thing obscuring his view is the hill further to the north called Witches Knowle.

Duncan and I make our way to Archibald's tent, where several dozen other nobles are already awaiting his first command. Sunlight glints off polished bascinets. Grim faces stare down at dew-slicked grass. The chink of rowel spurs sounds as more join us. Boots squelch in the mud with shifting weight. Here and there, a low murmur of greeting is exchanged.

No one smiles. No one raises their face to the morning light.

The moment the tent flap opens and Archibald walks out, silence drops like a bomb of foreboding. Everyone pulls back into a wide circle, giving him clear berth.

"Today is the day, then." Archibald forces a smile of encouragement, but the normal confidence is lacking in his demeanor. He pulls in a deep breath and draws his shoulders back as he looks from face to face. "King Edward steadfastly refused to acknowledge our relief of Berwick, even though we crossed the bridge and delivered much needed supplies. Several times, he has refused to abandon Berwick to protect his own cities and people. This morning I received a message from him again stating that the truce expires today. There are no more chances for negotiations, no possibility of relieving the town, no hope the English will leave until they either have what they came for or are beaten down for their arrogance. Many have criticized me for my unwillingness to act with haste." His gaze lingers on Alan, but only a moment. "Some have called me indecisive. A coward. But whatever you think of me matters not. The day is here."

I can't imagine the load he bears for his decisions or the judgment that has already been passed on him. Seven hundred years from now, the history books will portray him as a mere shadow of the man his brother the good James Douglas was. They'll refer to him as the Tyneman — the loser. Yet I know Archibald to be a good man, a respected leader.

If he knew how many lives are to be lost, would he avoid battle? Perhaps the opportunity to change fate rests not with me, but him? I have to say something. Maybe coming back here is my chance to avert tragedy?

Now or never.

I rush forward, my arm bumping his as I stop with my mouth inches from his ear. I keep my voice low, so only he will hear. "I beg you, my lord, do not take to the battlefield. This day will not end well for Scotland if you do. Thousands will —"

"Have you abandoned courage so readily, Roslin?" he whispers back. "The first arrow has not yet flown."

"And they will, Archibald. Flight after flight. He won't come down from Halidon Hill. I promise you that. He has no reason to. The moment you descend from Witches Knowle, your fate is decided. Scotland will lose Berwick. Thousands will die in the folly." Including me and you, I think but omit adding. "I have seen what is to come, my lord. Believe what I say."

He shrugs. "What do you propose then? We just … give up and walk away?"

"Yes." I lower my gaze. Even I, an out-of-place American from some other time, realize how ridiculous a proposal that is. I can't impose my twenty-first century thinking on any of them. These are proud men. They're soldiers. Robert the Bruce had brought their fractured groups together as one nation and defeated the mighty army of England time after time. They intend to do the same, no matter what the odds.

"Between the two of us, Roslin … I agree with you. It would save so much grief." Archibald places a hand lightly on my forearm. "But that is not up to me alone to decide, my friend."

Then he strides to the middle of the circle, hands clasped behind his back. He raises his chin, looking nobler than any man I have ever known. "So what shall it be, my lords? Do we stand down, cede Berwick, that city which we have fought so hard for since before our noble King Robert came to the throne? Or do we stand and fight?"

"Fight," Menteith replies. Then pounding a fist on his chest, he roars, "Fight!"

A pause follows. Some of them are hesitant. They know this is suicide. But unlike in my time, they see no honor in compromise. Nods of agreement spread. Then Keith and Atholl echo Menteith's cry. Moments later, it's a rumble of agreement.

Good God, I've never been surrounded by so much testosterone, so much … stupidity.

"We fight then," Archibald says. He holds his arms wide until they quiet. "The last time this many Scots gathered in one place … was at Bannockburn. No one thought Scotland would win the day, but we did — and we shall again."

History, so it seems, can't be changed. And in that case, my fate is determined, too. If I am to die this day — leave Mariota just as I had Claire — I no longer fear death. There will be another life for me, hopefully another love.

They cheer as he turns to go to his horse, held off to the side by a groom. As he passes me, I step toward him. "I wish to be in the vanguard, my lord."

He lets out a small laugh. "Is this because I questioned your courage?"

"I have only this life to give in Scotland's defense. Let me."

"Don't be so sure of your own death, Sir Roslin." The look he grants me is so intense, it sends a cold shiver down my spine. He raises a hand, palm down, to the level of the top of my head. "Touch your hand to mine."

I extend my left hand to tap the flat of his palm.

A half smile curves his mouth. "Now, the other hand."

Biting the inside of my lip, I try, but can't.

"How good are you at wielding a weapon with your left hand, Roslin? Not very, I presume. Could you even bear the weight of your shield with your right? I doubt so. No, you'll stay with the reserves in the rear, tend to the extra horses and supplies. When we defeat the English, we'll have need of you."

With that, he walks by me and mounts.

A LOT GOES THROUGH your head when death looms: the people you loved, the ones you hated, the things you're proud of, the chances you had but didn't take.

This day as I watch the army of Scotland — my brethren — advance down the slope from Witches Knowle, I sense the wisdom of seven lifetimes in every bone, blood vessel and sinew of my being. I'm still afraid of the pain that will come with dying, but not death itself, for I know my soul will carry on and that every word I have ever spoken, every action I have ever taken, will echo through the millennia. Like a pebble tossed into the ocean, one molecule displaces another, one action elicits a response, the word spoken is heard by another's ears.

If I do have another chance at life, I pray I can put this life's lessons to good use. For nearly thirty years, I've tried to make sense of my dad's harsh words and quick criticisms. I now realize it had nothing to do with me and everything to do with him. He was hurt early in life, although I'll never know how or by whom. The verbal weapons he lobbed at me and Mom were expressions of those inner wounds. But instead of drawing us nearer to him like a lasso reeling in the wild colt, they had pushed us further away and thus shielded him from more pain.

I have to let go of how he failed me and remember my love for my mom. I have to remember that being in that house where my parents fought constantly inspired me to be a better husband, to love Claire with all my heart, to cherish what was good about her and overlook her flaws. God knows I have my own. She loved me despite the fact that I arranged the books on my shelves by size and color one day, then by subject matter the next, never fully satisfied either way. I'm not that man anymore, the one who tried to control every insignificant minutia of his day. I know what matters now.

Sir Henry might never say he loves me, or is proud of me ... or that he forgives me for William's loss. But he risked his own life to save mine, and that's the greatest act of love there is.

And just when Claire was taken from me, Mariota was given to me. I shouldn't have ignored that. Maybe in the next life, I'll get it right.

A memory breaks free: the day Claire and I spent at Georges Square in Glasgow, eating our Indian food, watching people when an old couple caught our attention.

'Promise me something, Ross.'

'Anything.'

'If, for some reason, we don't both make it to that age, promise me you won't mourn me forever. That you'll find someone else to make you happy. I can't stand the thought of you being alone.'

Claire gave me full permission to move on, to love again, and I'd missed my chance.

Beside me, Christian leans against a sturdy, forked branch which serves as a crutch, gazing on as the three schiltrons — the left commanded by Lord Archibald, the center by young Robert Stewart, and the right by the Earl of Moray — descend onto lower ground. From here, their bristly spear points resemble the spines of a hedgehog. Each man in the formation is half an arm's length from the next. Those on the perimeter of the wedge shape hold their shields before them, edges overlapping. The rest clutch them high, ready to cover their heads. Christian was supposed to be one of the spearmen, but on his way back over the bridge that night, he'd leapt too soon. The fall had been far and he'd ended up with a broken ankle, unable to walk.

Sensing my eyes on him, he glances at me, a sneer marring his youthful face.

"You were very brave that night," I tell him.

He shrugs. "It made no difference, though, did it?" A mess of blond locks tumbles across his eyes as he returns his gaze to the impending battle. "I'm not sure any of it will."

He's right … but I can't tell him so.

The Scottish army, I estimate, numbers well over twelve thousand. More than the English, but it won't be enough. As I'd forewarned Archibald, Edward's army hasn't moved from its vantage point. The progress of our men slows as they enter the marsh. The rains have soaked the ground, making it like a sponge that can hold no more. Doubtless they're slogging through muck halfway up their shins. Even so, they maintain their lines, spears gripped firmly, shields at the ready.

There's a tug on the reins. My horse nickers and tosses his head. I remember earlier that morning, when Sir Henry mounted his own horse. The look in his eyes was grave.

"Your sword has saved many a Sinclair man," he said to me. "It was a gift from the King of Norway to my own great-great grandfather. Keep it close. Use it. Never let it from your sight."

For a moment, I thought he was going to yank me into his arms and give me a bear hug, but suddenly he turned away and was lost in the press of preparations.

On the opposite slope, the Welsh and English archers nestle arrows to their strings. They raise their bows. The Scots hoist their shields above their heads and forge onward. Black slashes cut across the sky, arcing high. Moments later I realize it isn't a flock of birds, but feathered arrows, seeking their targets.

Men crumple beneath the onslaught. Wherever one man goes down, another pushes forward to fill the gap. My stomach twists. I grip the reins of my horse, shut my eyes tight. Somewhere out there are my father, Duncan, Archibald, earls, knights, and nameless hundreds who I've marched beside, shared meals with, slept beside under the stars, laughed with. It's hard to imagine their lives being snatched away in an instant. Harder still to imagine being one of those marching on, while wounded and dead fall beside you, yet having to push on.

When I open my eyes again, I can barely fathom the horror unfolding before me. The Scots continue across the boggy expanse, then slog uphill, arrows raining all around. The right division, sorely depleted, is the first to collide with the English. The fight is fleeting. Like a tear through wet paper, the Scottish lines falter, then break. Whether Moray called on them to fall back or they simply lost heart, I can't tell. Men begin pushing back through the ranks, then fleeing downhill.

The center division continues to advance, but the left, led by Archibald, has already turned back. What began as an organized attack is quickly becoming a chaotic retreat.

The distance from the top of Witches Knowle on which I stand to the top of Halidon Hill is maybe half a mile, yet thousands and thousands of men are racing in our direction, desperate for safety, slowed only by the litter of bodies.

As the Scottish army collapses in on itself, the Earl of Ross, who commands the waiting rearguard at the top of the slope, makes the call for his Highlanders to stand their ground. I expect them to ignore his command — there can be only one outcome — but they don't. As men from the retreating divisions reach us, running for their lives, the Highlanders remain firm.

It's all unfolding too quickly. I can't watch any more. If I stay, I'll die, too. If I run, I have a chance — to live.

I whirl around, expecting to see Christian, but he's nowhere in sight. Gone. My first fear is that he's been trampled underfoot, but if that were the case, he'd be easy to find. No, he's gone to fight, even though he can barely stand on his own. If I can get to him, help him on my horse, I can get him out of here in time. So many soldiers are shoving past me, though, that I can't move forward. Only back. Away from the battle.

"Christian!" I yell. But there is no answer. Only the deafening roar of defeat.

My horse pulls his head back sharply. His black eyes are pressed wide, his nostrils flared. Gently, I try to reel him in, so I can steady him and mount. He resists, steps backward, then finally yields. Just as I slip my fingers in his halter, another panicked horse slams into his flank. My horse rears. The leather burns as he yanks away. I duck instinctively, fall to my knees. Feet pound around me. Behind me. Over me.

Through the crush of men fighting and fleeing, I glimpse Alan on his horse. He hooks his sword downward, his blade biting into the bare neck of a helmetless English solider. The man's head flops sideways; he sinks to his knees, then falls face down in a gurgle of bloody spittle ten feet from me.

Alan's eyes lock onto mine for the longest of moments. Then he spurs his horse sharply and gallops away.

A shield lands beside me with a thunderous thud. I grab its edge, pull it to me and huddle beneath it, waiting for my end.

This is it. This *is* the day after all.

I will die. But I have no fear. For I will live again.

Just, please God, hurry up. Be quick about it. I'm not good with pain.

A verse from Oscar Wilde flits through my scattered thoughts:

"And the wild regrets and the bloody sweats,
None knew so well as I:
For he who lives more lives than one
More deaths than one must die."

34

LONG, LONG AGO

Berwick, Scotland — 1333

I SWIM IN DARKNESS. COLD nothingness. All suffering — gone. I'm content. Glad to be free of my torment.

Torment?

The memory of a face appears through the mist of my dreams: translucent skin, eyes as green as the first unfurling leaves of springtime, hair like molten gold aflame. Her flesh beneath mine, warm, supple, my fingertips tingling. Her nearness stirring my blood.

Mariota.

I fight to wake. To climb from the airless void that entombs me and claim my own breath again. I gulp air, sputter and wheeze. My ribs scream in pain. The deathly clang of battle, broken by intermittent grunts, rings in my head. I cough, taste blood on my tongue. Or is it that I smell it in the air?

No. I don't want to go back. Not there. Not Halidon Hill.

I don't want to return to the future, either.

Just let me be dead, for God's sake.

The tang of damp iron curls inside my nostrils, overlain by an indescribably warm sweetness and the aroma of crushed grass.

Again — the ring of metal. Helpless dread gnaws at the pit of my stomach and seeps into my guts, filling me with panic, intensifying with each hammer of my heart. I try to sit up, to open my eyes, but I flail where I lay, enveloped by darkness.

One glimpse tells me all I need to know. It's over. We've lost.

I inhale again, long and deep, letting air fill my lungs, an assurance that I'm alive. For the moment, at least. Turning over, my right shoulder throbs with a habitual ache.

I tried to tell you, Archibald. Tried to tell you this would end badly. Tried to save you and the whole fricking army of Scotland. But you were too Goddamn stubborn to listen. And now you're dead, along with thousands of others.

Yet if it hadn't been Archibald and all the soldiers, the citizens of Berwick would have met a terrible fate, just like they had in Longshanks' time.

In the end, does it matter how the end comes? Fate is fate. There is no cheating it.

A sob convulses me, sorrow suffusing every inch of my soul like a black miasma. I don't want to live, knowing I've failed, knowing that these deaths hang on me.

If souls are allowed seven lives, like the Cathars believe, why can't I escape this one?

Overcome with exhaustion, I close my eyes again. Each breath becomes shallower, each heartbeat fainter.

Please, please let me die. Let me go.

If I could slit my wrists, hurry my passing, I would. If only I had a knife … My fingers twitch to reach for my belt, but I'm too weak. Can't move.

In the murky darkness of my dreams, I see Alan's face. See the way he had watched, triumphant, as the English soldier fell before me. The determined smile that had possessed him as he sped from the hill. North, undoubtedly. Toward Blacklaw Castle. Where Mariota is waiting — for me. He'll tell her I died. And then he'll … he'll …

Mariota!

Alert now, I gulp air in great shuddering heaves. It's long past nightfall, but even in the grayness, I can make out the scattered bodies, the heaps of dead in the distance.

I rake my fingers through the damp grass, trying to grab anchor so I can pull myself to my hands and knees. If I can't run from here, I'll crawl. Anything to escape this nightmare. To return to Mariota. And God help Alan if he does anything to her. I'll kill the bastard.

"Roslin?" someone croaks in a whisper. "God's bollocks, is that you?"

I look over my shoulder to see a man crouching some twenty feet away, a short sword held loosely across his knees. He looks around, then scoots toward me. As he comes nearer, I recognize the broken teeth, the scraggly beard of white.

"Duncan?" I push myself up on my good elbow. "Tell me — are you an angel, or the same old crusty turd you always were?"

"If I'm an angel, heaven's no better than hell." In front of me now, Duncan hunkers lower, looks me up and down. "Well you look a bloody fine sight. Ugly as ever. Whole … except for that crack in your skull where your brains are leaking out." He jabs rough fingers at my temple and I wince. A trace of warm blood seeps from beneath a fresh scab there. More gently then, he traces the edges of the wound. The skin is still there, mostly, the gash no more than an inch.

Sitting now, I clench his wrist. The blood drains from my head and I grip him tighter, trying to keep myself upright. "I need to get back to Blacklaw, Duncan. Will you help me?"

He twists his face in thought, turning his head from side to side as he peers into the darkness. "Can you ride?"

I nod, even though I'm far from certain I can. "If I fall …"

"If you fall, I'll throw you over my shoulder and carry you there like a sack of grain."

And he would.

"Good then." He lifts me up, but my legs are weak. I lean on him, for support as much as for courage. "Help me find a horse. Mine's dead and it looks as though you've lost yours."

HOW DUNCAN EVEN FOUND me is nothing short of a miracle. Thousands of ravaged bodies choke the marshy ground beyond Halidon Hill, sometimes stacked haphazardly in piles four or five deep. Even more than a mile from the worst of the massacre, there are bodies strewn about. The first few corpses we stumble past, I stop, turn them over and peer down into their faces to see if it's someone I know, or if perhaps, like me, someone else has lived and been left for dead. But they're all dead, many with limbs or ears missing, or big flaps of flesh torn loose to expose sinew and bone.

I slip on someone's entrails, or maybe it's brains, or both. Duncan latches onto my elbow, then puts my good arm over his shoulder.

"We don't have time for that." He yanks me forward. "'Twould be a pity for us to have survived this long, only to be gored by an English spear because you had to gawk."

Here and there I can make out shapes moving among the bodies: scavengers searching for valuables among the dead. Then I see a form stir, try to crawl away from one of the scavengers. A blade flashes in the darkness. A cry of mortal pain rings out, then fades to a dying moan. Had the wounded man been a noble, he might have been taken prisoner and ransomed, so that he would one day return to his family. But common soldiers aren't granted such graces.

Moon and stars are obscured by a broad veil of clouds. Our

further salvation comes as a mist descends over the land, first spilling into the low places between the hills and then reaching its milky fingers toward higher ground.

I struggle to stay awake as much as I do to stay on my feet. It's tempting to just stop, fold to the ground and sleep. If the enemy came upon us, I couldn't have fought them anyway. But Duncan drags me onward, babbling on about how he'll get me to Blacklaw and from there we'll go to Edinburgh, then something about how we have to save King David and ... At some point I can't make sense of his words anymore.

My foot catches on something and I tumble forward. Onto a body. A body missing its head.

"Shit!" Adrenalin blasts through me. I scrabble across the ground on my knees, hauling myself forward with my left arm.

Duncan growls, kicking me in the side of the leg. He shoves me down and squats before me, one hand twisting a hank of my hair to turn my head. "Our unfortunate friend left a horse behind, in case you hadn't noticed."

I bat his hand away and look. The horse is standing next to the headless man, its head hanging low, blood splattered on its white hide. In my fog of exhaustion, I didn't see the animal, so still it was. The beast was loyal to the end. The colors of its trappings match the knight's surcoat, although I don't recognize the emblem on his chest. He could have been either English or Scottish or a foreign mercenary, for all I know.

Tentative, Duncan stands, staggers toward the animal. It raises its head, snorts a warning. As he reaches toward it, the horse's ears perk, but it stays where it is. Duncan takes hold of the reins, slowly reeling the animal in as he speaks lowly to it.

A few minutes later, he climbs into the saddle, then slips his foot from the stirrup and offers me a hand.

I stare at his open palm. "I don't know if I can, Duncan. I'm so tired. So damn tired."

"Throw your arse up here, and live … or stand there like a simpering fool and die."

A dry laugh rattles in the back of my throat. "You said you'd carry me."

Muttering a curse, Duncan rolls his eyes. "If I did that right now, we'd *both* end up dead. First, we need to get away from this mess."

English voices drift through the fog. At first they seem to be fading in the opposite direction, but then another voice, closer to us, calls out and the others answer that they're coming.

Grabbing the cantle of the saddle, I wedge my foot in the stirrup and struggle to pull myself up. With a grumble, Duncan seizes my surcoat and hauls me behind him. I reach around him to slip an arm beneath the leather strap crossing his chest.

Carefully, he guides the horse around the fallen. Out in the open, he urges it to a trot. At that point, it isn't the threat of death from Englishmen on the hunt that keeps me alert, but the pain in my shoulder that shoots through my body with every stride of the horse.

35

LONG, LONG AGO

Blacklaw Castle, Scotland — 1333

BLACKLAW CASTLE IS LITTLE more than half a day's ride from Berwick. Under normal circumstances. It has taken us twice that long to reach it.

The castle beckons in the distance at the edge of the sea cliff, its stones flecked with the green and gold of moss and lichen. Not a large fortress, especially when compared to a place like Bamburgh in Northumberland, it's still imposing due to its height above the shore.

Duncan urges our lagging horse to a trot. Wearied by the pace he had demanded of it the last few miles, its gait is unsteady, but its obedience never wavers. The road dips low behind a hill and the castle disappears from view. I cling to Duncan's chest, my arm burning from the effort. I want to let go, to ask him to stop and rest, but I can't. Not now, not with Mariota so close.

When the road curves seaward and the castle comes into view again, it seems no closer than before. I cast a glance behind us to make sure we haven't been followed, then close my eyes to concentrate on the vision of Mariota.

I hear nothing but the constant roar of the sea and the rhythmic plodding of a single set of hooves on damp earth. Somewhere in the distance, seabirds jeer.

The horse stumbles and my eyes fly open. We're almost there. I gaze up at the keep. The wall appears empty of guards. The gate stands open. Then, toward the furthest edge of the headland where the cliff is highest, there is a movement. Someone, a woman, stands at the rim of the cliff, skirts flaring and snapping with the buffeting wind, her toes dangling over the precipice. She raises her face and spreads her arms wide, leaning forward into the wind.

"Mariota!" I cry. Duncan slows our mount to look, but I urge him onward, quicker. The horse lurches. Clamping my knees to the horse's ribs as I let go of Duncan, I cup a hand to my mouth and shout louder. "Mariotaaaa!"

She says something back, but her words are lost to the sea. She's not even looking our way. Her slender body yearns toward the ledge. Below, waves collide with a mass of jagged rocks, the spray exploding upward and scattering in the wind.

My heart vaults into my throat as I envision her falling, falling, falling.

No, no! Don't let me have come this far, lived through so much, only to witness her death.

I call her name again as the horse breaks into a full gallop, Duncan's spurs digging into its flanks. Again, again. My throat grows raw with the strain.

Suddenly, she turns her head toward us, but a gust slams her backward, away from the precipice. She crumples to the ground, her body heaving with sobs.

We clear the gatehouse without alarm, a pair of guards barely stirring at our entrance. With Duncan's help, I settle to the ground.

Then I run, my legs wobbling, through the small gate and along the path — to the point on the headland where Mariota kneels, waiting for me.

I PULL HER TO me and hold her tight, my right arm crushed between us. The ache in my shoulder eases with every heartbeat. Her arms hook around my neck as she buries her face against my chest. The wind beats at us, nudging us away from the edge. I lift her hand to my lips to graze her knuckles with a kiss, then turn it over and press the warmth of her palm against my cheek.

"Someone passed by after the battle and said ..." She gazes up at me, her eyes moist with tears. "I had given up. I thought ... that ..."

"That I was dead? So did I. Twice. But for whatever reason, I lived. I guess they wouldn't have me in heaven, or hell — or the next life, wherever it is that souls flee to when they leave this world. But I'm here now. Very much alive. Very much in love with you."

A smile graces her lips, but it's quickly replaced with a frown of concern. "Your arm."

"Hurts. I won't lie. But it'll heal in time." Although it will forever be my weakness. I know that already.

"And your head?"

"Looks worse than it is." The scar, I'm sure, will remain for all my life, a reminder of the horror I survived. Sadness creeps over me, threatening to paralyze me whole, and I shake it off quickly. No, I can't think about it. Not with regret. I tried to change the course of events, but all I did was change my own fate, to whatever end that might bring. Maybe that's all anyone has control over?

I trace a finger over Mariota's brow, the rose-pink rim of her ear, the exquisite line of her jaw. How had I not noticed the perfection of her features before? "Come. Let's go inside, Mariota. I need rest. I need you."

An understanding flickers in her eyes. She glances down shyly, taking my hand as we turn toward the castle. Her hand fits perfectly in mine. Her head is at the right height so that she can lay it against my shoulder. It is as if we were made from one mold. As if we have always known each other.

More than once in this life I had almost died. Yet Fate has preserved me. When I draw my last breath, it will be not on the battlefield, but in the arms of Mariota, the two of us grown old together.

MARIOTA WRINGS THE CLOTH into the basin, the trickle of water a sweet chiming in my ears. Leaning forward, she dabs at the skin around the gash at my temple, each stroke a mercy, cleansing.

"Where is Duncan?" She pours me a cup of wine and urges me to drink. "He is not hurt, I hope."

I down it in three gulps and ask for more. "Asleep in the gatehouse. Or flirting with the kitchen maids. But no, he's not hurt. Not seriously, at least. I wouldn't have made it here, if not for him."

The bedchamber in the southeast tower where I lay is small, scant on comfort, but tidy. A pair of candle stubs, an empty cup and a pitcher sit on a tiny round table, underneath which is a stool. Mariota's personal belongings are neatly tucked away in the rough-hewn chest next to the door. The bed itself is narrow, but comfortable and covered with a light woolen blanket.

"Why did you sleep here, of all places?" I ask her, as she hands me my third cup. "Surely there are grander rooms in this castle."

"Larger ones, yes." She inclines her head toward the window. "This one has the best view of the southern road. And the sea wind blows strongest through this window. I often couldn't sleep at night, so I would sit on the ledge and look out, to watch for you in the moonlight."

It takes an hour to carefully peel the layers of armor from my battered body and then more time for her to coax me to shed the clothing underneath. I can barely sit upright, let alone stand. I want to sleep, she knows, but if I let myself slip away before undressing and ridding myself of the blood and grime of battle, it'll dry to my flesh with the toughness of a rhino's hide. Sleep, although welcome, will have to wait.

Neither is this a time for many words. What would we talk about? My father? No, she must gather that since I have not spoken of him that he didn't make it. The battle? I'll never recount it to her. Better to forget it, to look forward. Should we talk of the future then? No, we don't need to. That's understood. We'll grow old together, have a herd of children.

With every loving stroke of her hand, every smudge of dirt and speck of blood wiped clean, I leave the past — and the future — behind.

Only this moment matters. Only her. Mariota. My wife.

In this life, she alone is my one true love.

She offers me more wine and bread. If I drink any more, I'll float away. My hunger, however, has returned in full force. Devouring the bread greedily, I take a few sips of the wine to wash it down. I lay back again and she resumes washing me. Time loses meaning. There is only this moment. Only us.

Wine flows warmly through my veins, not dulling my senses, but heightening them. The pressure of her fingertips is light, her movements meticulous as she sweeps over my body in slow spirals, beginning at my face and working her way down my neck, my arms and chest, pausing at the ridge of my hipbones. My lower waist is covered with a sheet. I'm beyond being modest, but I know now what I want: her. Yet I won't rush her toward the moment. It will happen when she's ready.

Which, evidently, is now.

She inches the sheet back to reveal my bare leg nearest her and dips the cloth in water again, then draws it slowly down my hip and onto my thigh. Every gentle movement sends a wave of energy pulsing through me. A few hours ago I could hardly stay awake. Wouldn't have cared if I had fallen to the ground and slept for days. Now, I am renewed.

A shudder spreads from my groin up through my abdomen and chest, finally settling in my shoulders. Each time she lifts the cloth and rubs it over my skin, I become more and more aroused. My shoulder still hurts like hell, but I want her, badly. And she isn't exactly being demure.

I take the cloth from her, dropping it to the floor. Her breath hitches as I pull the sheet back. She looks away a moment, then glances shyly at me.

"I would like to get to know my wife better," I say, trailing light fingers down her neck to her collarbone. "Let me prove I am no heretic, Mariota."

Slowly, she rises. She looks like she might bolt. God knows I'm in no state to chase her down. Counter to my fears, she begins to undress. With each garment she removes, her eyes flick to mine, lingering a little longer each time. Finally, she stands unclothed before me, intoxicating, perfect in every way.

Mariota takes a step, a single hesitant step toward me. Tears glimmer in her eyes. Is she afraid of how it will be this first time?

I flash my palm at her. "Is this what you want?"

She nods, smiling faintly. "I have wanted this since I first saw you. I have wanted this every time you were near, every time you drew away from me, every time you left, every night you were not with me. I always knew you would return to me, that we would be ... together." The last word suggests more than mere companionship. Her eyes full of wonderment, she looks me over. "All I had to do was wait for you." She climbs onto the bed and kneels beside me, stroking my cheek with her hand, bending so her mouth is close to mine. "I love you, Roslin. I will love you for all eternity, from this life onward."

36

LONG, LONG AGO

<u>Blacklaw Castle, Scotland — 1333</u>

M ARIOTA LAYS WITH HER head on my chest, her body still except for the gentle rise and fall of her ribs beneath my arm.

If only Claire could live long enough for the baby to be born, then there would be something of us left in that world. But I'll never know.

I've finally let go of hope. Hope that Claire had lived, that she would get better. Hope that I would ever return. I'll always love her, but there's no sense in mourning her loss, the child she carried, or my old life forever. *This* is my life now. I've found new courage in this crude lifestyle, learned to live by facing death, learned to love again by having lost.

Odd how we discover the strength within ourselves only when we need it as a last resort. I would have never thought myself so brave, so unbridled, had I never been thrown into this primitive madness.

Evening edges toward night and still I don't move. There's too much comfort lying here with her in my arms. Sleep tugs at my eyelids and I let them drift shut. But soon, the memory of battle echoes in my ears: the shouts building to a roar, the rumble of weapons striking shields, the cries of the dying.

I open my eyes and the sounds fade away. A breeze gusts through the window, rattling a wooden cup that sits on the ledge. The last candle sputters, then goes out. In a world of half-light, the edges of shapes blur with shadows. Night has passed and dawn arrived.

In the distance, I hear a shout. My heart jolts in alarm. Have the English come this far north? I sit up, causing Mariota to mumble at the disturbance.

"Shhhhh," I tell her. I slip from beneath the covers and begin toward the window.

"Roslin? Come back to bed."

Glancing out the window, I can see the road is clear, but from here the view to the gatehouse is obscured. I return to Mariota and tuck her hair behind her ears, whispering, "Someone's here."

Yawning, Mariota stretches her limbs. "The door is barred. They'll not disturb us."

"No, outside. At the gate."

She sits up, the sheet falling free of her body. "Who?"

The English, most likely. They've come for me. To take me back to England. But why? What use will I be to them now? Henry Sinclair is dead. So are Archibald and thousands more. The Scots are beaten. Many years will pass before we can hold our own against them again.

I reach for my clothes and begin to dress. "Can we defend the castle, Mariota? Can we keep them out?"

Slipping her chemise over her head, Mariota speaks rapidly. "There are only four guards left. The rest went to join Lord

Archibald. They never came back."

And never will. But I don't say it. She'll learn of the catastrophic losses in time.

We have to get out of here. Run.

Mariota is clothed before I am. She helps me into my shirt, taking care not to hurt my shoulder. I leave my chainmail and arm plates where they lie and claim my sword, pausing to run my thumb over the ruby-eyed serpent coiled in its pommel. There's no time for anything more.

Blood hammering in my ears, I unbolt the door and fly through the corridor. Mariota's lighter steps echo mine. I race down the spiral stairs, my sword held loosely in my left hand, my elbow stuck out to touch the wall as a guide, my vision barely adjusted to the darkness.

As I burst through the bottom door and into the morning light in the bailey, what strikes me is the odd quiet and lack of alarm. There are no English here. None. But the man who appears before me is just as much my enemy as any Englishman.

Alan struts toward me, pulling his sword free as he nears.

I level my weapon at him, but in my left hand it feels strange, unwelcome. "What are you doing here?"

"I've come to collect you, Sir Roslin." A wicked smirk crosses his face. Half a dozen men are seated on their horses behind him, including Malcolm, but they keep their distance, as if he's already informed them that this fight is his. "To take you to King David."

"For what? Can't you see I'm injured? I barely made it here. Go on to Edinburgh. I'll come when I'm able."

"There'll be no need by then. We must get David out of Scotland. Edward and Balliol will send their men throughout the country, demanding fealty. I imagine you'll be among the first to capitulate. That's why you want to stay here, isn't it? You're waiting for them to come so you can offer your services in return for promises of land and position. It's what your father planned all along."

"You're wrong, Alan. Now go to Edinburgh. Keep the king safe. I'd only slow you, as I am. For now, we all need to survive, what few of us that are left. In time, we can fight again."

"Help me get the king to France," — he closes the last few steps— "or I'll expose you for the traitor and heretic you are."

"I'm neither of those things. You know that. I went to Annan to help capture Balliol."

"Then you're a Cathar," Malcolm says with disdain. He slides from his saddle to stand behind Alan. "You have been since before you went to Spain with Lord James."

"Now come with us," Alan commands, thrusting his blade at me. "Renounce your faith before God and King David. If you re-fuse —"

"Damn it, Alan!" Anger explodes inside me. I knock his blade aside with mine with surprising strength. "I'm no bloody heretic. Let go of that, will you? Just ... just leave here!"

He retreats a step. His eyes skip to the point of his blade. Slowly, surely, he raises it again. "If you refuse to come, you will be proclaimed a heretic. Do you know what they do to heretics? Do you?" A tic jerks at a muscle in his jaw. "While a crowd gathers in witness to their sinfulness, they strap them to a pole atop a pile of dry kindling. Then they light it aflame and watch as his flesh melts from his bones. The agony you suffer in those few minutes will be but a glimpse of your eternity, Roslin. You see, there is no life after this one. There is only heaven ... or hell."

I glance at the soldiers behind him and at Malcolm. They're all wearing the same attire they fought in: blood-splattered, torn, muddied. They've had too little sleep and not enough food. Even so, the odds are stacked against me. To fight him would be futile. If he doesn't kill me himself, Malcolm will. My only chance is to reason with him, convince him it would be best if I stay here and provide refuge to those fleeing the English before going to Edinburgh. In truth, I haven't thought beyond the battle about what my future holds. I had believed my death was already scripted — and yet I survived. What if Father Murray was wrong about my death? What if I am to die today, at the point of Alan's sword, or in Edinburgh, at the stake? My prospects are looking grim.

"You have no proof," I say, even though I know I'm merely stalling.

A jagged smile distorts his mouth. "Then come. Simple, aye?"

Just as he lowers his sword, I catch a subtle movement out of the corner of my eye. Two of Alan's soldiers have dismounted and are encircling us. No, not us. Not Alan and me. They're watching Mariota, getting closer to her.

"Sir Roslin," Alan drawls, tilting his head, "perhaps I do have ... proof. A confession, of sorts. Tell us, do you believe we live more than one life? Have you ever admitted that you have?"

Only twice. First to Duncan in the storeroom at Lintalee. Then to Mariota, the day she came to camp at Berwick. But neither would have betrayed my secret. I was certain no one had overheard me at Lintalee, but Berwick ... The walls of tents are thin. Malcolm, maybe? If he'd heard, if he'd told Alan or anyone else, then that's all the evidence they'd need.

And as soon as I'm out of the picture, Alan can have Mariota all to himself. He doesn't need her permission. Her brother will gladly give it. After that, Alan will do everything in his power to become David's guardian now that Archibald is gone.

"Was it you, Malcolm?" I probe, looking past Alan. But Malcolm's features are granite, his mood unreadable. "Did you tell him something that would damn me?"

Triumph sparks in Alan's eyes. "You're asking if I have a witness to your confession? Maybe he did; maybe he didn't. What does it matter to you? Your sins are widely known and my word carries a great deal of weight with the king."

If I thought he might be bluffing, I thought it no more.

"Duncan!" I shout.

Laughing under his breath, Alan glances at Malcolm. He swings his sword before him like a pendulum. The blade gleams with blood. "Really, did you think I would let him live? He stood in my way. He won't again."

Behind me, Mariota's whimpering pleas escalate. "Malcolm, don't let him do this. Whatever you think you heard, it wasn't heresy. If you believe it is, then I am implicated, too. They'll have to deliver the same fate to me. Do you want me dead, as well?"

Malcolm gives no response, just glares back at her.

All at once, it's like I'm standing in a deep, dark pit and the walls are caving in on me, suffocating me, crushing me. If I confess, I'm as good as dead. So is Mariota. Alan could kill me on this very spot and suffer no repercussions. Murdering a heretic is no crime. It's a heroic deed done all the time in the name of God. If I deny it, he'll haul me all the way to Edinburgh and I'll die there — and not at all swiftly.

"So tell us," Alan repeats more slowly, ignoring Mariota's plea to her brother, "have you ever spoken of living another life ... to anyone?"

Feet slap over the cobbles behind me. I whirl around. Mariota's skirts whip about her legs as she darts through the postern gate. I run after her. Two of Alan's men have already followed her out onto the narrowing finger of land, but they stop dead when she spins around. Her back is to the cliff's edge, her heels but inches from a hundred foot drop.

"Mariota!" I call. "Mariota, no!"

Her eyes snap to me, and then to the gate as Alan rushes through, followed closely by Malcolm. She points a shaking finger at Alan. "If you take him ... if you kill him, Alan, I will step from this cliff. I would rather die than become your wife."

His arms drift wide, although he's still gripping his sword. "Mariota, don't be blinded by this sinner. He has deceived you. Woven a dark spell. Made you believe things that violate God's holy word. Please, my love, don't allow his trickery to dupe you further. Suicide is a mortal sin. Would you truly give up your life for him, knowing that you, too, would burn for all eternity?"

She raises her chin. The sea wind blows her hair across her eyes, tangles the strands into knots. Her countenance is a façade of passionate resolve. "Sharing your bed would be a worse torture than hell."

Alan clutches an empty fist to his chest, pain etched as indelibly over his features as if she has just shot an arrow into his heart. "Mariota, we have known each other since we were infants. Did we not once confess our love to one another? How can you speak to me thusly now?"

I want to interrupt, to tell him what a selfish bastard he is, but something in my gut begs me to hold off.

Mariota spreads her arms to either side, her flattened palms facing the sea, so that the wind buffets against them. She takes a tiny step backward. Her heels hang over the edge. "I was thirteen then and foolish. And yes, I thought I loved you. I even told you so, because I was afraid of being given away to a man I did not know and being taken from the only home I had ever known. But then ..."

Even from fifty feet away, I can see the tears streaming down her cheeks.

"Then, you raped me, Alan. That was not an act of love. It was an act born of jealousy and carried out in violence."

"No, no, no." With each word, Alan edges closer to her. "You remember wrongly, dearest love. We were both tempted. Our desires overtook us, that is all."

"Your lust closed your ears to my protests," she says. "I fought you, Alan. I gave you scars, so you might never forget."

His hand drifts to his neck, where the fingernail marks still stand out: three thin streaks of red.

"No, it was not love," she continues. "Not even carnal desire. Certainly not on my part. When you learned of my betrothal to Roslin, you wished to get me with child in hopes my father would renege on his agreement with Sir Henry and give me to you, instead. And along with my hand would come my inheritance. You knew Malcolm's wife had proven barren. You wanted land and the power that comes with it, so you won him over to your plans long ago, figuring that if anything ever happened to Roslin that Malcolm would grant his blessing. It was never about your love for me. What a blessing it was that as the months passed, no child came of your act upon me. Soon after, I was married to Roslin and left for Blacklaw. I thought then I had seen the last of you, but you would not leave me be, visiting my father-in-law on weak pretenses as often as you could. I feared for my safety every time I saw you. You sicken me even now."

In three angry strides, Malcolm swallows the ground between them. "You lied to me, Alan! You said Roslin had forced himself upon her, so that he could have her inheritance. But it was you."

"Shut up!" Alan shoves Malcolm to the ground, then turns back to Mariota, one hand outstretched, imploring. "Mariota, you don't understand. I *do* love you. I was desperate, that is all. I could not bear to think of you with him, or anyone. That is why I never married. I have been waiting for —" He stops himself in mid sentence. The secret is out. He has been waiting for me to die — in Spain, in England, at Berwick. He even came here expecting to find Mariota alone. Instead, he discovered the two of us sharing a bed.

"For years after Roslin and I were wed," Mariota says, "I would not let him near me. A man's touch, I thought, inflicted only pain and shame. Even so, Roslin was never anything but kind and patient. So very unlike you, who took what you wanted without care." She spits

~ 269 ~

at the ground. "Go from here, in peace. Take back your accusations of heresy against Roslin. I shall call you a liar and it will be my word against yours. Find yourself some other wife and make a life for yourself at King David's side. It cannot be between us, Alan. I was meant for Roslin. He is my husband. I ... I love him. I always will."

A burst of wind swirls around her, snapping at her skirts, nudging her. Her body wavers. She leans forward to steady herself.

Alan lurches.

"Wait!" I cry.

He whirls around to look at me, every muscle in his body tensed as if he's torn between saving her and wanting to murder me.

"I'll go with you," I tell him.

"No!" Mariota bolts forward, directly into my arms. She grabs at the front of my shirt, bunching it in her hands. "You cannot, Roslin. Do not put your life in his hands. He will kill you if you give yourself up to him."

I have no doubt she's right. But better my life than hers.

She brushes the back of her hand against my rough-whiskered cheek. I close my eyes, touch my forehead to hers and simply breathe, inhaling the scent of her: ocean and earth, pennyroyal and cloves, damp stones and moss ... I can even still smell on her fingertips a hint of the lavender-infused oil she had massaged into my aching muscles last night.

"You'll have a son, Mariota," I whisper, opening my eyes to look into hers. Then I lift my right hand just enough to briefly touch her belly before white hot pain flames through my shoulder. I clench my teeth, swallow the pain. "*Our* son."

A bittersweet smile flits over her lips. I lean in to kiss her, but just as I do, the space between us opens up.

Alan thrusts her from me and she tumbles to the ground, landing hard, her elbow striking a stone. His sword whooshes through the air, metal dividing sky. I flail my left arm outward. Our blades collide. The force of the blow travels up my arm, jarring my bones from skull to heel.

Before he can recover, I strike again and again, throwing an anger-fueled strength into my attack that I never knew I possessed. Step by step, he retreats toward the cliff. Wielding a sword left-handed, I'm clumsy, all force, no finesse. The effort is rapidly draining me. I pause, hoping to gather more strength, but my limbs are growing heavy, my head light.

Bodies rush at us and I'm suddenly reminded of his reinforcements. To my amazement, Alan warns them off with a roar. "Stand back! By God, the man wants to die, then die he shall — on the point of my blade." He extends his sword straight at me, then dips the end at the ground. "Down on your knees. Make your peace with Our Almighty Father, now, Unbeliever. Repent of your sins. You shall not get another chance."

"I have nothing to confess." My lungs are on fire, my energy fading fast. I can barely breathe to speak. "The only untruths spoken here today are the ones you have uttered."

Screaming, he barrels at me. I slash downward, but my balance and timing are poor. My blade glances off his arm plate and is ripped from my grasp.

"Roslin!" Mariota screeches.

Moments unfold like minutes as I watch his blade slide cleanly into my gut, just above my hip bone. I suck my torso back, but he holds his arm rigid. Then with a wrench of his elbow, he yanks it free, the point twisting inside me as he does so.

I collapse to my knees. A dark red stain on my shirt spreads rapidly, wetness seeping down my groin, over my thigh, pulsing away my life. The sound of my own heartbeat drums in my ears — or is that the sea crashing rhythmically against the shore? I can't tell. Can't feel the wind anymore, don't sense any pain. Only coldness washing over me, sucking me slowly into a downward spiral.

Alan's laughter breaks through my fog. It's the last sound I hear before everything goes silent.

I slump onto my side. Scattered stones softened by clumps of grass press through my clothing and into my flesh, but even that awareness is fading. In a sideways world, I think I see the red of Mariota's gown sweep across the ground. Her feet tangle in her hem. She falls. Then a startled look flashes across Alan's face as Malcolm's hulking form crosses between them.

Shapes collide, twisting. A slash of metal. Then light.

Malcolm stands alone at the verge of earth and sea.

And where Alan had been, only feet from the edge … there is nothing but sky.

Mariota comes to me, bends down. Her voice breaks through the silence, a frail thread. "Shhh, shhh. Rest now, my love."

My eyes go shut. I can't open them, no matter how hard I try.

PART III

Would the happy spirit descend
From the realms of light and song,
  In the chamber or the street,
  As she looks among the blest,
Should I fear to greet my friend
Or to say "Forgive the wrong,"
Or to ask her, "Take me, sweet,
  To the regions of thy rest?"

From Alfred, Lord Tennyson's *Maude*

37

HERE & NOW

Near Berwick, Scotland — 2013

"ELLO." A TENTATIVE FINGER pokes me in the ribs. "You awake?"

What?

I ignore the voice. Keep my eyes closed. Something's different. I can no longer hear or smell the sea. Instead, the musky scent of earth and crushed grass floods my nose. Then another smell intrudes. I inhale more deeply and cough, fighting the urge to gag. Engine oil and gasoline.

I force my eyes open. My vision is blurry. I can barely make out a guy about twenty-years old with dyed black hair. He hovers over me, his gloved hands braced on his knees. He's wearing a pair of grimy jeans and a leather jacket hung with chains.

"Good to see you're alive," he says.

"I ... I'm not dead?"

"I'd say not. If you were trying to kill yourself, next time pick a taller bridge, eh?"

I feel utterly drained, disoriented. The sun is low on the horizon, but is it morning or evening? This is no seaside cliff or wooded glen, but open hills covered in grass. Up above a low rise is the road I'd bailed from when the lorry forced me off on my way back to Aberbeg. Not far away is a meandering stream and maybe twenty feet above it a narrow bridge. I remember it clearly, as if it just happened.

"What year is this?" I mumble. I can see a little better now, but not perfectly.

He laughs and I'm momentarily distracted by his lip barbell piercing. "That bad, are you? Must be pished. Or taken a pummeling. Still 2013, if that helps."

Shock rolls through me.

No, it doesn't. I don't want to be here. I want to be with Mariota. I want to go back.

Digging my fingers into thick grass, I try to pull myself up, but the world spins around me. My muscles are like Jell-O. My shoulder blazes with pain. A groan escapes my throat. Warm dampness spreads along the waistband of my jeans.

The punk rocker or Goth or vampire … whatever he is pushes me gently back down. "Stay where you are. I called an ambulance already. They're on the way." He lifts the bottom of my shirt, grimaces, then puts it back down. "Bleeding a wee bit there. Ugly gash on your head, too. Nothing serious, though. Probably just got scraped up when you took a tumble. I think you'll be all right."

"What day is it?" I ask.

"I should probably ask you that. Do you remember?"

I think hard. My head is foggy. What day, what day? Our flight home was supposed to leave in two days, on the 21st of July. "The 19th?"

"Close enough." He straightens. "Ah, just down the road. Almost here."

The wail of a siren rises above the rustle of a light wind until it comes to a stop on the road above. Doors slam. My rescuer hails them. Soon two EMTs are scurrying down the hill with a stretcher.

They ask me simple questions: what's my name, where am I from, how did this happen, does anything hurt, what day is it? I'm not sure I answer everything correctly, because I'm too tired to think and they ask me some things more than once. I just want to go to sleep, hoping I'll wake up back in 1333.

Because if this is real, if I'm stuck here now, I've not only lost Mariota forever, but I'll soon lose Claire, too. Or already have. If that's the case, I don't even want to be alive. The next truck that comes along, I'll be sure I plant myself squarely in front of it.

It seems like forever before they finish checking me over and begin to carry me uphill. Every stride jars me back to wakefulness. When we finally reach the road, the biker rushes to one of the EMTs and hands him something.

"This must be his." He drops it into the man's outstretched hand. "I stopped to take a piss over the bridge when I heard it ringing. Found it part way down the hill, then saw him. Looks like someone's been trying like mad to reach him."

The last thing I hear is the boom of the ambulance doors as they fling them shut and the piercing scream of the siren.

A PINPOINT OF WHITE light blinds me. I jerk my head sideways and hear the crinkle of a stiff pillowcase. A quick look at my surroundings tells me I'm in a private hospital room.

"There now," comes a voice crackled with age. "Remain calm. Everything's going to be fine, just fine."

An older man with ragged gray sideburns and Coke bottle glasses smiles patronizingly at me. Great, I'm being attended to by an octogenarian.

He clicks his pen light off and listens to my heartbeat with his stethoscope. "You must have skidded across the pavement when you fell off your bike."

"I was run off the road by a moron."

"Of course. Did you get a license number?"

"I was a little more concerned with not getting splattered under his wheels, actually."

He moves the cold metal around on my chest, then jots a few notes on the clipboard beside my bed. "No internal injuries, thank goodness. We had to put a few stitches by your temple there. You have some abrasions along your ribs and hip, consistent with the accident you described. And a dislocated shoulder, which we've already set. It will be sore for a bit, but you should have full mobility within a week or so. "

That's the first time I notice the sling on my right arm. I hadn't felt the pain before. Don't feel it now, thanks to the drugs zipping through my bloodstream.

"We couldn't find any identification on you. Is there someone we can call for you?"

I remember leaving my wallet behind when I left for the kirk. But I'd had my cell phone. "My phone. The guy who found me gave them my phone. Where is it? I need to call Parker."

"Ah, I'll see if it's at the nurse's station. Who's Parker? A relative?"

"Brother-in-law. He's here with my wife."

"Wife?" His unibrow folds in confusion, then lifts. "Ah, why didn't you say so? How do we contact her?"

A lot of good that would do. Yet he'd asked the question in all innocence.

"She lapsed into a coma while we were on our honeymoon here. They don't think ..." The realization that this isn't a dream wallops me with the force of a hurricane wind. If this is reality, then what had I just been through?

A memory. A memory of a life lived long ago.

"Sir?" he prompts.

Damn it. I can't say it. But I have to face it. I have to. There's no more escaping to the fourteenth century. "Is this Berwick Infirmary?"

"Aye, the only."

I swallow, force the words out. "Coma. They don't think she's going to make it."

"Ah." He tilts his head back. "Yes, I know who you are now. Let me get your phone for you."

A few minutes later he's back with my phone.

"I can't make out the numbers without my glasses," I say. "Maybe you could —?"

"Ah, yes." He steps toward the bed and retrieves a pair of glasses from the adjustable table next to it. "Here you are. They found these on the road. Luckily, they weren't damaged too badly. Nurse Stephens managed to straighten the frames for you."

I slip them on and stare at the display, scanning through the missed calls. Parker has called twenty times. What the heck? I've only been gone a few hours. Why didn't he just text me?

Then I see the date. It's the 21st. The day Claire and I are supposed to be going back to Ohio. A sinking feeling tugs at my stomach.

Oh God. Is she …?

A knot forms in my throat. I slam the phone against the bed and bite down. If the doctor doesn't leave, I'm going to break down in front of him.

"It seems one of the nurses took a call not long ago for you," the doctor says. "It was your brother-in-law. She told him what room you were in. He said he was on his way, but he wanted you to call him right back as soon as you could."

"Sure." I gulp in several breaths, turn my head toward the window. "Could you leave?"

"Yes, of course. If you need anything, the call button is on the left rail there. The nurses are only two doors down."

I wait until the door clicks shut, then scroll to Parker's name and hit 'Send'.

"Hello?"

"Parker? It's me, Ross."

"Ross! Where in the hell have you been, man? I've been trying to reach you."

"Run off the road by a truck. Guess I fell down a hill, hit my head. Dislocated my shoulder again, too. But I'm going to be okay." *Physically* I'm going to be okay. Mentally I'm about to fracture into a million pieces.

"Ross, I need to tell you about Claire."

I don't want to hear it. Sooner or later though, I'll have to.

"You won't believe this." He laughs. He actually *laughs*. Sick bastard. "She woke up yesterday. She's a bit groggy, can't remember some things. But they say she should make a full recovery in time. God, I can't believe it, can you?"

The phone drops from my hand onto the pillow. I try to process it all, but can't. How do you go from accepting the loss of your first love and moving on, to falling in love with another, to this?

"Ross? Ross, are you there?" His voice sounds muted coming from the tiny speaker. I retrieve the phone and press it to my ear again.

"Yeah, I'm here. Just in shock, that's all."

"Hey, I had to go back to the hotel and grab a change of clothes, but I'll be back in fifteen minutes. I told the nurses to have a wheelchair ready for you. I'll take you to see her when I get there. Okay?"

"Sure, okay." But the enthusiasm in my words is lacking. I'm not sure what to feel just now. Joy? Loss? Relief? Maybe it's the guilt that's eating me up?

In my fists, I ball the sheets up so tight my hands begin to cramp. Tears slick my cheeks and roll onto the pillow.

I need more than fifteen minutes to sort this all out, to get my head on straight. But I don't have more time. And I can't just spit out everything that's happened to me. They'd all think I was insane. Instead, I have to jump back into this life as if nothing ever happened.

I don't know how I'm going to manage that.

PARKER PUNCHES THE DOOR open and wheels me through. There on the hospital bed is Claire, just as I'd last left her: flat on her back, her tousled blonde hair spread around her puffy face, her eyes closed.

For a second I think she's slipped back into the coma before I could see her again. Then Parker flips the switch by the door. The light blinks to life, humming for a moment as the bulb warms up. She doesn't move, not even when Parker clears his throat.

He bends closer to me. "She's tired. Still sleeps a lot. Come on, let's say 'hi'."

When we reach her, I take her hand, careful to avoid the IV needles taped to the back of it, but that brings no response. Her skin is cool, her fingers limp, her whole body sunken down into the mattress like she hasn't moved from it in days.

They had warned me she might have brain damage. Am I going to spend the rest of my life caring for someone who doesn't even know who I am? Can I be that strong, that selfless? I want to shake her awake, hear her shout my name and feel her throw her arms around me.

Face toward the ceiling, Claire's lashes flutter open, then quickly drift shut again.

"Claire? Claire? I'm here." I clutch her hand more firmly. "I came back for you, Claire. I came back."

She squeezes my hand back so lightly I almost don't notice.

"About time, Ross Lyndon Sinclair." She turns her head toward me. A faint smile pries apart lips that are thin and cracked. "Took you forever."

I kiss her knuckles, try to swallow back my tears, but they come anyway. "Yeah, it seems that way."

38

HERE & NOW

Berwick, Scotland — 2013

EVERY DAY, CLAIRE IMPROVES steadily. They had released me after twenty-four hours, but only after Parker insisted that he'd stay with me for a few days. My shoulder had been set, my gashes sewn up and my abrasions liberally swabbed with iodine. Claire was poked with more needles than a lab rat, as they ran test after test on her, took x-rays and did more MRIs, and woke her up every three hours to take her vital signs. By the fourth night of this, she was so irritated, she tells me, that she threw a half-filled water pitcher at the door when one of the nurses knocked. It makes me wonder if I'll have to deal with personality changes and volatile mood swings, but fortunately she seems fine except for that one incident. It's all for a good cause, though. They're going to write her up in the medical journals as a modern day miracle.

A week plods by before they'll even talk of letting her go home. I worry that we'll eventually get swamped with a mountain of medical bills between the two of us. But since we're in the land of social health care, I decide not to let it bother me. For now.

For now, I only want to remind myself how damn lucky I am. But that's hard to do, because I still ache for Mariota. And I feel guilty about it, about having slept with her after resisting for so long, even though I shouldn't. That was another life, I tell myself. I was someone else back then. There was no Claire. Only Mariota.

Yet I miss that life. The simplicity, the rawness of it. And I miss Mariota, terribly. She's gone now, though. I have to go on. It should be that simple.

Yet it's not.

Still, something else troubles me. Something I can't quite put my finger on. Like there's a piece missing.

CLAIRE POSES IN FRONT of the hospital bathroom mirror, pulling a brush through her hair in long strokes, a distant look on her face. She doesn't even notice me coming through the outer door. I lean around the doorframe of the lavatory, gazing at her. Several seconds pass before she gives a startled reaction.

"Oh!" The brush falls from her hand to land in the sink with a clatter. Startled, she looks at me in the mirror. "My God, Ross. You scared me to death."

"Did you forget I was coming to take you home?" I slide my arms around her waist and kiss her neck. "You looked far away just then. Where were you?"

Sighing heavily, she wriggles out of my hold, then marches to where her suitcase is on the bed. She's wearing her favorite flowered sundress and a pair of strappy low-heeled sandals. Her hands flutter over her skirt, smoothing the wrinkles as she stares down at her painted toenails.

"Have you ever had a dream," she says, "that seemed so real you believed it?"

"All the time." I cross the room and sink into the vinyl chair in the corner.

"I mean like … like you were actually *there?*"

"Did you have a dream last night?"

"Not last night, no. When I was unconscious." Her dark eyes flick to me, then down again. "I always thought that being in a coma you'd just be thinking of nothing. Or you'd hear people around you and not be able to respond. But it wasn't like either of those things."

"What was it like?" I have to admit, I'm curious. So far I haven't asked her about it because I figure she'll tell me if there's anything worth telling.

"Most of it didn't make sense at first," she says. "It was here, in Scotland, and yet it wasn't. The land looked the same, the hills, the forests, the glens. But the people were different, the way they talked, what they wore. It took me awhile to realize it was a different time. A long time ago. But it wasn't so much like a dream as a —"

"Memory?"

"Yes." She nods vigorously. "A memory."

A shaft of sunlight divides the space between us. Half-blinded by the brightness and barely able to see Claire, I lean forward into the light, my elbows on my knees. "And what do you remember?"

"That I was standing on a cliff, with the sea below. There were birds everywhere, and a strong wind in my face. I was waiting for someone to …" — she struggles for words, her forehead creased in concentration — "to come back to me."

"Your husband. You were waiting for your husband to come back from a battle."

"Yes … yes. And then I learned that thousands had died and I was sure he hadn't survived, but I still hoped." Her mouth slips into a frown, her shoulders weighed down with sadness. Suddenly, her head snaps up. "Wait. How did you know that?"

In that moment, everything makes sense. To me, at least. Grief and remorse are expunged in an instant. I rise, my heart pounding so hard I feel like it might explode. "Because I was there with you, Claire."

She comes around the bed, staring at me in disbelief. "But how? It *was* only a dream — wasn't it?"

I take her face in my hands. "It was real. As real as you and I standing here together now."

"How do you know that? How can you be sure, Ross?"

"Your name was Mariota."

Her eyes go wide. She clamps her hands over mine and whispers, "Roslin?"

I laugh with relief. For weeks, I had tried to deny my feelings for Mariota, thinking that I would somehow be betraying Claire if I gave in. But my heart had been right all along: Mariota *was* Claire. "Yes, that was me. Do you understand now? We've lived before. We were together even then, almost seven hundred years ago."

She arches a skeptical eyebrow at me. "Excuse me if this is all a little hard to swallow."

"I know, I know. But how else do you explain it?"

The whine of cart wheels is followed by a thump. Nurse Stephens has steered the meal cart into the doorframe.

"Oh," the nurse remarks in surprise, backing the cart up to maneuver it into the hallway, "leaving this morning, are you? Well, we'll miss you something fierce, Ms. Forbes." She unhooks the clipboard from its hook on the wall and scans it once. "They can't stop talking about you in the staff room. The doctors say it's a miracle you snapped out of that coma as if it had never happened. They can't explain it. Please send us a letter when you get home, love, let us know how you're getting along, won't you?"

Claire rushes to her to give her a quick hug. "Of course, I will. I'll never forget what good care you took of me. Although I can't say

I'm unhappy to get out of here."

"Home is where you belong." Nurse Stephens tilts her head, her lower lip quivering. She dashes a tear from her cheek. "You two look so perfect together. After all you've both been through … I'm so happy to see you like this. Just think of the stories you'll have to tell that wee one of yours someday."

"Yeah, someday." Claire turns Nurse Stephens by the shoulders and guides her out the door with a sudden urgency. "I'll write, okay? I promise."

"And send pictures of the three of you?"

"Sure, sure." Claire urges her out into the corridor, then yanks the door shut. Before I can ask her what they were talking about, she ducks into the bathroom and makes a big commotion as she collects her makeup bag and other toiletries.

"Um, Claire … dear." I poke my head around the door, but she won't meet my gaze. "What's wrong?"

She fishes around in her makeup bag. "Nothing."

I lift her chin and force her to look at me. "The truth, Claire."

"It's just that … that …" And then it all comes out in a torrent. "It's all my fault, Ross. I know we had it all planned out, that we'd start trying for a family six months from now. I was being careful. I really was. Then we got carried away that one night and, and, and I suppose I just forgot, but I figured maybe luck would be on my side, so I didn't say anything to you… Oh God, how stupid was I to have that whiskey? What kind of mother am I going to be? What if our baby has problems? It's my fault. I'm so dumb and I've ruined everything and you should just divorce me right now because —"

"Stop, stop, stop." I pinch her lips between my fingers, then wrap my arms around her and pull her into me. I kiss the top of her head. If this is her hormones talking, we're going to be in for a long, bumpy ride. "I knew about the baby before you woke up. And I believe you didn't know. It's going to be okay, Claire. It really is. So we're going to be parents a little early. Big deal. We'll be fine. We're smart people. We'll figure it out. You're going to be a great mom. The best. Me, though? You'll have to be patient. I'll try hard, every day. I didn't have a very good example for a father, but at least I know what not to do."

"Are you going to tell your dad about the baby, Ross?"

"I suppose so." To others, it's natural to tell your family you're going to have a baby, knowing they'll be happy for you. But every time in my life I told my dad about something I thought would make him proud of me, he had ridiculed me, found fault, or flipped it all inside out to make it into something bad. Not this time. Not ever again.

"Do you want me to do it?"

"No, this is something I have to do myself. I need to stand up to him. Set limits. My whole life I've kept quiet, swallowed the hurt, and run away. But not anymore." I start to help her put the last of her things in the overstuffed suitcase. "If there was one thing I learned while I was 'away', it was that if someone's always finding fault with you, sometimes it's because they're still fighting something in their past. I can't be part of that fight any longer, whatever it is. He has to understand that or he just can't be a part of my life, our lives, ever again. I know that seems harsh, but you can't change someone unless they want to change."

"It makes perfect sense to me." She cups my jaw in her palm, smiling in that gentle, understanding way that has always melted my heart. "So you've checked out of the B&B?"

"Yeah. Dermot says bye and next time we come back, he'll give us a couple nights free."

"That's nice of him. Are we on our way to the airport, then?"

"We have a few hours before we need to check in, so if you don't mind, I'd like to swing by St. Joseph's Kirk. I never did get to talk to Reverend Murray again. I already called and he's expecting us.

Something he told me doesn't quite add up and I wanted to see if he learned anything new about the Sinclairs."

39

HERE & NOW

<u>Near Berwick, Scotland — 2013</u>

WE MEET WITH REVEREND Murray at the pub in Aberbeg. The man behind the bar greets him heartily. I assume they know each other from church services or community functions, until the barkeeper asks if he wants 'the usual'.

"This happens more often than I'd like to admit, but it seems I confused a few facts." Reverend Murray pulls a dark frothy drink toward him and takes a sip. "It was Sir Henry Sinclair who died at Halidon Hill."

"I'm aware of that, but his son died just days later, didn't he?" I say. "From wounds received during the battle, perhaps?"

He looks at me with utter befuddlement. "Oh no, no. Not at all. I contacted my cousin's friend in Kirkwall and asked him to look into family records there. There's a small graveyard on one of the northern islands, near where a castle once stood. It's nothing but ruins now, the markers on the graves barely legible. But he said there was clearly a Sir Roslin Sinclair buried there whose birth date matches this one." He spreads out the paper and points to the name. "He had a son named William, but also a brother by that name."

"And Sir Roslin's date of death?" I ask.

"Some thirty-five years after the battle. About a year after the death of his wife."

"Mariota," Claire says.

"Yes." He hooks a finger over the edge of his glasses and slides them off his nose. "How did you know her name? It's not written here. Only on the gravestone."

Claire and I look at each other.

She slips her hand in mine atop the table. "You wouldn't believe us if we told you."

"Reverend Murray," I say, "do you believe we only live once?"

He gazes up at the soot-darkened rafters, contemplating the question. "When I read from the Holy Gospel at a funeral, I recite the words 'Ashes to ashes; Dust to dust.' It means that our bodies are nurtured by the earth and when we die, we return to it. Become a part of the soil, so to speak."

Then leaning across the table, he places his hand over both of ours and smiles knowingly. "But our souls ... our souls are eternal."

Columbus, Ohio — 2013

WE'RE SITTING ON A pair of plastic chairs halfway between our gate at the Columbus airport and the luggage carousel. I've had a lot of time to think on the flight home. No matter how long I turn things over in my mind, it will never get easier. It's been over ten years since I've spoken to him. But there's a part of my past I need to leave behind and until I address a few things, it's always going to be there. Hell, I could let it eat me up for ten more years and what would I gain from that?

Claire squeezes my knee as I press the numbers on my keypad. It rings on the other end five times, six, seven … If he doesn't answer, I don't think I can get up the nerve to do this again.

Finally, the ringing stops. I hear the soft crackle of air on the other end. And then his voice.

"Hello?"

"Hey … Dad." My words come out high-pitched and soft, like I'm ten. I try to swallow, but my mouth feels like it's stuffed with cotton. I pop open the tab of my Coke and take a swig. "It's me."

"Ross?" A long pause follows. My stomach clenches. If it wasn't for Claire sitting next to me, I'd snap the phone shut and pretend this never happened. But it's his tone that keeps me on the line. It's not what I expected. He sounds almost … cheerful, if that's possible. "Ross. It's been a long time. Good to hear from you, son."

"Yeah, um …" Everything I'd planned on saying is suddenly lost in a haze of amnesia. I should've written it all down. And then, being the wimp I am, I blurt out, "Look, I'm sorry I —"

"No, Ross." There's a hitch in his voice. "I'm sorry."

I lower the phone for a second and look at it, then press it to my ear again. "What?"

"I said *I'm* sorry." He's more insistent this time, like he doesn't want to repeat himself and I'd better listen up.

"Oh. About what?"

"You know … Things I said. Did." Another long pause follows.

A couple of weeks ago, I would have blasted my anger at him, pressed him for a more thorough answer and accepted nothing less than him blubbering tearful regrets while he prostrated himself before me. My perspective, however, has changed a lot recently. Truth is I'm not sure he could tell me exactly what he's sorry about.

He *does* seem to understand that he bears some responsibility.

What will happen if I let my guard down? Will he revert to the same old behaviors? Will his words still hurt as much as they used to?

The fact that he's apologized, however vaguely, well, that's a huge step on his part. He can't erase all the things he's said and done. But I can allow him a fresh start. I can give him a chance.

In this life, there won't be any heroic acts of valor or self-sacrifice. Just those two little words: 'I'm sorry.'

Two words. And yet they hold so much power. So much potential to heal.

"So, I was thinking," I say, bridging the silence, "of coming back to Indiana to visit some friends. Thought I'd stop by the house, if that's okay. There's someone I'd like you to meet."

Historical Note

The Battle of Halidon Hill was fought on July 19th, 1333. It is estimated the Scots numbered 13,000 strong, while the English army had 9,000 men.

Lord Archibald Douglas has been criticized for not acting more quickly when Edward Balliol entered Scotland in early March and laid siege to the city of Berwick. Rather than raid into England immediately, Douglas chose to focus on gathering a large enough force to outnumber the opposition. Meanwhile, Balliol dug trenches and cut off the water supply to Berwick, placing its citizens in an increasingly desperate situation. In May, King Edward III joined Balliol. Berwick was forced to negotiate. Douglas set out south to attack Bamburgh, where Queen Philippa was staying, but upon Edward's hanging of the first of the hostages offered up by Berwick, he returned there. Battle was inevitable.

King Edward had two undeniable advantages and used both of them to overwhelming effect. The first was his positioning on Halidon Hill to the north of Berwick, the only open land route to the city, which is surrounded to the west and south by the River Tweed and to the east by the sea. In order for the Scots to relieve Berwick by force, they had to break through the English lines. If they failed, Berwick would surrender. Edward had no intention of abandoning his superior vantage point. He would force the Scots to come to him.

The second was his use of the longbow. Basically, the moment the Scottish army crossed over the marshy ground at the foot of Halidon Hill and Edward employed his archers, Berwick's fate was decided.

Scottish casualties were staggering. Numerous nobles lay dead on the battlefield, decimating Scotland's leadership for years to come. In English eyes, the humiliating defeat at Bannockburn had at last been avenged.

A few months later, Edward Balliol held a parliament in Perth. His hold on the crown, however, did not last. A year later, he was deposed.

Young King David was sent to France for safety and did not return to Scotland until 1341, at the age of seventeen. Five years later, he invaded England, but was captured at the Battle of Neville's Cross. He remained a prisoner of Edward III's for eleven years. In 1357, he was released under the terms of the Treaty of Berwick, which demanded heavy payments. David died childless in 1371 and was succeeded by his nephew Robert Stewart, the first of many Stewarts to rule Scotland.

The Cathars were a sect of Christianity existing from roughly the mid 12th century to the 14th. Rigorously persecuted by the Catholic Church, they believed the Universe was ruled by two powers: good (God, the spiritual) and evil (Satan, the flesh). One of their primary beliefs was that the Soul would be born again seven times, until spiritual growth and perfection had been achieved. The Cathar Perfects, believed to be closest to the end cycle of reincarnation, often took great pains to offer the *Consolamentum* or Consolation to the dying, which was thought to help purify the Soul and assist it on its journey. Credentes, those just beginning their spiritual journey, were not expected to maintain the severely austere lifestyle that Perfects did.

In 1244, the Cathar stronghold of Montsegur in southwestern France was the site of a siege and the eventual surrender of over two hundred Cathars, who were put to death by fire. Afterwards, the fortress was razed, but rumors that the Holy Grail was once housed there persist to this day, as evidenced by the numerous books and movies containing elements of the siege and the castle's ties to the sacred relic.

About the Author

N. Gemini Sasson holds a M.S. in Biology from Wright State University where she ran cross country on athletic scholarship. She has worked as an aquatic toxicologist, an environmental engineer, a teacher and a cross country coach. A longtime breeder of Australian Shepherds, her articles on bobtail genetics have been translated into seven languages. She lives in rural Ohio with her husband, two nearly grown children and an ever-changing number of animals.

Long after writing about Robert the Bruce and Queen Isabella, Sasson learned she is a descendant of both historical figures.

If you enjoyed this book, please spread the word by sharing it on Facebook or leaving a review at your favorite online retailer or book lovers' site.

For more details about N. Gemini Sasson and her books, go to:
www.ngeminisasson.com

Or become a 'fan' at:
www.facebook.com/NGeminiSasson

You can also sign up to learn about new releases via e-mail at:
http://eepurl.com/vSA6z

Acknowledgments

Heartfelt thanks go out to the members of Team ITOK, who helped bring this story to its final stages: Sarah Woodbury, Lisa J. Yarde, Julie Conner, J.S. Colley and Reini Brickson. Your wisdom, honesty and encouragement have been invaluable.

Lightning Source UK Ltd.
Milton Keynes UK
UKOW05f2008260913

218042UK00004B/409/P